Dear Reader,

In many ways, writing Sadie's story was a bit like coming home for me. I currently live on the other side of the world in southern Africa, but Colorado will always be my second home.

I first visited the state over twenty-five years ago with my college sweetheart in order to meet his family for the first time. It didn't take long for me to realize that not only had I fallen in love with my future husband and his family, but also with the snow-capped mountains, golden aspen trees, and green forests of this beautiful state.

Over the years, I've enjoyed visiting Colorado's small towns and national parks, which is one of the reasons why Silver Peak is the kind of place I'd like to settle down in one day. I love the homey feel of ambling down Main Street with the majestic mountains rising up in the background and familiar, friendly faces—like Sadie, Roz, and Edwin—greeting me.

Writing *A Lode of Secrets* brought me back to that familiar feeling of community. And as someone who loves a good mystery, helping Sadie find out the truth behind what was going on in the old silver mines made my job even more enjoyable.

So I hope, as you read this story, you'll enjoy being swept away for a few hours to the beautiful town of Silver Peak with Sadie and her friends.

Best wishes,
Lisa Harris
writing as Carole Jefferson

Mysteries of Silver Peak

A Mountain of Mystery
Nobody's Safe
Silver Surprise
Wildfire
A Lode of Secrets

A Lode of Secrets

CAROLE JEFFERSON

Guideposts
New York

Published by Guideposts Books & Inspirational Media
110 William Street
New York, New York 10038
Guideposts.org

Acknowledgments

Every attempt has been made to credit the sources of copyrighted material used in this book. If any such acknowledgment has been inadvertently omitted or miscredited, receipt of such information would be appreciated.

Cover and interior design by Müllerhaus
Cover art by Greg Copeland represented by Deborah Wolfe, Ltd.
Typeset by Aptara, Inc.

Printed and bound in the United States of America
10 9 8 7 6 5 4 3 2 1

A Lode of Secrets

Prologue

My dearest Raymond,

Sometimes I wonder what would have happened if I hadn't decided to walk into the Depot that July afternoon. If I hadn't let Julia convince me that we both needed an ice cream sundae to beat the summer heat. What would have happened if I hadn't looked across the row of tables and diners and noticed you?

Funny how I remember that moment as if it were yesterday. The instant you looked up and caught my gaze, with those blue eyes that seemed to see right through me. I'm certain my heart stopped in that instant. It also became a point of no return when I somehow knew my life was about to change forever.

And change it has.

At that pivotal moment, though, I didn't even know who you were. It wasn't until a week later that I learned you'd grown up in Denver and had lived the past two years working in a New York office. Yet there you sat in the middle of our small town, laughing with an old friend across a couple of root beer floats as if you'd lived in our tiny town of Silver Peak your entire life.

I share these memories with you, because even I must play them over in my mind to ensure myself that they are real. That you are real. You swept into my life, reminding me that I didn't want to spend the rest of my life in a predictable fashion. You showed me that my heart longed for adventure beyond the confines of Silver Peak—beyond what anyone I've known up to this moment will ever be able to offer me. You asked me to trust you completely. And I want you to know that I do.

Because meeting you again yesterday confirmed everything I had hoped. Your devotion to me. Your love for me. But I also know that you worry about how my family feels about you. That my father and brother have reservations over my marrying a man I've known for such a short time. (Though I must say, my mother seems to have no such reservations. You've completely captivated her with your charm!)

Still, you must understand that my family has expectations for the person I will marry. My father, in fact, has stated more than once that marrying for position is far wiser than marrying simply for love. He sees the notion of marrying for love as frivolous. Even foolish.

Because of this, I have been cautious, even afraid, for far too long. I have been unwilling to accept your marriage proposal for fear it might in the end divide my family. But your continual declarations of love give me confidence.

Which means that now, I have decided that I don't fear as much the repercussions of our actions as I fear losing you, my dearest Raymond. And I have made a decision. It is time that my family accepts the truth about us, and allows me to follow my heart.

Forever yours,
Abigail Chaplin

1

SADIE SPEERS HUMMED ALONG WITH A DELMORE BROTHERS SONG playing in the background of the Antique Mine as she sorted through a collection of late-nineteenth-century drawer pulls and accent knobs.

Her best friend, Rosalind "Roz" Putnam, picked up one of the clear glass drawer knobs and held it up to the light. "Marilee's going to love these, Sadie."

"I think you're right." Sadie nodded in agreement across the counter where Roz stood. "I left Marilee a message to drop by the shop as soon as she could."

While the majority of Sadie's sixty-two years had been spent teaching business and history at the local high school, she'd always loved antiques. Which was why, after retiring from teaching, opening up the Antique Mine had been the perfect project for Sadie. Located on Main Street next to Arbuckle's Coffee, the building she owned was big enough to rent out the upper levels for apartments and offices, while still allowing plenty of room for her antique business—which was excellent for Sadie's need. The store's original high pressed-tin ceiling, with fluorescent lighting, created a bright and cheerful space, making the store a popular stop with the tourists and locals alike. More often than not, she felt like a modern-day treasure hunter, as she searched for valuable collectibles she knew her clients—like Marilee—would appreciate.

"I wish you could have gone with me yesterday to this estate auction," Sadie said, adding a pair of brass knobs to the keeper box as she continued sorting. Roz often attended estate sales with Sadie, but this past week she'd gone to visit one of her sons in Phoenix. "You would have loved it."

"I always miss something when I go out of town, but I did see that small antique table you set out in the front." Roz replaced the knob she'd been examining, then tugged on the hem of the flowing multicolored tunic she wore. "I think I might have to pick that piece up for myself."

"You know I'll give it to you at cost." Sadie smiled.

"I might just take you up on that. There's an empty spot in my entryway I've been waiting to fill," Roz said. "What about this box?"

Sadie's attention shifted from the drawer pulls to the box of vintage perfume bottles that sat beside them on the counter.

"The auction also featured this collection of perfume bottles gathered from all over the world by an elderly couple." Sadie held up one that was made from Italian glass. "Some of them are cracked, unfortunately, so I'll need to sort through them. But most are in beautiful shape."

"They're beautiful, though not exactly my taste. I think I'll stick to the table for now."

Roz's answer wasn't unexpected. While the two of them tended to be opposites in many ways, that fact had never stopped them from being fast friends. Sadie wore her thick, wavy hair short and barely reached five-foot-four, while Roz playfully claimed to be five-foot-twelve, and wore her gray hair in a bob that framed her face. Roz also favored flowing bohemian clothes in bright colors and lots of jewelry, while Sadie tended to dress like someone who'd spent most of her life in the mountains, preferring North Face vests and hiking boots in the winter and Teva sandals in the summer.

But it wasn't just their appearance that set them apart. Roz was nearly always calm, collected, and ready to handle a crisis, while Sadie had a tendency to jump headfirst into things if she wasn't careful. Those very differences, Sadie was convinced, were part of the reason why their friendship had continued to blossom over the years. Roz was, as Sadie had said on more than one occasion, the string to her kite.

The bell above the front door jingled, interrupting Sadie's thoughts. She looked up to see her fourteen-year-old granddaughter toting a large black garbage bag that clanked beside her as she made her way through the middle of the store.

"Why, Sara, what a nice surprise." Sadie set the box of knobs under the counter for safekeeping, then rounded the counter to greet her granddaughter. "I wasn't expecting to see you today."

"Morning, Grandma. Mrs. Putnam."

Sara's braces sparkled as she gave them a self-conscious smile. A typical teen, Sara spent as much time as possible texting her friends and shopping for clothes, but she also had a deep compassion for injured animals that had inspired her to build a makeshift wildlife sanctuary in the backyard for the animals she was always nursing back to health, and Sadie prayed her granddaughter's empathy and compassion would continue to develop as she grew older.

"Good morning, Sara," Roz said. "What on earth are you carrying?"

Sadie winced as Sara plopped the large bag on the front counter between the box of perfume bottles and her old-style brass cash register. "Mom sent Theo and me into town to pick up a few things from the store and drop these off for you."

"Is this what I think it is?" Sadie asked, starting to open the bag.

"A dozen milk jugs. Mom says she's happy to collect things for you as long as you keep them."

Roz laughed. "I don't blame her. Your grandma's collections are threatening to take over her house."

Sadie's eyes twinkled. "Oh, Roz. I have plenty of room for these at my house."

"Maybe, but what is Claribel going to think when she comes to clean?"

As a penny-pincher, Sadie had been reluctant to hire Claribel to help clean the five-bedroom farmhouse she'd inherited from her parents. But it was one of Sadie's few indulgences, and given her work at the Antique Mine and her involvement in her community, it was one she'd found to be an absolute godsend. Claribel had an almost irrational love for cleanliness and organization that kept in check Sadie's love of antiques, knickknacks, and books that easily could fall into disarray and clutter.

"It's all for a good cause." Sadie waved her hand in the air as if shooing away Roz's concern. She removed the bag and set it on the floor behind the counter until she could take it home. "When the Campfire Chapel puts out another appeal for paper towel tubes, milk jugs, and empty pizza boxes for their upcoming Vacation Bible School, I'll be ready."

"Why am I not surprised?" Roz said.

Sadie laughed at her best friend's comment. Roz knew all too well her penchant for thrift and collecting things that might one day be useful.

Sara laughed. "I think Mom's just happy they're not being stored in our house."

"I'll call her later to thank her, but be sure to tell her for me."

"I will, Grandma."

Sadie looked toward the plate-glass windows in the front of the shop to see if her late husband's 1960 Cadillac convertible was parked outside. She'd agreed to let Theo drive it while his car was in the shop, since she knew how much he loved the car and it normally just sat in her garage anyway. She much preferred her red four-wheel-drive Tahoe. "Where is Theo?"

Theo was Sadie's oldest grandchild, named after his grandfather, Sadie's late husband.

"Theo said I could wait here while he does Mom's shopping. He shouldn't be that long." Sara leaned against the counter and caught her grandmother's gaze as a thought occurred to her. "Grandma, I heard you were going to be on a TV show."

"I'm not actually going to be on a TV show, Sara. Have you heard of *American Treasure Chest*? I'm the historical consultant for a documentary TV series they're putting together."

Roz's face lit up. "Still, it's so exciting, Sadie. Roscoe and I love that show." She turned to Sara. "They go behind the scenes to re-create unsolved mysteries from America's past."

Roz was married to Roscoe Putnam, who owned Putnam & Sons, next door to Sadie's shop, an old-school hardware store where Roscoe was known for being able to find just about anything a customer might need for repairs, plumbing, or gardening, and on top of that, he could fix just about anything that needed fixing.

"Right now," Sadie explained, "they're working on a six-part series on mines around the country, and one of those six just happens to be right here in Silver Peak."

Sara's eyes brightened. "So what does it mean that you're a consultant?"

"For starters, I've spent the past few weeks corresponding with the director to answer his questions, researching details of the story, and ensuring the script is as accurate as possible."

"Though not everyone was thrilled with the fact that Abigail and Raymond's story is being told," Roz added.

Sara gave Sadie a puzzled look. She was clearly intrigued—and perhaps as starstruck at the thought of a TV crew in town as Roz, but she waited to see what her grandmother had to say.

"Well, Priscilla Hewitt told me she didn't want to be involved in the documentary, even though it centers on her mother's story," Sadie explained. "She believes that there are some secrets from history that should stay that way."

"Are you going to be there during the filming?" Sara asked, leaning against the counter.

Sadie went back to sorting through the perfume bottles. "Well, I'll be providing the majority of the props and costumes for the reenactments, and they've asked me to help them be sure the historical clips woven into the documentary are accurate." Sadie pointed to the stack of boxes she'd lined up by the back door, ready to be loaded into her Chevy Tahoe. "I've got carbide lamps, a miner's lunch pail, folding candlesticks the miners used, and other blasting-related items. The costumes are already up at the mine."

"Where did you get all of this?" Sara asked.

"A lot of it comes from here"—she motioned around her shop—"but other items I was able to borrow from Ol' Sam at the American Mining Museum. Greg and Evelyn Winston, the mine owners, offered some things as well."

Greg and Evelyn Winston, along with their fifteen-year-old son, Craig, lived near the Silver Peak Mine, where they ran tours of the silver mine that had been in the family for three generations.

Sadie grabbed one of the perfume bottles, a beautiful clear blue one. "I just had another thought. This will be a perfect addition to Abigail's dressing table."

"And who, exactly, was Abigail?" Sara asked, picking up one of the bottles.

"You remember that skeleton Greg Winston found up in the mines a few weeks back?" Sadie began.

Sara nodded.

"Of course she does. Everyone in town knows about the skeleton Greg found. And now the police claim that the victim had been murdered." Roz leaned in and lowered her voice, as if she were divulging a tantalizing secret. "It was a tragic love story. A vanishing fiancé presumed dead by the hands of Abigail Chaplin's brother, though no one really knows the truth about what happened up in the mines that fatal night."

Sadie laughed at her friend's flair for the dramatic. "And since it happened over half a century ago, no one probably ever will know."

"What *do* you know?" Sara asked.

Sadie glanced at her friend, wondering how much of the story needed to be repeated in front of her granddaughter.

"Grandma." Sara rolled her eyes and let out a huff of frustration. "It's not like I'm a kid anymore. And if everyone in town knows the story, I'll hear it all anyway."

Sadie weighed her granddaughter's logic. "I suppose you're right. But no one knows for sure who Greg discovered up in the mines. The crime lab is trying to identify the body, but most people assume it's Raymond Butler."

"And who's he?" Sara sounded impatient.

"Back in the mid-1950s, a young woman who lived right here in Silver Peak, Abigail Chaplin, fell in love with Raymond, a handsome stranger, the story goes, who waltzed into Silver Peak and swept her off her feet."

"How romantic," Sara said.

"So it would seem. But Abigail's family was wealthy, and her father and brother in particular were convinced that Raymond was simply after her money."

"Was he?"

"No one knows for sure. Supposedly Raymond and Abigail's brother, Philip, had a big argument right in the center of town at the library where Abigail volunteered." Sadie could remember the old library building, now replaced by a modern glass-and-steel structure that she privately thought looked out of place with the rest of Silver Peak.

"What happened?"

"Words were flung back and forth at each other," Sadie continued, "along with a few punches. After the fight was over, Philip threatened Raymond that he would kill him if he didn't stay away from his sister."

"And did he?" Sara asked.

"No. Because Abigail's family was against the marriage—and Raymond was afraid for his life—he tried to convince her to elope with him. But before they did, Raymond disappeared."

"What happened to him?"

"That's the problem," Roz cut in. "No one knows for sure, but it was rumored that Philip made good on his threat, killed Raymond, and hid his body up in the mines."

Sara's eyes widened. "What happened to Philip?"

"Philip was taken in and questioned by the authorities, but even though there were witnesses to their fight in town, they weren't able to tie him to Raymond's disappearance. Nor did they have a body," Sadie said. "And without a body, it was impossible to prove there'd even been a murder."

"How about Abigail?" Sara's phone buzzed beside her on the counter, but in a rare display of indifference, she ignored it. "What happened to her?"

"Her parents sent her to Europe for a few months to stay with a relative, hoping it would get her mind off the incident. She eventually returned to help out the family when her father become very ill. Philip died a few months later in a car crash on his way back to Silver Peak from Denver. Her father died right after that."

"What a sad story." Sara shook her head. "What do you think happened to Raymond?"

"I wish I knew." Sadie glanced at her watch. "But for now, I need to get going. I'm supposed to meet the TV crew up at the mines in less than an hour. If the two of you wouldn't mind helping me finish loading up my car with the props, I'd be grateful. Julie's on her way right now to watch the store while I'm gone."

Sara tapped her fingers against the counter. "Grandma..."

"Yes?"

"Would it be okay if I came along with you?"

Sadie set the box she'd picked up back on the counter. "To the mine?"

"Yeah. I was just thinking how Theo likes to hang out with you, but since he's busy with summer school for his honors class, maybe I could help you with the props."

Sadie studied her granddaughter, wondering where her motivation to "hang out" with her grandmother had come from. "Did the story intrigue you that much, or does your wanting to help out have more to do with the fact that there will be TV crews and cameras?"

"Well..." Sara's gaze shifted. "It's more interesting than hanging around the house all day."

"You're two weeks into summer break and already bored?"

"I'm not bored," Sara countered. She gave her grandmother a mischievous grin. "This would be...educational."

"Educational, huh?" Sadie laughed.

"I'm serious." Sara drummed her fingers against the counter, then glanced at her reflection in the dark screen of her cell phone and tucked a strand of hair behind her ear. "And if they happen to need an extra, then I'll be available."

"So now the truth comes out." Sadie couldn't really blame her granddaughter, though. Something told her if she was Sara's age again, she'd think the same thing. "What about your mother? The mine isn't the safest place."

"I asked her before I left the house. She said if it was okay with you, it was okay with her."

"You're sure?" Sadie asked.

Sara nodded, her eyes wide with excitement. "When she told me what you were doing, I hoped they might need some extras. It would be fun."

Sadie weighed her options. Maybe spending the week with Sara wasn't such a bad idea after all. Not only would she get some quality time with her granddaughter, but she'd have an assistant. What could go wrong?

"Do you think Theo would be interested in coming too?" Sadie asked.

"I don't think he has time, with this class he's taking."

Sadie made her decision. "They've hired a small number of actors for the main parts, but I understand they're looking for some extras, especially for the town shots. And I could always use an assistant."

"Yeah!" Sara clicked a button on her phone and the screen lit up. "I'll let Mom know."

"Hold on... Not so fast. There are two rules, make that three."

"Rules?" Sara's smile faded slightly.

"You have to wear a helmet when you are in the mine, and"—Sadie glanced at her granddaughter's cell phone—"no cell phones or other electronic devices that might distract you. The director will expect anyone who works on the set to be completely professional."

"No problem."

"And third, while the mines are set up for tourists, they still can be dangerous if you don't follow the instructions."

"Grandma, I promise I'll be careful."

"Great. Call your mom and let her know I said you could come, then let's load up the car. We've got a documentary to shoot."

When they reached the mine, Sadie and Sara carried the last two boxes up to the wood-framed house that had been built back in the late 1800s. Plans were for the documentary to be filmed in two main locations, including the mine and surrounding area and in town where Raymond and Philip had their infamous fight. Greg had offered the empty house that sat on his land as a base for the filming equipment, props, and dressing rooms.

The house needed a paint job and some TLC, but the rustic patina of the old place would look great on camera, which was one of the reasons why the site had been chosen for inclusion.

"It's beautiful up here, isn't it?" Sara exclaimed.

"A view I don't think I could ever get tired of," Sadie agreed, looking out on the stunning spread of aspens and evergreens that surrounded Silver Peak below them.

Sadie's cell phone rang as she set her box inside the house next to the rest of the props she'd brought earlier. She checked the caller ID, about to dismiss it, when she noticed it was Edwin.

Sadie felt her heart flutter. Long before she'd met her late husband, T.R.—more than four decades ago—she'd gone steady with Edwin Marshall, until he'd left Silver Peak to pursue a career as a circuit judge in Chicago. Now, all these years later, following his retirement and the loss of his wife, Rose, he'd returned to Silver Peak. Sadie had never imagined a second chance at love—not at her age—but that was exactly what she'd been given with Edwin.

At first, she hadn't been quite sure if his visits to the Antique Mine were to see her or simply an excuse to stop by Arbuckle's Coffee for one of Luz's thick slices of homemade apple pie. Her daughter, Alice, had been convinced his frequent visits both to the Antique Mine and Campfire Church were motivated by the fact that he wanted to be her beau again. The pie, Alice insisted with a chuckle, was just the icing on the cake.

It had turned out that Alice was right. He'd managed to steal her heart the same way he had all those years ago. And after a frustrating day—or any day for that matter—there was something calming and comforting about Edwin's presence.

Sadie glanced at Sara. "Would you mind moving these boxes to the corner while I take this call?"

Sara nodded in assent as Sadie quickly showed Sara where she'd begun organizing the props yesterday, then stepped out into the sunshine.

"Just called to wish you luck," Edwin said as soon as she answered. "Though I know you, of all people, don't need an ounce of it."

Sadie laughed. "I admit to being a tad nervous that everything goes smoothly, but mainly just excited."

"You'll do a fantastic job. You know I have every confidence in you."

Her smile broadened, making her feel like a schoolgirl again. "The crew isn't here yet, but that will give Sara and me time to unpack the rest of the props."

"So you've got your granddaughter involved in the project?"

"I'd love to say that it's just that she loves to spend time with her grandmother, but I suspect there is at least one ulterior motive in this case."

"Let me guess. Lights, cameras, and a film director."

"How did you know?"

"I remember Noelle at that age," Edwin said, speaking of his daughter who lived in Atlanta. "She would have jumped at a chance to be involved in something like this."

"Sara's hoping she can be an extra."

Edwin laughed. "Well, I won't keep you, as I know you have lots to do, but enjoy yourself today."

Sadie smiled. "I will."

Greg Winston, owner of the South Ridge Mine, walked up to the house as Sadie hung up the call.

"Good morning, Greg."

"Hey, Sadie. Ready for the big day?"

"All the props are here, and just about organized, so yes. I believe so."

Greg leaned against the railing at the top of the stairs. "I was kind of surprised when I heard you were going to be involved in this project, knowing how busy you are in your store."

"I think it'll be a lot of fun. Is the documentary crew here yet?" she asked, brushing the dust from her hands.

Greg's gaze slid to his watch. "They're going to be late, actually," Greg said, as Sara stepped out onto the porch. "They called and said they'd had a flat tire twenty miles out of Denver. But there's no reason why I can't start the two of you off with a tour of the mine and a little history. How's that sound?"

"Sara?" Sadie asked her granddaughter. "What do you think?"

Sadie caught a glimpse of disappointment in Sara's eyes flash before she shot them both a smile. "Sounds great to me."

Sadie chuckled inwardly. Apparently, touring an old mine didn't rank quite as high as hanging out with a film crew.

Fifteen minutes later, with all of the props and costumes tucked away in the house for safekeeping, Sadie ducked into the narrow rock passageway that led into the mine, careful to watch her step as she crossed the cart rails running along the horizontal shaft. She shivered behind Greg and Sara, wondering if her chill was as much from the sharp drop in temperature or the thought of what had happened in this very mine a half a century ago.

She'd taken this tour before—run by Greg and his employees—but this time she was looking at it from an entirely different light. She could imagine Raymond and Abigail meeting outside these mines, with the Rocky Mountains in the background as they declared their love to each other, and tried to decide what they should do. Until the fatal moment when something had happened to change everything.

"Watch your step, ladies." Greg stopped in an open section of the cavern that was filled with old mining equipment and rubbed his hands together. "Our tunnels are lit by solar panels, but it's still pretty dark in here. Especially when it comes to filming. The crew is bringing in extra lighting, though, which they've assured me will solve that problem."

"It sure is cold in here." Sara brushed up against Sadie.

"True, but you won't find a better air-conditioning system. And in the winter, believe it or not, this will seem warm compared to outside." Greg's enthusiasm came through in his voice. "This is the section where we normally do our tours. We also have a place outside down the hill where people can pan for gold."

"Anyone ever find anything?" Sara asked.

"We've had a few small finds over the years." Greg stopped in the middle of a small cavern where there was more space to move around. "Back in the late 1800s, there weren't the big blasts like you might imagine. Instead, they would hand drill in a spiral fashion to bring down the rocks." Greg showed them an example in the wall. "There are tales of men finding deposits of silver the size of a grapefruit. Boys as young as seven earned seventy cents a day as powder monkeys to carry the dynamite into the mine, which, let me tell you, was good money back then."

"Sounds dangerous," Sara said.

"It was. And it was just as dangerous for the miners," Greg continued. "Most miners back then died before they were thirty-five from breathing in the granite dust, which is like glass on the lungs."

"That's awful!" Sara said.

"You don't have to worry about that today. We do regular oxygen checks to ensure they're safe, so you don't need to worry about anything other than watching your step and your head. That and stay out of the tunnels marked with the warning signs. Those areas of the mines aren't safe." Greg hit the beam above him with his fist. "Right here, though, it's solid as a rock."

Greg rushed on with his speech, clearly in his element. "At the height of the silver rush, over a hundred years ago, two brothers arrived from Europe and staked their claim in this very spot. Silver Peak became a boomtown overnight, driven by mines like this and the others dotting the area. They built up the town with large Victorian-style houses, shops for commerce, and even the opera house, where the educated brought music and plays to the stage during the long winter months. Silver Peak put itself on the map. Before long, people from all over came to jump on the bandwagon, certain they, too, would find their fortune. And some of them did. Others, unfortunately—most, in fact—ended up leaving with nothing. Which is why—"

The lights above them flickered. Greg paused. Seconds later, Sara screamed next to Sadie as the tunnel plunged into darkness.

2

SADIE FROZE IN THE DARKNESS OF THE CHILLY TUNNEL. SHE FELT behind her until her fingers touched the cold wall. Up until this moment, she hadn't minded the claustrophobic feel of the tunnels. Now, however, her instinct was to bolt. But bolting through the pitch-black passageway wasn't exactly an option.

"Hold on, ladies. There's nothing to worry about." Greg's voice pierced through the darkness. "Give me a second, and I'll get the lights back on in a jiffy."

"Sara?"

Sadie realized she wasn't at all worried about herself, but she had promised Alice she'd take care of her granddaughter. And she had assured Alice that hundreds of tourists explored these very tunnels every year, and that there was nothing for her to worry about.

Sara grabbed Sadie's hand. "I'm right here, Grandma."

"Are you all right?" Sadie asked.

"I'm fine, but it is creepy. Especially when you think about how they found that old skeleton in here."

Greg's flashlight clicked on, casting eerie shadows against the gray wall. Sadie shivered, agreeing with her granddaughter. Was this how Raymond felt the night he'd died? Had he been left to suffer in the total darkness while his murderer escaped? Maybe the scenario playing in her mind was melodramatic, but this definitely wasn't a place she wanted to be left alone and dying.

"Please stay exactly where you are for safety reasons until I get the lights back on." Greg's voice interrupted Sadie's thoughts. "It will just take a few seconds."

Greg was true to his word. Thirty seconds later, all the lights were back on again.

"Are the two of you all right?"

Sadie turned to Sara, who nodded.

"I'm sorry I screamed," Sara said, the relief evident on her face. "The moment the lights went out, something brushed up behind me. I thought... I thought it was a rat or something."

"I'm the one who should apologize," Greg said. "Normally, everyone wears headlights, but since this was going to be a quick tour, I thought the hard hats would be enough."

It was clear to Sadie from his pained expression that Greg was probably more upset over the incident than she or Sara were, though any lingering thoughts of glamour in regard to gold fever had completely evaporated from Sadie's mind.

"We have the occasional glitch in the lighting from time to time," Greg continued, "but please let me assure you that this isn't anything to worry about, as long as you obey the signs in the tunnels. I've verified the safety of the ones we use myself. But you will need to remember that not all the tunnels are safe. Men have been caught in a collapse in these tunnels in the past, and in the pitch darkness as you just saw, well, just take my word for it. Be careful and you'll be fine."

Sadie followed Sara and Greg toward the tunnel exit and felt a wave of relief wash over her.

"I couldn't help but think," Sadie said out loud, "how quickly we glamorize gold fever in novels and movies. But while some men might have made their fortunes here, the reality is that many, many more left empty-handed."

Sadie walked out into the bright morning sunshine beside Sara while Greg took a call on his cell phone. It wasn't the first time she'd wondered what it would have been like living in the late nineteenth century. The only problem was, while she definitely preferred the simpler things of life, she wasn't sure she was willing to trade in some of the perks of the twenty-first century. Which was one of the reasons she was perfectly content to be right here, in this town, in this century. Running the Antique Mine, active in her church, spending time with family and friends, and participating in an occasional project like this was enough to keep her both busy and fulfilled.

"Good news," Greg said, shoving his cell phone back into his pocket. "Looks like the cast and crew from *American Treasure Chest* are back on the road again. They'll be here in the next thirty to forty-five minutes."

Sadie turned to Sara and nodded. "Which should give us just enough time to finish organizing the props and costumes."

Fifty minutes later, the cast and crew joined Sadie, Greg, and Sara. Most arrived in rented vans to transport both the cast and the equipment, while two of the cast members pulled up in their own vehicles.

Sara stood beside Sadie as the director, Tom Wilson, a tall, energetic man with curly dark hair, took charge and made the introductions.

"Sadie, I'd like you to meet our cast. Just so you all know, Sadie Speers lives here in Silver Peak and has worked with me over the past few weeks as a consultant. She's here to ensure we get things right historically." He turned to the man standing beside him. "This is Darren Rogers. He'll be playing the part of Abigail's love interest, Raymond Butler."

Darren was tall, handsome, and suave in an expensive-looking dark suit. If everything she'd heard about Raymond was true, the man fit the part perfectly.

Sadie shook the man's hand. "It's nice to meet you, Darren."

"Caleb Waters will play the part of Philip Chaplin, Abigail's brother," the director continued.

While the man was somewhat older than Sadie had imagined him, his smile and hardy handshake convinced her he was going to be the one keeping the crew smiling when they were off camera.

"And last but not least is Nicole Fountain, who will play the part of Abigail Chaplin."

Sadie shook the woman's hand and smiled. "I'm so happy to meet you, Nicole."

"I'm excited to see the costumes you've come up with. The director told me you've done an amazing job."

Sadie smiled at the compliment. Nicole's face was fresh and makeup free, while her dark blonde hair had been pulled back in a ponytail. At the moment she wore a pair of skinny jeans and a pink T-shirt, but Sadie had found a number of outfits at a recent estate sale she'd attended that would transform her into a young woman from the fifties.

"We also have a number of cameramen who are busy unloading the van at the moment. Rob Tannehill is our tech man," Tom said, nodding at the man standing in the background, "and Mary Michaels rounds out the crew as our makeup artist."

Sara's eyes widened as she shook the director's hand. "It's nice to meet you, Tom."

"Sara is my granddaughter," Sadie began. "She was wondering if you needed extras for any of the scenes."

Tom rubbed his chin. "There are a few cameo parts for Abigail's sister, Ruth, and you are about the same age."

"Cool," Sara said, her voice barely above a whisper.

Sadie smiled down at her granddaughter's sudden shyness, thankful for her decision to let Sara come with her. She also noticed that Sara's phone, normally always in her granddaughter's hand, had vanished from sight. One would have thought Sara was meeting Steven Spielberg and not the director of a low-budget documentary TV series.

"This is fantastic," Nicole said inside the wood-framed house a few minutes later where Sadie and Sara had organized the vintage clothes on two long racks. "They're stunning."

"I was hoping you would like them," Sadie said. "I own an antique store, so a lot of my time is spent searching for antique furniture and collectibles. I was excited for the opportunity to search for a few pieces of vintage clothing."

Mary, the set's makeup artist, walked into the room with her silvery eye shadow, fake eyelashes, and southern accent that seemed out of place high up in the Rocky Mountains, but her smile was completely genuine, which was why Sadie couldn't help but be won over by the woman's charm.

"I can't wait to see the costumes y'all came up with," Mary drawled as she picked one of the dresses off the rack and held it up.

Sadie held her breath as she waited for the women's reaction to the burgundy satin dress with its black lace overlay and circle skirt.

"It's stunning," Mary said after a moment, looking at Nicole. "What do you think, Nicole?"

"I love it," echoed Nicole.

Sadie let out a sigh of relief at their reaction.

"Okay, people, we've got a tight schedule and two scenes to shoot today, and we're already running late." The director's voice boomed across the prop room, interrupting their conversation. "I want everyone ready for rehearsal in full costume and makeup in thirty minutes."

"Looks like we need to hurry then," Mary said, scooting Nicole into the makeup chair.

Twenty minutes later, the men were finished dressing—Philip in a tailored blazer and Raymond in a leather jacket and flattop, while Mary worked to finish Nicole's hair they'd decided to leave in a classic fifties ponytail. For the first scene, they'd chosen a simple floral dress for Nicole, with a flowing skirt and a pair of heels.

Sadie put a hand on her hip and turned to Sara, who had just tried on a dress for her role as Abigail's younger sister. "What do you think, Sara?"

Sara spun around in the red polka-dot dress with the full skirt Sadie had found for her, grinning from ear to ear. "It almost makes me wish I lived back in the fifties. I love these clothes."

In a few minutes, they'd rehearse their first scene, and while this was a nonspeaking role, and she would only be shot in the background, Sara clearly couldn't have been more excited.

"It might not be the most glamorous role," Sara gushed, "but Mia and my other friends are going to be so jealous when they find out what I'm getting to do. They're not going to believe I might be on a TV show."

"I saw the director speak with you briefly about your part," Sadie said, adjusting the skirt. "Do you know what you're supposed to do?"

"He said that essentially I'm the chaperone, though I'm not sure exactly what that means, except to sit quietly on a blanket, for example, in the picnic scene they're getting ready to shoot first."

"According to my research," Sadie explained, "Abigail Chaplin religiously read Amy Vanderbilt, the fifties authority on etiquette, and treated her advice like it came straight from the Bible. Which was why her younger sister often accompanied her and Raymond on their dates."

"Sounds awkward to me," Sara said, slipping into a pair of saddle oxfords.

"Perhaps in this day and age, but 'avoiding the appearance of evil' was a rule that many, including Abigail herself, took very seriously. And if you ask me, that's a rule that would do many good if it were followed today."

Sadie took one more glance at Sara, then fished a velvet pouch from her front pants pocket before pulling out the brooch she'd slipped into it before leaving the shop. "One more thing. I keep this on display at the shop, though it's not for sale. I decided to grab it when I knew you were coming with me. This was my mother's."

"Really?" Sara ran her fingers across the sterling-silver bow that had been covered in small crystals on the brooch. "It's beautiful."

"It's not worth a lot of money. Just sentimental value, but you're right. It is beautiful."

Sara reached up and gave her grandmother a hug. "Thank you."

"You're very welcome." Sadie took a step back and pinned it onto the bodice of Sara's dress. "I guess all I can say now is go break a leg, as they say in show biz."

Sadie sat in the background, watching the small cast rehearse the story of Abigail and Raymond while the cameramen decided the best angles, first on the lawn beneath the towering shadows of the Rocky Mountains, then in the small confines of the mine. Unlike Sara, she was quite sure she wouldn't enjoy being in front of the camera, but the behind-the-scenes process fascinated her. She'd spent the morning working with the clothes of the cast, and with the director, ensuring the props he wanted were in their rightful place.

Despite the crew's early flat tire that morning, the blackout in the cave, and more recently, a missing battery, rehearsals seemed to be going smoothly.

The backdrop for the first scene was stunning. Set up on a large, grassy field, they were surrounded by white-tipped mountains full of aspen trees and evergreens. In the forefront, Abigail and Raymond stood together looking into each other's eyes, while Abigail struggled to find the courage to agree to Raymond's proposal because of the opposition from her family.

"It's not that simple," she began, her gaze lowered. "My family has expectations of me, and now..."

"Are you telling me you don't love me, Abigail?" Raymond grasped her shoulders. "Because if that is true—"

"No. You know I love you. It's just that they don't approve of you. And..." Abigail took a step back, sobbing.

Raymond didn't look convinced. "Philip's a big boy, Abigail. And your family, all they want is for you to be happy. Isn't that what really matters in the end? That you and I are happy? We just need to give them some time. Once they get to know me better, they'll realize that we're perfect for each other."

"Abigail?"

She swung around at the sound of her name. "Philip?"

Abigail's brother stormed toward them, pulling them apart. "I thought our last conversation was clear, Abigail. Father told you to stop seeing this man. Did you think we wouldn't find out?"

Abigail's chest heaved. "I was going to tell you—all of you—but I just...I just didn't know how. You have to understand—"

"Understand what?" Philip shouted. "You don't even know this man, and you're so blinded that you can't see the truth. All he wants is your money."

"That's not true!" Raymond shouted.

Philip pulled out a gun and pointed it at Raymond, then tossed his sister his car keys. "Abigail, take Ruth to the car and drive back into town. I'm going to do what I should have done a long time ago."

"Philip, don't do this." Abigail grabbed on to Philip's arm, but he pulled away. "People can't control who they fall in love with."

Philip shoved her away, the gun still pointed at Raymond.

"Good," the director broke in. "Cut."

Sadie let out a deep whoosh of air as the director walked toward the actors, realizing she'd been holding her breath. While no one really knew what had happened that day at the mine—the day Raymond disappeared—the scriptwriters had taken Sadie's research and chosen this scenario as one of the options.

"Everyone on their feet," the director shouted. "Let's move inside the mine and block out the final fight scene between Philip and Raymond."

Sara ran up to Sadie, her cheeks flushed from excitement as the cast headed toward the mine. "I'm not in the next scene, but I'd like to watch."

"So would I," Sadie said.

They followed the group into the mines to the open cavern that gave just enough space to film the scene, and stood in the background beside Mary and Nicole. Five minutes into rehearsing the fight scene between Raymond and Philip, the lights in the tunnel dimmed.

The director turned to Rob, the tech intern. "What's wrong with the lights?"

Rob fidgeted with one of the bulbs. "Looks like the solar lights in the mine, but also one of our lights went out, sir."

The director dumped the script he held onto his chair. "If we can't get these lighting issues fixed, we're never going to get this shot filmed. Get what we need out of the supply van, so we can film this scene."

Sadie watched as the director continued blocking out the fight scene while Rob hurried to replace the light.

She turned to Sara. "What do you think about all of this?"

"It might not be Hollywood," Sara said, "but it's exciting to me."

Rob reappeared a few minutes later and stopped in front of the director, his head down. "I can't find the replacements, sir. We must have left them in Denver."

"You're not serious..." The director called a ten-minute break, then scrambled out of the mine with Rob following on his heels.

Mary let out a low whistle beside Sadie. "Sparks are about to fly."

"Maybe Abigail doesn't like having her story told," Nicole said on the other side of Mary.

"That sounds a little superstitious," Mary said, starting toward the exit of the mine with Nicole and Sadie following.

"Flat tires...burnt-out bulbs...not to mention that missing battery this morning," Nicole continued. "Maybe it's just the fact that we're shooting a scene near where they found a dead man, but the whole thing gives me the creeps."

"Me too, although I assume there's a perfectly logical explanation for every single one of those incidents," Sadie said.

"Maybe, but if I really were Abigail Chaplin, I'm not sure I'd be happy to have my story told," Nicole said.

Sadie stepped back into the sunshine with the other women to wait for the director to return—she hoped with the equipment he needed. The idea that Abigail herself didn't want her story told seemed silly, but the cast and crew had seemed plagued with problems since their arrival.

Loud voices around the corner caught Sadie's attention.

"What's going on?" Sadie asked.

The director rounded the corner with Rob.

"If we can't find a replacement in Silver Peak, we'll have to go back into Denver." The director shoved his hands into his pockets. "We're calling it quits for the day, but we'll start again at eight sharp in the morning. And Rob, if something like this ever happens again, you're fired."

"Yes, sir."

Sadie turned around to find Sara, realizing for the first time that she wasn't there. Which was strange. They'd been standing together inside the mine, watching the rehearsal of the fight scene.

"Sara?" Sadie called out.

"Is something wrong, Sadie?" Nicole asked.

"I'm not sure where my granddaughter is."

"She was with us inside."

"I know."

Sadie frowned. Surely she wasn't still inside the tunnels. The cameramen and the last of the crew had come out as the director and Rob had gone off looking for the light bulbs.

"Greg?" Sadie caught the attention of the mine owner. "You haven't switched off the lights inside the tunnels, have you? Sara was in the mine with us a few minutes ago for the filming, and now I can't find her."

"The lights are still on, but I thought everyone had come out." Greg glanced at the doorway into the tunnel. "But don't you worry, Sadie. If she is in there, she couldn't have gone far."

Someone screamed from inside the mine.

Sara?

Sadie felt her heart race, as she rushed into the chilly tunnel behind Greg. "Sara!"

The small caravan where they'd filmed was empty.

Where was she?

"Sara?"

Greg stopped in front of one of the *Do Not Enter* signs. "It sounds to me like she could be down this tunnel, but you'd better wait here, Sadie. One wrong step and the entire shaft could collapse."

3

Sadie waited at the entrance to the adjoining shaft, her heart frantic with worry. If anything happened to her granddaughter...

"Sara? Greg? What's happening? Have you found her, Greg?"

Several of the cast gathered around Sadie as she waited for a response.

Please, God, please. Let Sara be okay.

"I've got her, Sadie."

Sadie let out the breath she'd been holding in an abrupt *whoosh*. A moment later, Greg carried Sara from the blocked-off tunnel and out into the late afternoon sunlight, where he sat her down in one of the chairs the cast had been using.

Sadie's emotions quickly switched from fear to relief to frustration. "Sara, are you okay?"

Sara's gaze dropped. "I'm fine. I think. It's just my ankle."

"What were you doing, going down that blocked-off tunnel?"

"I'm sorry. I saw something, and I thought if I was careful and didn't go far..."

Sadie shook her head. "Not only did Greg tell us to stay together, but there is a sign here that clearly marked that it was dangerous. Do you know how many people have been injured in these mines?"

"I'm sorry." Tears formed in Sara's eyes as she tried to get up.

"Can you walk?" Sadie asked.

Sara took a tentative step. This time silent tears rolled down her cheeks. "I think I can."

"I'll run and get an ice pack from the kitchen up at the house," Nicole said.

"Thank you, Nicole. Then we need to get you back to town to see Doc Conroy and find out if it's broken."

"I'm sorry. I'm so sorry. I just thought—"

Sadie wrapped her arm around her granddaughter. "We'll worry about that later. For now, we need to make sure your ankle's okay and then we're both going to have some explaining to do to your mother."

Sadie forced herself to stay under the speed limit as she drove down the winding two-lane road toward Silver Peak with Sara beside her in the front seat, balancing a bag of ice on the injury. Her fingers gripped the steering wheel, trying not to focus on what could have happened. The list of accidents in the mine was as long as the history of mining itself. Back in 1884 the deaths of fifty-nine miners in Gunnison County had become the catalyst for the State of Colorado to pass legislation requiring mining companies to report accidents. That horrible loss had started with an explosion ignited by a lamp. Throughout the years, fire, water, explosions, and caving in of shafts for starters had taken their toll on the miners risking their lives for the chance to strike it rich.

She shifted into lower gear as the road took a sharp curve to the left. Injuries in the mines weren't only problems of the past. Just last fall three people had died from carbon monoxide poisoning, which was a by-product of the explosives used in the mines.

Thankfully, Sara's injury wasn't life-threatening, but that didn't mean Sadie wasn't concerned. Even though she didn't think Sara's ankle was broken, it had started to swell and Sadie wasn't going to take any chances. Simply icing it and waiting until morning as someone had suggested wasn't an option. Against her better judgment, she'd also called Alice. Knowing Alice the way she did, she knew her daughter would be worrying right now, but if she was going to be upset anyway, it would be better to have her at the doctor's so she could get the report firsthand.

"I am sorry, Grandma." Sara's words broke through Sadie's rambling thoughts.

"I know." Sadie's gaze shifted briefly at her granddaughter. "How's the pain?"

"It hurts, but I don't think it's broken."

"We'll have to let Doc make that judgment, though I hope you're right."

Sara sank back into the seat. "Did you call my mom?"

"I called while Nicole was getting you the pack of ice. She was at the Antique Mine, filling in for Julie, who had an appointment to take her twin sons to the dentist for cleanings. Your mom was with a customer, but she'll close up shop as soon as she's done and meet us at Doc Conroy's office."

Sara's fingers gripped the armrest. "What did she say?"

"Not much. She's worried, but I assured her that you're okay, and it's probably nothing more than a sprain."

"Trust me. She'll have plenty to say once I'm there. Especially when she realizes I was where I wasn't supposed to be."

"She's your mom, and moms worry about their kids. But no matter what happened, your well-being will be her first concern."

"I know, and that's why I'm so sorry about this. I wasn't paying attention. I thought I saw something flash down the tunnel and I wanted to take a look. I didn't expect it to be so slippery and uneven."

Sadie felt some of her frustration begin to melt away. "I remember what it was like to be fourteen and curious. And to be honest, that curiosity has never gone away."

It was that same curiosity—combined with an empathetic nature—that had compelled her more than once to seek out the truth in a situation. A truth she always hoped would in turn uncover God's light and ultimately bring hope and healing. Sara just needed to curb that curiosity with a little common sense.

Sadie caught her granddaughter's frown and wondered how she could convince her of that truth.

"I suppose if Theo had been up there with us," Sara began, "he wouldn't have gotten himself into trouble."

Sadie slowed down as the speed limit dropped coming into town. "I love your brother, and thoroughly enjoy spending time with him, but like the rest of us, he's not perfect either."

Sara's frown deepened. "He's close enough to perfect."

"What does that mean?"

"He gets good grades, he's awesome at sports. Even the girls think he's *all that.*"

Sadie laughed. "And what would *all that* mean?"

"You know. He's tall and has that hair that flops into his face so he has to push it out of the way. Mom wants to cut it off, but trust me. The girls love it. They're always calling him and texting him..."

Sadie hesitated, uncertain how far she should push. "Is that a hint of jealousy I'm hearing?"

"I suppose, because then there's me. You know? Braces and strawberry-blonde hair that never looks right."

"Fourteen isn't always an easy age, but I promise it will get better. And besides, I love you just the way you are, Sara Macomb."

"You have to." Sara let out a soft laugh. "You're my grandmother."

"True enough, but I still mean what I say."

Sadie drove into the city limits and headed toward Main Street, where she pulled into the small parking lot outside Doc Conroy's office. The lights were still on even though it was just past closing.

Sara hesitated before opening the car door. "I have a feeling my mom isn't going to let me go back to the mine."

"That's up to your mother." While Sadie loved being a grandmother, one thing she believed strongly was that she should never interfere with her daughter's parenting. "Though there were certain rules—"

"I know, and I am sorry."

Sadie reached over and squeezed Sara's hand. "As far as I'm concerned, you're forgiven."

Sadie went around to the other side of the car to help Sara out. She grabbed the ice pack, then wrapped her arm around her granddaughter's waist. "Do you think you can make it, or do I need to find someone who can carry you?"

"I think I can make it."

At the door of the small reception room, Rita Dodd, Doc's receptionist, shuffled them into the clinic with a broad smile on her face. Sadie had known Rita since high school, and while she'd never married, she clearly loved mothering the patients who came into the clinic. She also loved buying different colors and styles of eyeglasses. This week, she peered out over the top of a pair of red plaid, horn-rim glasses. "It's a good thing you called when you did, Sadie. We were just getting ready to close up."

Sara winced. "I'm sorry to keep you from going home, Miss Dodd."

"Not a problem at all." Rita's voice softened as she helped Sara hobble toward the back of the reception area. "Can't have one of my favorite patients in pain, now can we? How are you doing, darlin'?"

"My ankle hurts pretty bad, but I think it'll be okay. The ice has helped."

"You did the right thing coming in." Rita smiled at Sara, who seemed to relax slightly. She'd always had a knack of putting nervous patients at ease. "Doc's back in the examination room, ready to take a look at you."

Sadie had known Dr. Tom Conroy, or "Doc" as everyone called him, for as long as she could remember. He had delivered Alice, while his father had delivered Sadie. His daughter, Lucy, had followed the family profession, and now lived in Boulder and had a family medical practice there.

"Oh my." The friendly physician, with his silver hair and green eyes, was pushing seventy, but from the way he acted you'd never know it. He helped Sara onto the examination table and frowned. "What happened here, young lady?"

"I think it's just twisted," Sara said as she scooted back on the table, tears pooling in her eyes.

"We were up in the mines working on the documentary," Sadie began explaining. "Sara slipped and twisted her ankle pretty badly. We're hoping it isn't broken."

"Well, you wouldn't be the first person who was injured up in those tunnels. A century ago, things were a whole lot more dangerous up there. Thankfully, nowadays, things like tunnels collapsing and poisonous gases escaping are far more rare, though I remember the last serious accident in a Colorado mine."

"I remember that one too," Sadie said. "Over in Pitkin back in the early 1980s. Fifteen were killed in that accident."

"That's terrible," Sara said.

"It was terrible. Affected a lot of families. But . . . " Doc chuckled. "I definitely think you'll survive this one. Let's take off your sock and have a look." Sara winced as Doc slid off her sock.

He studied her ankle, then asked, "Did you know that around twenty-five thousand people sprain their ankles every day?"

Sara's eyes widened. "Twenty-five thousand? Every day?"

"Crazy, isn't it?" Doc started slowly moving her foot. "How did it feel walking on it?"

"It hurt pretty bad, though I could still walk."

"Sara?" Alice rushed into the room. The exam room door swung back and hit the wall behind them. "Rita let me in and told me you were back here. Are you okay?"

"Mom." Sara rolled her eyes, clearly embarrassed. "It's nothing, really. I just twisted it."

"If you give me another couple of minutes, I'll be able to tell you exactly what's wrong with it," Doc said. "Does that hurt?"

A minute later, Doc was done with the exam. He stood back, folded his arms across his chest, and looked at Alice. "The good news is, the ankle isn't broken, but I still recommend staying off it as much as possible. You should also ice it for twenty to thirty minutes three or four times a day until the swelling and pain is gone. If you have any more issues, or feel like it's not healing, come back and see me."

"And the bad news?" Alice asked.

Doc shot Alice a wink. "Who said there was bad news?"

"I thought..."

"Give it a couple days, and she'll be back to normal again, I promise." Doc scribbled a few notes into Sara's chart, then flipped it shut. "And in the meantime, I'll wrap it and give you some medicine for the swelling. But she's going to be fine."

"Thanks, Doc. I appreciate your staying late to see her," Alice said, the relief clear on her face as the doctor wrapped Sara's ankle.

"There," Doc said, standing up. "Alice, why don't you go ahead and help Sara put her sock back on. The shoe is optional, though probably better kept off for the next day or two."

Doc followed Sadie and Rita back into the reception room.

"I've heard quite a lot of talk about that documentary TV series they're filming," Rita said. "Most people think it will bring in extra tourists to Silver Peak, which certainly won't hurt the town."

"You're probably right," Sadie said. "You know how popular those kinds of shows are these days."

"I know I have a couple favorites I watch from time to time," Rita confessed, taking Sara's folder from the doctor and refiling it in the wooden cabinet.

"This one is looking at America's buried treasures," Sadie said.

Doc tapped a pen against his prescription pad on the counter and shook his head. "I often wonder what my father would think about how much life has changed over the past few decades. Even I have a hard time keeping up. Between technology, computers, and the Internet, now people want to read good old-fashioned books via some electronic-fangled device."

Sadie laughed. "I admit to having a laptop and a smartphone, but even I'm not ready to give up my books, Doc."

Rita shut the file cabinet and turned back around. "I heard that crew has had quite a few mishaps since their arrival."

How fast news travels! she thought, though she really shouldn't be surprised. News seemed to be almost instantaneous in small towns. "There have been a few issues."

"I read about it on the *Chatterbox*," Rita continued. "From flat tires to technical issues, and now Sara—"

"Sara's mishap is on the *Chatterbox*?" Sadie laughed. Sara might be getting more exposure than she'd intended.

"Oh no," Rita said. "There isn't anything about Sara on the blog, and I doubt whoever writes it would write about a minor."

Sadie turned back to Doc. "You said your father delivered Abigail. He must have known the family. Did your father ever talk about what happened up there when Raymond disappeared?"

Doc's eyes twinkled. "How old do you think I am, Sadie Speers?"

"You know, I'm not even going there, Doc," Sadie said.

"I'm teasing. I was still a boy the summer Raymond disappeared, though I do admit I remember the adults whispering about some scandal up in the mines that apparently little ears didn't need to hear."

"Did you believe that what they thought happened?" Sadie asked.

"I don't think anyone ever really knew what actually happened. Which makes it perfect fodder for speculation when you add together a romance with a missing person and now a dead body."

A minute later, Sadie, Alice, and Sara said good night. Rita locked the door after them and changed the sign in the window to Closed.

Alice turned to her daughter. "I still am not sure how this happened, Sara. I thought those mines were safe with all of the tourists coming through."

"It's just a sprain, Mom."

Alice frowned. "Humor me. I like details."

Sara limped to the end of the sidewalk to lean against the car before glancing at Sadie, then back at her mom. "I wandered off the main tunnel into a shaft that's closed to the public."

Alice's brow furrowed. "Wasn't it marked with some sort of sign?"

Sara hesitated. "Yes."

Despite her granddaughter's choices, Sadie felt a sliver of guilt slide through her. She *had* promised to look after her granddaughter.

"And you went down there anyway?" Alice asked.

"I'm sorry, Mom. I was just curious. I thought I saw something flash down the passageway. It wasn't too far, and I was—"

"Curious." Her mother finished the statement for her. "In case you've forgotten, curiosity killed the cat. Do you realize how dangerous those mines can be? Do you know how many people have died falling into a collapsed mine shaft?"

"But I didn't, Mom. Doc said I'd be fine after a few days. And besides, it wasn't the mine. I was clumsy and tripped."

"Because you were somewhere you weren't supposed to be."

"Alice—" Sadie started.

"We'll talk more at home, Sara. Get in the car please." Alice rubbed the back of her neck as if trying to rub away a headache. "I want to talk to your grandmother."

Alice turned to Sadie after Sara had slid into the car, clearly unhappy. "I'm overreacting, aren't I?"

"Tough day?"

"Sort of." Alice shoved her hands into the backs of her jeans pockets. "Theo told me that his father went on a date. Which is fine, really, but it just . . . rubbed me wrong. And yes, I know I worry too much about my kids and can definitely be overprotective."

Sadie felt a stab of sadness for her daughter. Her marriage had ended, leaving Alice with anything but the fairy-tale ending all mothers want for their little girls. Sadie had always liked Cliff, Alice's ex-husband, but to this day, she'd never understood how he'd given up his family so easily. Thankfully, the divorce had been amicable and Cliff lived in Denver, close enough to be able to see the kids. But even with her ex-husband's support, raising children in this day and age was difficult.

And Alice wasn't the only overprotective mother.

"All mothers worry." Sadie smiled. "Trust me."

"I try not to. Really, but sometimes raising teenagers isn't like when I was a teenager. I spent my summers reading books and going to the library or hanging out at the Depot with my friends eating ice cream."

"I'll be the first to admit that you have a tougher job than I did."

"Today, they prefer texting, video games, and shopping. You have to worry about online predators and who they might run into on social media."

"That might all be true, but Sara and Theo are good kids, Alice. They might not always make the right choices, but they have a growing faith, and they are respectful, well-adjusted kids."

"I know, but I still worry." Alice let out a deep sigh. "Life doesn't always turn out exactly the way one plans."

"You could consider dating." Sadie threw out the suggestion, knowing her daughter would more than likely dismiss it.

Alice laughed. "I feel far too old to start dating again."

"I'm sixty-two and it hasn't stopped me."

"Touché, Mom."

"All I'm saying," Sadie continued, "is that I can think of a couple single men in town who, if given the right encouragement, might decide to make their feelings known." Sadie knew her daughter probably wasn't ready to start dating again, but surely a little nudge now and then couldn't hurt.

Alice blushed. "Mom. Stop."

"That's all I'm going to say on that subject. But back to Sara, don't be too hard on her. It's a sprained ankle. She's going to be fine."

Alice looked up and caught Sadie's gaze. "I'm sure you're right, but I'm still not sure I want her back up there."

"At the moment, I think she needs to take Doc's advice and stay off of it for the next few days, which might solve the issue of her returning without your having to tell her she can't go. Natural consequences often work the best."

Alice nodded at Sadie's advice.

"Let her rest tomorrow in order to give the swelling a chance to go down, and after we're done filming, if it's not too late, I'll come by and pick her up," Sadie offered. "Maybe take her out for ice cream. I really enjoyed spending the day with her and was looking forward to the rest of the week together."

"I know Sara would enjoy that." Alice reached for the car handle, then paused. "I know you're right about all of this, but don't you think the whole idea of finding a skeleton in the backdrop of those dark tunnels and a deserted mine is sort of creepy?"

Sadie felt an involuntary shiver race up her spine. "There was a glitch in the lights today while we were in the tunnels, and I have to admit, at that moment, I felt pretty uneasy."

Alice bit the edge of her lip as if she were trying to decide if she should continue with her train of thought.

"What is it?" Sadie asked.

"Probably nothing, but when I was helping Sara put her sock back on, she told me that there had been a number of strange things happen up at the mine today—the lights you just mentioned included. She said she overheard comments made by the cast about Abigail not wanting her story told."

"You know as well as I do that there is no truth in a statement like that, especially considering the fact that Abigail is dead." Sadie shook her head. "Trust me, it was nothing more than a few odd...coincidences."

"Or sabotage," Alice threw out. "Someone was murdered up in those mines and the murderer was never caught. Maybe someone doesn't want the truth to come out over what happened the night Raymond disappeared."

"You read too many mystery novels," Sadie said, laughed, then hugged her daughter good night and headed for her car to go home. She'd meant it when she told Sara that the sheriff was the one who had to discover the truth, but that didn't mean she could completely dismiss the questions rising to the surface. But the glitches up at the mine were nothing more than a string of coincidences. Because why would anyone want to sabotage the documentary? Surely there was no reason to cover up a murder that took place over half a century ago.

4

SADIE PARKED HER CAR IN THE SMALL GRAVEL LOT OUTSIDE the mine the next day, disappointed Sara hadn't been able to come with her. She'd called Alice before leaving town, who told her that Sara had slept fine and the swelling in her ankle was down. Thankfully, she should be back to normal in the next few days.

Sadie swung her purse over her shoulder, then tried to balance the two boxes of goodies she'd picked up on her way.

"Hi, Sadie. Let me help you with that." Nicole slammed the door shut on the car, two slots down, and hurried over to help.

"Thanks, Nicole."

"I'm not sure what you have stashed in here," Nicole said, taking one of the boxes, "but it smells heavenly."

"There seems to be plenty of snacks on hand for the cast and crew, but I thought you all might appreciate these. I asked Luz Vidal, from Arbuckle's Coffee in town, to whip up an extra batch of cinnamon rolls so I could bring them in this morning."

Hector and Luz Vidal ran Arbuckle's Coffee, a small coffee shop next door to the Antique Mine. It had become one of Sadie's favorite places to grab a cup of coffee and something sweet, though the constant temptation wasn't good for her waistline if she wasn't careful. It didn't help that there was a door between the two shops.

"Wow, these smell heavenly. I think you're about to make a bunch of friends for life." Nicole headed with Sadie toward the old wood-framed house. "How is Sara doing, Sadie?"

Sadie appreciated the younger woman's interest in her granddaughter. "She's feeling better today. Thank you for asking. I think she'll be completely back to normal in a few days."

"I feel sorry for her having to miss the rest of the filming. I know she was so excited about it. In fact," Nicole said, starting up the porch steps, "she reminds me a lot of myself when I first started in the business. Full of energy, and in awe over everything. And perhaps convinced she'll be discovered, as well."

"Discovered like you?" Sadie asked.

"Hardly." She waved a dismissive hand. "My résumé consists of a few parts you'll only see if you watch infomercials in the middle of the night, along with a couple of cameo shots in films where even my mom can't tell it's me."

Sadie stopped on the rambling porch and laughed. "So this is your first big break?"

"If you can call it that." This time, Nicole was the one to laugh. "Not that they were knocking at my door, nor will I be up for an Oscar, but there was something about Abigail's story that tugged at me when I read the script."

Sadie could see Nicole's emotional connection to the part thirty minutes later when she—as Abigail—tried to stop Philip and Raymond in their fight scene inside the mine. Thankfully, Rob had managed to source what was necessary for the lighting, which meant that things were going smoother than yesterday in regard to technical difficulties.

"Perfect." The director called cut, then slid off his chair. "Take a ten-minute break, people."

Nicole hurried over to where Sadie had stood watching, her full skirt rustling with each step inside the cold tunnel. "Sadie, the next scene is the one where Raymond gives me the brooch, but I can't find it anywhere."

"That's strange. I know Sara went through the list of jewelry yesterday afternoon, and everything was there."

Sadie started with Nicole out of the mine toward the wood-framed house and slipped off the sweater she'd worn while inside. The sun shone brightly today, a stark contrast to the low temperatures inside the mine.

At the house, Sadie searched for the vintage red glass brooch with diamonds from back in the twenties among the other jewelry. According to the script, Abigail often wore the piece that had been a gift from Raymond, and it was supposed to be worth quite a lot of money. Sadie had found the brooch Nicole was supposed to wear at an estate sale a few months ago. It wasn't worth nearly as much as the original, but the match was close.

According to the photos and notes Sadie had from her research, Abigail had clearly adapted a look that tended to be more formal and tailored than fashion was today. Sadie knew how important it was for women in the fifties to dress like ladies, which to them meant elegant and sophisticated. And which was exactly how Sadie was attempting to dress Nicole for the role with tailored suits and full pleated skirts. For one scene, she'd even found a full-length gown with elbow-length gloves and jewelry to complete the outfit.

But where was the brooch for today's scene?

"Mary." Sadie turned to the makeup artist, who was looking at shoes with Nicole for the next scene. "Have you seen the brooch Nicole is supposed to wear with the burgundy and black number?"

Sadie kept looking through the leather travel jewelry box that had made transporting the jewelry easier and was supposed to help keep the pieces together and organized. But there was no sign of the brooch.

"Here it is." Nicole said a minute later, holding up the brooch. "It must have fallen into the shoe box."

Sadie let out a sigh of relief.

"Just in time," Mary said. "Because we need to quickly get your makeup freshened up."

Sadie closed up the jewelry box. Keeping an inventory, as she'd learned from her own shop, was important. And in this situation, because she was using items from a number of other sources, it was especially crucial. Having Sara here yesterday had been a huge help in keeping things organized. Maybe Alice would consider letting Sara return tomorrow if she was feeling better.

A scream from across the room jerked Sadie from her thoughts.

"Nicole?"

Nicole stood frozen in front of the dressing mirror, clutching a piece of paper between her fingers. Even with the makeup she was wearing for in front of the TV camera, her face had paled to a chalky white. She fell back onto the wooden seat behind her and let the paper she'd been holding flutter to the floor.

"Nicole?" Sadie grabbed the young woman's hand. Her pulse was racing like a jackhammer. "Nicole, what's wrong?"

"It's . . . it's a warning."

Sadie reached down to pick up the piece of paper Nicole had dropped and read the brief message.

Stop filming or someone else will get hurt. Abigail

"What is this?" Mary asked.

"Some kind of warning," Nicole said, her voice shaky.

"Where did you find it?" Sadie asked.

"It was…it was taped to the mirror of my dressing table. I noticed it just now when I started to sit down."

Sadie looked up to the mirror, where remnants of tape were still adhered, then glanced back to reread the letter.

Stop filming or someone else will get hurt.

"Who's it from?" Mary asked.

"From her," Nicole added, her hands shaking in her lap.

"Who?"

"Abigail. Who else?"

"From Abigail." Mary took the letter from Sadie. "How is that possible? The woman's been dead for over a decade."

Nicole was still shaking. "Then you tell me why it's signed by Abigail."

"I'm sure it's simply someone's idea of a stupid prank," Sadie offered.

"Well, I for one don't think it's funny," Nicole said.

"I certainly agree."

Nicole reached back to rub her neck. "I never should have taken on this role. She doesn't want us here. Doesn't want us poking around in whatever happened that night."

"That's ridiculous," Mary countered.

"Ridiculous?" Nicole shook her head. "Just yesterday I jokingly said that it seemed as if someone was sabotaging the documentary. The flat tire. Technical issues. Sara's injury. And now this? You can't tell me it's ridiculous."

Sadie stood between the two women asking the same questions Alice had asked yesterday. She might not believe that Abigail had actually written the note, but someone had. Which possibly put a different light on what had been going on. Were the technical issues coincidences or intentional? Still, Sara's injury wasn't enough to stop the documentary, and to think it had anything to do with covering up a murder that happened decades ago seemed silly.

"What's going on?" Director Wilson entered the room and addressed Nicole. "I'm ready to shoot today's last scene, and you're not even changed. We're already behind schedule after yesterday's problems. I need you on set now."

"There's been a development you should know about." Sadie crossed the room and handed the note to the director.

"A development?"

"'*Stop filming or someone else will get hurt*'?" The director read the paper out loud, then shook his head. "Who wrote this?"

"It's signed Abigail," Sadie said. She could hear the doubt in her voice even as she spoke.

"I can read that, but why? Is this supposed to be some kind of joke?"

"More than likely," Sadie said. "Nicole found it on her dressing table."

"It's not a joke," Nicole said. "It's a warning."

The director frowned. "To even consider that Abigail wrote this note is ridiculous, and you all know it. Someone's probably having a good laugh over your reaction right now."

"And what if they're not? What if someone really does want us to stop filming? What if someone else gets hurt?" Nicole took a deep breath. "Then what? This place is already creepy enough with dead bodies, dark tunnels, and unsolved murders."

"It's a TV documentary, Nicole." The director's frown deepened. "Most of the script is based on nothing more than speculation over what might have happened. Someone heard your comments yesterday and thought they'd have some fun. Besides, everyone involved in this story is dead."

"Like I said earlier." Nicole glanced at the director, her expression dead serious. "Maybe Abigail herself doesn't want us doing this."

"Nicole. I know you're upset, but you can't honestly tell me you believe that."

"All I know is that there's been a lot of weird things going on around the set." Nicole continued, "Technical issues with lights and batteries, Sara's injury, and now this? What am I supposed to think?"

Sadie tried to look at the matter objectively as the two clashed over their opinions of who had left the note. Nothing that had happened seemed to be enough to stop the filming, but whether Nicole truly thought Abigail had really written the warning, one thing was clear. The young woman was scared.

"I'm not sure who's behind this, but one thing I can guarantee is that this note isn't from Abigail." The director crumpled the note between his fingers and thrust it into the plastic trash can. "Someone is trying to scare you."

"Well, if that's what they wanted, they succeeded." Nicole's gaze slipped to the crumpled note. "I need to get some air."

The director flung up his hands as she ran out of the house. "This is crazy. We have a show to shoot."

Sadie reached into the trash can for the letter. The entire scenario might sound ridiculous, but she wasn't sure they should simply brush away the warning.

"That's evidence the sheriff might need," Mary stated matter-of-factly.

"Evidence?" the director countered. "It's a stupid prank."

"And if it's not?" Sadie asked.

She and Mary both looked to the director for an answer. He let out a sharp sigh.

"Please don't tell me that you're falling for this nonsense. We're reenacting a sixty-year-old crime. Almost everyone connected with Abigail and Raymond is dead by now, and I certainly don't believe in ghosts, which means this is a prank."

"All the same, I think we need to call the sheriff and let him make that decision," Mary said.

"Call the sheriff?" The director shook his head. "If I called the sheriff every time someone played a prank on the set, they'd have started ignoring me a long time ago. Clearly someone overheard Nicole and decided to have a little fun."

"Maybe so," Mary said, "but it's not our call. The paper might hold evidence."

"Evidence of a practical joke that is costing me time and money." The director started toward the door. "I appreciate your concern for the crew, but if the sheriff starts asking people a bunch of questions, it will imply that there's some nut on the loose and the entire cast will be worried."

Mary took a step toward the door. "That might be true, but even you have to admit that there have been some rather...odd things since the filming started."

Sadie had to agree. She might not believe Nicole's version, but should they simply dismiss the letter as a joke?

The director's shoulders dropped. "Fine. I'll call the sheriff, but we aren't going to let this letter stop the filming."

"What about Nicole?" Sadie looked toward the open door. "Maybe we should hold off shooting for a little while. Give her a chance to calm down."

"Absolutely not. Which means that one of you better talk some sense into her, because we have another scene to rehearse and shoot before the end of the day."

Sadie looked outside to where Nicole had run off. "Let me try. The note just scared her. I'm sure she'll be fine if we give her a few minutes to calm down."

"I'll give you fifteen."

Sadie walked out into the bright afternoon sunlight, hoping that the connection she'd felt early with Nicole was enough to talk some sense into the girl. Nicole was only a few years older than Sara, and Sadie understood that emotions could be difficult to control in a young woman. The note probably would have upset Sadie at her age, as well.

She started down the path looking for where Nicole might have gone, thankful for her sturdy shoes. A few clouds had settled in against the Rockies in the distance. By nightfall, the temperature would drop, but for now the warm sun felt good on her face.

The questions stirring in the back of her mind wouldn't stop. *Who would have had a reason to leave a warning note to the cast and why? Was it just a prank as the director insisted, or was it something more serious? And was it connected somehow to Sara's accident yesterday?* The very thought seemed ridiculous. There might have been a number of strange events happen over the past few days, but most of them—on their own—could be explained away as accidents.

All except for the letter.

Sadie found Nicole halfway to the mine, sitting on a large rock that overlooked the tree-filled valley below, and shoved away the questions for the moment. Sadie took a deep breath and prayed that God would give her the words to say.

"Nicole?"

Her eyes were red as if she'd been crying. She blew her nose into a tissue, then shoved it back into her pocket.

"I guess you won the short straw," Nicole finally said.

"To come find you?"

Nicole nodded.

"I wanted to come. To make sure you're okay."

"It was a stupid note. A prank, I'm sure. I don't know why I overreacted."

"You have every right to be upset."

"You really think so?"

"Definitely."

Nicole didn't look convinced. "I think at this point I'm mainly embarrassed."

"That's understandable, as well."

"But you don't think Abigail had anything to do with this..." Nicole shook her head. "Never mind. You don't have to answer that. It's just that this experience has been strange. When I took the job, that's all it was, a job. Now I want to know what she was thinking, and what really happened that night. When I put on one of those dresses, it's like stepping back into another century. It's like I'm her."

"It shows in your performance. You've connected with the character. That's what great actresses do."

"Yes, but maybe I've gotten too close to the situation. Abigail was my age. Knowing that makes me wonder what I would have done in her situation. In love with a man my family didn't approve of. Not knowing who I should listen to. She had to be scared and alone, not knowing who to talk to." Nicole drew in a sharp breath, then let it out slowly. "So what do we do now? Ignore the warning?"

"I agree with the director that it's probably just a prank, but I don't think we should simply ignore it. I'll make sure the sheriff knows what is going on. And in the meantime, I'll try to see what I can find out as well."

Nicole looked up and caught Sadie's gaze. "Do you think this was nothing more than a prank to scare us?"

"Honestly, I'm not sure. Why try to stop the filming? It doesn't make sense. The murder took place decades ago, and it was so long ago that most of those involved are dead."

"Which means it was just a prank to scare me."

Sadie wished she could give Nicole a definitive answer, but for now, there was nothing she could do but to encourage her to push through the rest of the day and get her job done, she hoped with the same amount of focus and passion she'd demonstrated so far.

"The director is ready to shoot the next scene. Can you do that?" Sadie asked.

Nicole slapped her hands against her thighs and nodded. "I'll need to change, and I'm sure my makeup will need a touch-up."

Sadie smiled. "Maybe just a bit."

Nicole wiped some of the smudged mascara from under her eyes with the back of her hand. "Thank you."

"For what?" Sadie asked.

"For listening, and not thinking that my reaction was totally crazy."

Sadie smiled. "You're not crazy. Forget about the note for now. You're needed on the set."

They'd just finished shooting the last scene of the day, when Sadie saw Sheriff Slattery drive up in his sheriff's car. Sheriff Mac Slattery and his wife, Anita, had moved to Silver Peak a few years ago after he'd retired from his job on the Denver Police force. According to Anita, the opening for the sheriff's position had appealed to both of them, since they were looking for a slower way of life.

Which was exactly what the sheriff and his wife found. Because of Silver Peak's low crime rate, Sheriff Slattery ended up spending much of his time searching for lost hikers on the mountain and helping stranded motorists.

Officer Kenmore, who had once been one of Sadie's students, slipped out of the passenger side and joined the sheriff, hands on his holster as he walked toward her as if he were investigating a murder, not a possible prank. It was hard to remember sometimes that Kyle wasn't a squirrely senior itching for the lunch bell in Sadie's Introduction to Business class anymore, but a sworn officer for the State of Colorado.

"Sadie Speers." Sheriff Slattery smiled as he shook Sadie's hand. "I was surprised by the director's call, considering most everyone involved in Raymond's disappearance is dead."

"It's probably nothing, but there have been a few strange things happen since filming started," Sadie said, hoping this wasn't going to turn into a bigger issue than it should be. She reached out to shake Officer Kenmore's hand. "Good to see you, Kyle."

"It's always better to be safe than sorry," Officer Kenmore said, reassuring her hesitation.

The three of them started walking toward the wood-framed house where the crew was putting away the equipment and costumes for the day.

"I understand that one of the cast members received a threatening letter," Sheriff Slattery began.

Sadie stopped to pull the letter from her pocket and handed it to the sheriff. "I think most of the crew believes it's a prank to scare Nicole. A joke that backfired. It really scared her."

"You've been around the cast and crew the past few days. What do you think?" the sheriff asked.

Sadie hesitated before giving her answer. "Honestly, I'm not sure, but there have been a number of things happen that individually, one wouldn't think anything about. But collectively, one starts to wonder."

"Such as?" Officer Kenmore prodded.

Sadie drew in a deep breath of mountain air that was beginning to cool as the sun dropped. "A flat tire and a number of equipment issues. Then last night, Sara sprained her ankle pretty badly. Granted, she was in one of the restricted tunnels, but when you add to that a threatening letter . . ."

"I can understand the concern," the sheriff said. "Has anyone mentioned seeing someone hanging around who shouldn't be here?"

Sadie shook her head. “Not that I know of. The crew and cast are small. They shut down the tours for the week. The tour guides are still here, using the free time to do some repairs.”

“So anyone who showed up on the set unannounced would be noticed?” Officer Kenmore asked.

Sadie nodded.

Officer Kenmore turned to the sheriff. “Well, at least that narrows down the suspect list.”

“Yes, but it still doesn’t make any sense.” Sadie shrugged. “What’s the motivation?”

“Maybe it is a prank,” Officer Kenmore said. “Someone trying to scare Nicole, and they didn’t expect anyone to call in the sheriff.”

“I hope you’re right,” Sadie said.

“We’ll look into this, talk with the mine employees along with the cast to see if anyone saw anything. I can also check to see what fingerprints might be on the paper, but I’m not sure I’ll find anything.”

“I understand.” Sadie knew that finding out who’d left the letter would be difficult if not impossible, but she was still glad they were willing to at least investigate the matter.

“In the meantime,” the sheriff said, “call me if anything else strange happens.”

“You know I will, Sheriff.” Sadie nodded, praying that all of this was simply a prank, and not—as the letter implied—something far more sinister.

5

SADIE FOUND ALICE BURIED IN A MYSTERY NOVEL ON THE FRONT porch of her house, outside Silver Peak. She was happy to see her daughter take some time off to relax. So much of Alice's time was spent teaching elementary school, keeping up the house as a single mom and, of course, raising two teenagers.

Sadie walked across the porch that overlooked the big front yard bordered by a long row of evergreen trees. "Alice?"

Alice jumped in her chair, then pressed her hand against her heart. "Mother! I didn't hear you walk up."

"I'm sorry." Sadie laughed as she slid onto the padded chair beside her. "I didn't mean to startle you."

Alice's auburn hair and green eyes, both legacies from her father, shone in the late afternoon sunlight that filtered through the trees. "The heroine had just stepped into a trap, baited by the villain, when I realized someone—you—were standing over me."

"Sounds almost as exciting as my day," Sadie said.

"What happened?"

Sadie had debated whether or not she should share what had happened with Alice, not wanting her daughter to worry. But knowing how fast news traveled in Silver Peak, it would more than likely be on the *Chatterbox* blog by morning and then all of the town would know about the letter.

"It was probably nothing more than a prank," Sadie began. "But a warning note was left on one of the actor's dressing tables."

"What did it say?"

Sadie hesitated with her response. "Stop filming or someone else will get hurt."

"Someone else . . . like Sara?" Alice's frown deepened.

"Most people think it's just a prank by one of the cast or crew members."

"It doesn't sound like a prank to me. Sara was injured up there—"

"Which is why I called the sheriff to investigate, just in case," Sadie said, wanting to play down the situation. "But I'm sure when all of this is over, we'll discover it was nothing more than someone's bad practical joke."

"Maybe." Alice didn't look convinced.

"Which reminds me," Sadie said. "How is Theo's class going?"

Alice tapped on the edge of her book. "Changing the subject, Mom?"

Sadie shot her daughter a smile. "Yes, I am."

"It's going very well, actually. Theo has really stepped up and is working hard on this class. I'm proud of him." Alice jutted her chin toward the street. "Speaking of Theo . . . "

Theo pulled into the driveway in T.R.'s convertible, turned off the engine, and jumped out of the vehicle.

"You're home early, Theo," Alice said as Theo sprinted across the yard toward the porch.

"My teacher let us out so we can work on the new assignment he gave us today, an ancient civilization timeline." Theo set down his backpack, then kissed Sadie on the cheek. "Hey, Grandma."

"Theo, I was just asking your mother how your class is going. You've been so busy this summer, but I'm thrilled to hear it's going well."

"I wasn't sure at first I wanted to spend most of my summer studying, but it's ended up being a fun class a lot of the time and is going okay," Theo said, leaning against the porch railing. "And I wanted to thank you again for letting me use Grandpa's car to go back and forth to class this week."

"I'll have to add my thanks to that one," Alice said. "Shuffling the kids from one activity to another can become extremely time consuming."

Sadie smiled, thankful—not for the first time—to have her grandchildren living so close to her. "You know you're both very welcome."

She glanced at the car, knowing how much Theo loved the convertible, and hoped it would be his one day. And one day, she might very well give it to him.

"Wish I could hang around, but I want to get started on that timeline." Theo picked up his backpack and chuckled. "And I was worried about getting bored this summer."

"Don't forget we're going to Mia's mother's birthday party tonight for dinner at Los Pollitos," Alice added as he headed for the house.

"I won't, Mom. I'm always in the mood for Mexican food. Trust me."

Los Pollitos was run by Sara's best friend Mia's family. A Mexican restaurant on Main Street with a terra-cotta tile floor and a relaxing outdoor dining patio, it had become one of Sadie's go-to spots for comfort food.

"He's just always in the mood for food, period." Alice laughed as Theo stepped into the house. "You should see my grocery bill."

"He's growing up," Sadie said, proud of the young man he was becoming. She turned back to Alice. "What would you think of Sara coming with me to visit Priscilla this afternoon? I know she's not happy that her mother's story is being told, and I thought it might help if I invited her to watch some of the filming. She might even change her mind about the documentary."

"Until she finds out someone is threatening to stop the filming." Alice set her book down on the small end table beside her and glanced at the front door. "And as for Sara, I'm not sure I want to let her out of the house."

"I'll be with her, Alice, and it would give us a chance to 'hang out,' as she so eloquently puts it. I won't take her up to the mines. Just down the road to one of the local B and Bs."

"I don't know, though she is feeling rather cooped up." Alice glanced up at the doorway. "Though speaking of your granddaughter, why don't you go ahead and ask her, Mom?"

"Ask me what?" Sara said, slipping through the screen door and plopping down onto the chair across from them. "I didn't know you were here, Grandma. I was in my room reading."

Sadie turned to her granddaughter. "I'm on my way to visit Priscilla Hewitt, Abigail's daughter, and wondered if you'd like to come with me. I thought it might be nice to invite her to watch some of the filming."

"Even after what happened today?" Alice said.

"What happened today?" Sara asked.

Sadie glanced at Alice before answering Sara's question. "There was a letter left on Nicole's dresser today, and I'd like to ask her a few questions."

"What kind of note?"

"It said *Stop filming or someone else will get hurt* and was signed by . . ." Sadie realized she'd left out that detail when she'd told Alice earlier.

"Signed by who?" Sara asked, her eyes widening.

"Abigail."

"Abigail Chaplin?" Alice asked. "You didn't tell me that."

"Man, I always miss everything exciting," Sara said.

"Like I said. I'm sure it's just a prank."

Sara leaned forward, her eyes begging her mom for permission. "Please, Mom. I'm tired of sitting around the house."

Alice didn't look convinced. "You're finished icing your foot?"

"I've had the ice pack on it the last thirty minutes while I've been reading, and yes, it's feeling better."

"Fine," Alice finally said. "You two go, but be careful. This whole situation has me nervous."

Fifteen minutes later, Sadie and Sara were driving down Main Street toward one of the local B and Bs.

"Thank you for rescuing me." Sara leaned back in the passenger seat.

"It's barely been twenty-four hours."

"I know, but being up on the set was so much fun. I can't believe I'm stuck back at home again."

Sadie wondered if she should remind Sara that the reason she was back home with a bum ankle was because she'd made a bad decision, but she decided not to bring it up for now. More than likely her ankle was enough of a reminder that she'd been somewhere she shouldn't have been.

"I am sorry about yesterday," Sara confessed.

"I'm just thankful you didn't break anything. Your mother would have been furious with both of us."

"My mother worries too much."

"Which—like I said yesterday—is completely normal. I worried about your mom when she was your age, as well."

Sara giggled. "It's hard to imagine my mom as a fourteen-year-old."

Sadie pulled up in front of the large Victorian house, then shut off the engine. "Just wait. Your daughter will say that about you one day."

Sara grasped the car handle and then stopped. "Can you tell me more about Mrs. Hewitt before we go in?"

"I tried to find out more from Priscilla while I was doing research for the director, but she insisted she didn't want to get involved." Sadie pulled the keys from the ignition. "What I do know is that about two years after Raymond disappeared, Abigail met a man named Jacob."

"Was it love at first sight, like it was with Raymond?"

"I'm not sure about that, but Jacob was well respected, and they made a good match. As far as I know, they stayed in Silver Peak the rest of their lives and had been married close to fifty years when Jacob died."

"Wow. That's a long time."

"Abigail died a few months later. Priscilla was their only daughter." Sadie nodded to the house. "Jacob and Abigail bought this place shortly after they were married, named it the Painted Daisy for the colorful assortment of painted daisies growing in the gardens, and turned it into a bed-and-breakfast."

"It's beautiful."

"Yes, it is." Sadie dropped the keys into her lap and rested her hands on the steering wheel. "In the late 1800s, when Silver Peak was a boomtown, the population grew rapidly, which created a huge demand for hotels and places for people to stay. There was also a lot of money changing hands. It was during that time that large Victorian houses, many of them right here on Main Street, were built."

"Who built this one?"

"If I remember correctly, it was built and first owned by a doctor."

Sadie had toured the house once, many years ago, and had been impressed with all of the original fixtures to the brass and crystal lights, a fireplace with Florentine tile, beveled mirrors, maple and mahogany inlaid flooring, and stained glass.

Sadie and Sara got out of the car and headed for the sidewalk, Sara's limp definitely better than the night before.

"It's for sale?" Sara asked, passing a real estate sign.

"Priscilla and her husband are retiring after twenty-five years of running the bed-and-breakfast."

Sadie had known Priscilla for years, first meeting her at the Campfire Chapel, where they both attended church. While Priscilla wasn't much of a talker, Sadie had often been impressed by Priscilla's spiritual knowledge, and had quickly come to realize that when the woman did speak, there was almost always value in what she said.

Sadie followed Sara up the brick walkway to the house, then knocked on the door. A moment later, Priscilla opened the door, wearing a purple gardening apron covering jeans and a blouse.

"Why, Sadie, you just caught me. I was on my way out to the backyard to catch up on some gardening. I never hear the bell when I'm out there."

"Priscilla, sorry for stopping by without calling first."

"To be honest, I enjoy company far more than I do gardening." Priscilla pulled off her gardening gloves and dropped them into one of the apron pockets. "Honestly, it's been quite an adjustment closing down the B and B, as I mentioned to you before. I've become so used to fixing breakfast every morning for our guests that I don't quite know what to do. For as much as I've been looking forward to retirement, I'm afraid the quiet is going to drive me crazy."

"I don't know about you, but I'm convinced that retirement doesn't have to be boring." Sadie smiled, then turned to Sara. "You've met my granddaughter, Sara, haven't you?"

"Of course. It's nice to see you, Sara." Priscilla set her hands against her hips. "Is everything all right?"

"Everything is fine."

Priscilla hesitated. "Why don't you come in and join me for lemonade and some cookies that I just pulled out of the oven. I'm going to gain twenty pounds if I'm not careful without guests to help eat the goodies I'm used to making, so you might as well join me."

"That would be nice, but we won't stay long," Sadie assured her. "And we certainly don't want to be a bother."

"You're not a bother at all. Like I said, I need someone to help me eat these cookies I just made."

Sadie stepped into the cozy Victorian-styled kitchen behind Priscilla and Sara.

"It does smell delicious, Mrs. Hewitt," Sara said.

"I tried making my niece's recipe for Flourless Chocolate Pecan Cookies, and I have to say, after already sampling one, they are delicious."

Priscilla waved them into the kitchen to the antique table in the corner of the room that boasted a large picture window looking over the well-kept gardens. Something told Sadie that if she had sat here a hundred years ago, the scene would look almost identical.

While Sadie did have some specific questions to ask Priscilla, she decided to ease into the conversation about her mother. "Any nibbles on selling the house?"

"A young couple from Denver have been by three times now, but Jack and I feel like we need to sit down with them to discuss the realities of running something like this, as it is obviously much bigger than simply buying a house. It's like having company year-round. You end up having to deal with all sorts of guests, friendly and rude, guests that arrive late, and on top of that, you still have to wake up before the sun to prepare breakfast with a smile. They are supposed to give us an answer at the end of the week."

Sadie thought of her own two-story ranch house located on the edge of town. It had originally been a part of a huge, family-owned ranch until the Depression, when her family had been forced to sell off large sections of the property. Today, the five-bedroom house sat on a small, two-acre plot, the only remnant of the ranch she still owned. And while she loved having people over for dinner, along with the occasional overnight guest, she wasn't sure she'd enjoy having a full house year-round.

Priscilla set a plate of cookies on the table in front of them, along with glasses of lemonade.

Sadie took a bite of one of the cookies. "You were right. These are delicious."

"Thank you."

Sadie glanced out the window. "Your view here is stunning."

"It's one of the things I'm going to miss about this place."

"I heard you and Sam were planning to move to Dallas?"

"As soon as it sells. We have a daughter there and three granddaughters." Priscilla took a sip of her lemonade. "Something tells me you didn't come here just for a social visit. Am I right?"

Sadie nodded. It was time to cut to the chase. "Please know that I don't want to put any pressure on you, but I thought you might enjoy coming up to the mine and watching some of the filming."

Priscilla waved her hand in the air. "Like I explained to you before, Sadie, I might not have been alive when all that happened between Raymond and my mother, but it's still the story of *my* mother they're trying to re-create. And it just seems too…too personal. I can only imagine what my mother would think about the fact that they're planning to air her story across the United States. What happened back then is something even she never really spoke about."

"I can assure you, the main story is the mystery of the skeleton that was found. I've read the script, and I did my best to ensure it was as accurate as possible. No one has any intention of harming your mother's reputation."

Priscilla pushed her glass away and leaned back in her chair. "I didn't mention it to you, but the producer came by after I spoke with you. He implied that they're making it into some sappy love story."

"I knew he wanted your input," Sadie said, "but I told him clearly that you had asked not to be involved."

Priscilla shook her head. "He told me they wanted to tell my mother's story. Her falling in love with Raymond...why her family was opposed to her marriage to Raymond Butler, and, of course, to find out what really happened in those mines the night Raymond disappeared. Whether or not my mother's brother had killed Raymond, or if my mother had been somehow involved."

Sadie hated the fact that she was dredging up painful memories, but it seemed as if the writers of the documentary had already done that. "I told them I wasn't interested in being a part of this story. I won't be involved in anything that might smear my mother's name. Or my uncle's. No one was able to prove he killed Raymond."

"I am sorry, Priscilla. If I would have known..."

"It's not your fault. He said he had spoken to a sister of Raymond who was living in Denver when he disappeared. Claimed the two of them were close."

Sadie took a sip of her lemonade. "Her name's Sandra O'Conner now. She married a lawyer. She lives in an assisted living complex in Denver."

Sadie knew Priscilla didn't want to get involved, but if someone *was* really threatening to sabotage the film, it made sense that it was someone connected with what had happened back then.

"Aren't you afraid whatever Raymond's sister said would be biased toward the Butler family?" Sara asked.

"Probably." Priscilla shook her head. "But what was I supposed to say? The truth is that Raymond either left on his own accord, or was murdered, presumably up in those mines. And the only people who knew what happened are dead and can't tell us. Even I don't know what happened that night. All we really have is rumors that have been passed along for over fifty years. I don't know what's true or what is merely an overgrown fabrication based on gossip, because my mother refused to speak of it."

Sadie fingered the edge of the table, wondering how far she would go to stop a film if she believed someone was speaking against her mother's reputation. Or would it matter after all these years what had really happened on that night? If she could find the motivation, she might be able to find out what was truly going on.

Sadie took a deep breath and tried to choose her next words carefully. "Please believe me when I say that I have no desire to do anything to hurt your mother's name. In fact, the director doesn't even know I'm here, and my reason to be here has nothing to do with the show's script. I knew your mother for years, and she was a wonderful part of this community. And besides that, she made the best plum jelly in the county."

"I remember when I finished her second to last jar of plum jelly after she died. It was as if it was gone forever with her. In fact, I still have one in the freezer that none of us will ever eat." Priscilla gave them a slight smile. "But if you're not here to convince me to tell my side of the story to the director, then why are you here?"

"Because I thought you might want to be on the set and see what they are doing. I think you would be pleased." Sadie glanced at Sara. "But also because some strange things have happened up in the mines on the set these past few days."

"I'm sorry." Priscilla reached for another cookie. "I'm not sure I follow. What kind of things?"

"Sabotage is the only way I know how to describe it. There have been strange technical things, along with a written warning that if we didn't stop, someone was going to get hurt."

"Sabotage? You think someone is trying to stop the filming." Priscilla's head tilted as if suddenly everything clicked, and her eyebrows rose. "You think I'm the one trying to stop the filming?"

"Of course not, Priscilla." Sadie reached out and squeezed her friend's hand. "I could never think that about you."

"The truth is that my mother was a good person, but whatever happened that night changed her forever."

Priscilla stood up and started scrubbing down the already spotless counters.

"Did you make this rug?" Sara asked.

"My rug…" Priscilla turned back to them.

Sara pointed to the colorful rug on the kitchen floor. "I think it's cool."

"Thank you."

"Do you make them yourself?"

"I…no…my daughter does, actually. It's crocheted. I probably have a dozen of them throughout the house. She likes trying out new patterns, then ends up giving them away."

"She should sell them, shouldn't she, Grandma? I think people would love them."

"I might even have a place for them in my shop. Not exactly an antique, but I do, on occasion, sell things on consignment."

"You said there was a letter," Priscilla said. "Was the sheriff contacted about the threat?"

"Yes."

"Have they stopped the filming?"

"I think most people are convinced it was nothing more than a prank," Sadie said. "And maybe they're right. No one knows at this point."

Priscilla sat back down at the table. "I'm guessing that it won't be long until I have another visitor—the sheriff—so I might as well tell you what I do know, though I'm not sure it will help."

Sadie leaned forward, interested in what the woman was about to say.

"You have to understand," Priscilla began, "that this filming brings up a part of my past that I'd always preferred left buried. I wasn't born, of course, when the first rumors swept through the town, but I must say I always found them quite disturbing. My mother never completely recovered from everything that happened that summer, even though she went on to marry my father and make a good life for herself. I think she always felt guilty that she could have been involved in a possible murder."

"Did she ever talk about that summer and what really happened between Philip and Raymond?"

Priscilla stood up again and stared out the window before turning around and facing them. "No. I remember when I was in college one Thanksgiving. We were all sitting around talking and somehow the name of Raymond Butler came up. That was the first I'd ever heard about the man. My mother was upset, but when I went to ask her about it later, she refused to talk about it. She told me that sometimes the past needs to stay in the past and this was one of those times. So I never brought it up again. And she never volunteered.

"And after that... I don't know. It didn't seem to matter. My mother had a family and the rumors about Raymond Butler's disappearance began to fade." Priscilla shook her head. "I've been going through some of her things as we've been packing and have found cards, letters, and correspondence with old friends. Everything I find confirms that my mother was a sweet, kind woman who somehow got involved in a difficult situation, but you knew her. She certainly wasn't capable of murder. Nothing will ever change my mind about that fact."

"Priscilla..." Sadie's mind began to spin. The art of letter writing might be dying out as people today use e-mail and texts, but she'd found a number of letters, poems, and photographs in antique trunks and desks she'd bought over the years. "Did you happen to ever find any letters between Raymond and your mother?"

"I..." Priscilla hesitated, then walked across the room to a small desk where she pulled out a small stack of papers. "I wasn't going to share these with anyone, but you seem to have a knack for discovering the truth about things in the past. Maybe, just maybe these hold the key to the truth about my mother."

A wave of guilt swept over Sadie. "Are you sure you want me to look at these?"

Priscilla laid a stack of letters on the table in front of Sadie. "In spite of the fact that I haven't wanted to get involved, maybe I've been wrong. Maybe it's time the truth of what happened that day came to light. And you knew my mother. You know she'd never hurt anyone. And besides, if she was planning to run away with Raymond, she never would have hurt him."

"These are beautiful," Sara said, tracing her finger across the top of the letters, which had been tied with a red satin bow.

"I think so too. I always knew about the relationship, but these letters—like I said—prove to me that my mother didn't have anything to do with Raymond's death. She truly loved him. But maybe I've been wrong in wanting to keep the past in the past." Priscilla looked up at Sadie and shook her head. "If you can find a clue in them, something I missed when I read through them, maybe then we can put the rumors surrounding my mother to rest."

6

Sadie and Sara walked into Arbuckle's Coffee, which was located next door to the Antique Mine. Sadie breathed in the aroma of fresh-roasted coffee—something she tended to drink constantly, at least according to Julie, who enjoyed teasing her for her love of coffee.

Arbuckle's had been remodeled into a cozy space filled with tables, padded armchairs, and love seats. Colorful throw rugs covered the wood floor in the seating areas, adding both warmth and style to the shop. The high ceiling, with its exposed ductwork and beams, gave a modern edge to the historic atmosphere of the shop.

"I don't know about you, but I could use a pick-me-up," Sadie told Sara as they stepped in front of the glass counter filled with mouthwatering pastries. "What would you like?"

"I wouldn't mind another lemonade."

Sadie greeted the owner, Hector Vidal. "The cast loved the cinnamon rolls, Hector."

"You know I'm always glad to hear news like that. Do you want your usual today?" he asked.

"You know me too well. One of these days I'll surprise you and order something completely different." She chuckled. "But not today."

Hector laughed. "You got it. What about you, Sara?"

"A lemonade please."

"Anything else?" Hector asked.

Sadie shook her head, passing on the temptation to indulge in a thick slice of the fresh apple pie on display since they'd just had homemade cookies with Priscilla. A few minutes later, Sadie finished chatting with Hector, then took their order to one of the comfy corner chairs, where Sara already sat, resting her foot.

Sadie handed Sara her lemonade, then sat down beside her. "I was impressed with how you spoke with Priscilla."

Sara wiggled back in her chair and shrugged off the compliment. "I knew she was upset, and I really did think the rug was cool."

"Smart thinking. And I saw you reading through the letters in the car on the way here. What do you think about them so far?"

Sara tapped on the letters she'd set at the end of the small table nestled between them. "You have to read them, Grandma. They are so romantic. Listen to this."

Sara picked up one of the letters from the stack and began reading.

My dearest Abigail,

It might have only been since yesterday, but every hour we are apart I can't help but imagine the next time we are together. I need your answer, not sure how much longer I can wait for you.

Sara held the letters against her chest and sighed. "This is better than any romance novel I've ever read."

Sadie's eyes widened dramatically. "Your mother lets you read romance novels?" she teased.

"Oh, Grandma!" Sara leaned forward. "Today, if a boy likes you, he sends you a text. Forget flowery, romantic words like these."

Sadie laughed. "It's like Doc was talking about last night at the clinic. Technology and communication have definitely changed over the years. Not too long ago, for example, if you forgot your grocery list at the store, you couldn't call home to have someone read it off for you."

Sara echoed Sadie's laugh. "Mom does that all the time."

"And a hundred years ago—before my time, by the way," Sadie added with a grin, "there was both the telephone and postal service, but they operated much slower, so obviously there simply weren't as many ways to communicate as there are today. So because letters took so long to reach their destination, people tended to write lengthy ones."

"Personally, I can't imagine life without my cell phone or being able to text my friends."

Sadie nodded at Sara's phone resting beside her on the arm of the chair. "I've noticed."

Sara shrugged. "I like having the world at my fingertips—literally twenty-four hours a day. And as for Raymond Butler, he might have lived eons ago, but he was a true romantic."

"I'm afraid that the art of letter writing is a lost art today."

She'd mentioned it to Roz recently. She couldn't remember the last time she'd received a handwritten note in the mail from anyone who wasn't over sixty. Personally, she still enjoyed sending out thank-you notes and get well cards, but today's world made it too easy to just shoot off a simple e-mail with a quick note.

"It's sad, though." Sara let out a deep sigh. "To think that they were in love and then their romance ended."

"Which brings us back to the warning note Nicole found today," Sadie said. "And the question of who would want us to think that Abigail didn't want that story shared."

"I still can't believe I missed all of the excitement, but that would have creeped me out. I mean, a letter from a dead woman?"

"We all know it wasn't really from Abigail. What we don't know is who—and why—someone would do something like that. Who would have enough motivation to want to stop the filming of her story all these decades later, and what are they trying to hide?"

"Do you think Priscilla was telling us the truth?"

Sadie considered Sara's question. "I'd like to think so."

"What do you know about Abigail's family?"

Sadie took another sip of her coffee, enjoying her time with Sara. "Their family has lived in Silver Peak since the start of the Silver Rush back in the late 1800s, and they were, in fact, a part of the founding of the town. Her father was the president of the bank, and they lived on Main Street in the Victorian house where Priscilla lives now. Her grandfather made quite a windfall in the mining business, then later moved into bank management after selling his shares."

"They were here before Harry Polmiller," Sara observed.

Sadie nodded. Harry Polmiller was the oldest member of Campfire Chapel, and of Silver Peak for that matter. Yet despite his age and stooped stature, the man was still quite active and had one of the biggest vegetable gardens in town.

"So what do we do now?" Sara asked. "We know that Mrs. Hewitt isn't happy about the filming, but as far as we know, she wouldn't go as far as sabotaging the documentary."

Sadie pondered the question, unable to figure out what was niggling at her in the back of her mind. "If it wasn't a prank, I can't help but question who might have been behind it. I think we need to pay a visit to the library."

Sara finished up the last of her lemonade and frowned playfully. "The library? Whatever is that?"

"Oh, you know… It's that big building on the corner of Main Street filled with books," Sadie said with a laugh.

"I know where the library is, Grandma. And yes, I do like to read, but it's summer, which was why I was so excited about the chance to hang out with the TV crew up at the mine. I thought I could avoid the library for a while."

"This is strictly about us finding some answers." Sadie downed the last of her coffee. "I think we should look through news articles from around the time of Raymond's disappearance. We might be able to find out something."

After some initial reservations about the building, Sadie had grown to love the Silver Peak Library. A few years ago, it had been renovated by a local benefactor who'd turned the once-multiuse building into a gorgeous, lofted, high-ceilinged library that was, in fact, the most modern building in town. Light oak woodwork and local art lining its walls made it the perfect place to disappear for hours among the stacks of books.

But today, it wasn't the books on the shelves Sadie was interested in. It was the microfiche machine located on the second floor of the library that she hoped held an answer to some of the questions they were asking.

Sadie and Sara, who hobbled slightly beside her, stepped up to the front desk where Kimama, the librarian, sat. A beautiful

Native American woman, Kimama was an expert in local literature and had, more than once, helped Sadie to find elusive pieces of information. She was about as creative and resourceful a person as one could find. Which was exactly why Sadie had wanted to come.

Kimama smiled when she saw Sadie. "Hi, Sadie, Sara. How are you folks?"

"We're great, thanks. You?"

"Keeping busy, as usual. I hear you were asked to be a consultant for that documentary being filmed up at the mines."

"That's why I'm here, actually. I'd like to do some more background research around the time when Raymond Butler disappeared."

"That would have been around 1955," Kimama said. "Around the same time that the Chaplins sold the mine to Greg Winston's father."

"I'd forgotten about that." Sadie's interest piqued. "There was a trend back in the fifties to find uranium deposits, which is the only reason I can imagine wanting to invest in a mine like that, as the price of silver had dropped at that point."

"You're right," Kimama noted. "If I were you, I'd start upstairs. The microfilm machine should be free. Let me know if you have any problems finding what you need."

A couple of minutes later, Sadie had the reel she needed to view. She switched on the power to the microfilm machine and sat down in front of it.

Sara slid into the empty seat beside her. "I know you're not *technically challenged* like some people your age, Grandma, but this thing looks like it came off the ark with Noah."

"Really?" Sadie chuckled, deciding to take her comment as a compliment. "Just because something is a little out of date doesn't mean it won't work. Sometimes the good, old-fashioned way is the best way."

Sara scrunched up her lips. She didn't look convinced.

"I tell you what. How about we make a deal?"

"What kind of deal?" Sara asked.

Sadie began loading the reel onto the machine. "I'll use this while you go on the Internet browser on your phone. We'll see which way really is the fastest. Microfilm or the Internet."

Sara smiled. "Okay, you've got a deal."

Sadie used the directional buttons on the machine to advance the film. She really did try to stay current on what was happening in the world of technology, but even she knew that she'd never experience it the way her grandchildren did.

Sara was right about one thing. Going through the reel was like stepping back in time. Sadie scrolled through the current news for that time period, interspersed with ads for products like 7 Up, Sears, and Armour Star's Corned Beef Hash.

On a national level the first McDonald's opened, while TV dinners became more popular, and the first cans of Coca-Cola had just been released.

"Are you finding anything interesting, Sara?" Sadie asked after fifteen minutes had passed. She'd skimmed through the local news during that time, but hadn't yet come up with anything that she thought would help them.

"Maybe." She handed Sadie her phone. "What about this photo? I Googled the Chaplin family from here in Silver Peak and came up with some photos. Is this Abigail?"

Sadie studied the black-and-white photo. She'd seen photos of the young woman, but she didn't think that was her. "Where was this taken?"

"According to the article, it was at Philip Chaplin's funeral."

"Abigail and her family would have been there."

A year after Raymond's disappearance, Philip had died in a car accident up in the mountains.

"I could be mistaken, but I don't think that's Abigail."

"Then who is it?" Sara asked. "I know a funeral is a sad time anyway, but this woman looks totally devastated in this photo. It's sad."

"I don't know. This is from the *Sentinel*, so it's local. You stay here and rest your ankle, and I'll run downstairs and ask Kimama for the yearbooks from that time period. Abigail was nineteen when Raymond disappeared, after graduating the year before. Maybe we'll be able to find something. We can start with 1953 through 1957."

Sadie returned a few minutes later with the stack of yearbooks.

"This should cover it." Sadie held up one of the books. "Did you know that in 1953, Silver Peak High School won the state basketball championship?"

"Grandma, it's on the water tower on the west side of town," Sadie said. "Don't you remember?"

Sadie laughed. "I might be old, but I'm not that old."

They each took a yearbook and started flipping through the pages, trying to match the photo on Sara's phone to a photo in the yearbook. Of course, it was possible that whoever was in the photo hadn't gone to high school in Silver Peak, but at least it was a starting place.

"What about her?" Sara asked, pointing to one of the photos.

"Granted the photo in the paper is not only in black and white, but kind of blurry too. But I still don't think that's her."

Sara wrinkled her nose as she studied both photos side by side. "I think you're right. The person we're looking for has a much narrower chin."

They kept flipping through the class photos.

"Like her," Sara said.

Sadie held up the photo and nodded. "This time I think you're right. Which would mean if we're not mistaken, that's a much younger version of Lucile Knight."

"Do you know her?" Sara asked.

"She lives about five miles out of town on a small piece of property. Maybe we should pay her a visit."

"People call her Loopy Lucy."

"Loopy Lucy?" Sadie tried not to smile. "That's not very nice."

Sara dropped her phone next to the row of yearbooks they'd been using. "I'm just saying what I've heard. Apparently she's sort of crazy."

"I confess I don't know her well. She and her family moved away when I was young, then she moved back a couple of years ago, but I don't think the woman is crazy. She definitely keeps to herself."

"What we do know is she clearly felt something for Philip."

"You think she was in love with him?"

"I don't know, but it's possible."

Sadie scrolled through the details of the funeral, but as far as she could tell, Abigail wasn't in any of the photos.

"Here is the obituary." Sadie started reading out loud. "Philip James Chaplin, twenty-three, of Silver Peak, died in a fatal car crash while driving home from Denver. He was born February 17,

1932, in Denver. He was survived by his parents, James and Evelyn Chaplin, and his sister, Abigail."

"What about you, Grandma? Did you find anything?"

"An article on Raymond Butler right after his disappearance," Sadie said, adjusting the reel before reading it out loud.

"The search for Raymond Butler who went missing two weeks ago continues, but at this point the police don't have any conclusive evidence to his whereabouts. Several people have been brought in for questioning, including Philip Chaplin, who, according to witnesses, got into a fight last month with Butler while in town.

"Police are looking for anyone who might have information about Butler's disappearance, and asks them to please come forward. The last time anyone claims to have seen him was Friday afternoon in Silver Peak. There has been some speculation that Butler was killed and his body dumped in one of the local mines, but so far the police have refused to give more details as to why they suspect he might have been murdered."

Sadie sat back in her chair as she sorted through the facts. "So Raymond Butler disappeared, but there was no hard evidence of what happened."

"He could have run for some reason," Sara offered.

"Or, as the article implies," Sadie began, "he could have been murdered."

"But either way, what does that have to do with the filming up on the mountain? Why would someone want to stop it?"

Sadie sighed. "That's the question, Sara."

It was a question she didn't have the answer to. What reason was there for stopping the truth from getting out? Was someone trying to cover up Raymond's murder?

"Do you think we should go visit Loop—er, Miss Knight?" Sara asked.

Sadie glanced at her watch. "For now, we call it a day. I promised I'd get you home by suppertime, and it's already half past five. Your mother told me that you had a birthday party at Los Pollitos to go to tonight."

"Oh, I almost forgot." Sara started gathering up the yearbooks.

"Sounds like fun."

Sara picked up the pile of yearbooks and paused. "You could come with us."

"Well, I appreciate the invitation, but I'll probably just stop by the shop, then call it a night. It's been a long day."

"That doesn't sound nearly as exciting as a plate of enchiladas, Grandma."

Which was true, but if she was honest with herself, she needed a quiet evening, along with some time to sort through everything that had happened. Because while she still felt that the warning in Nicole's dressing room had been a prank, it was too early to make an assumption that could end up with someone else getting hurt.

7

Sadie put away the leftover salad from her dinner, then finished cleaning up the kitchen of the spacious farmhouse, glad to be home. While she'd enjoyed her day, especially going out with Sara, tonight the quiet house had helped her begin to sort through the day's events in her mind.

Hank, her golden retriever, named after Hank Williams, one of her favorite country music singers, nuzzled against her leg, leaving a trail of hair on her dark pants.

"I think we'll skip our walk tonight, Hank. It's been a full day." Sadie reached down and scratched his head, before sitting down with the letters Priscilla had given her. "Though it looks to me as if I need to take you in to the groomer."

Brushing Hank herself helped, but it certainly wasn't enough to keep him groomed. Especially in the heat of the summer.

Sadie pulled out one of the letters on the top of the stack. She wasn't sure they'd give her the answers she was looking for, but after all of the research she had done for the documentary, holding actual letters written between Raymond and Abigail had her heart racing with excitement.

Dear Raymond,

I received your last letter and have read it at least a dozen times until the edges are crinkled. I only wish it were you speaking the words on the page to me in person rather than just ink upon the page. In my mind, I go over and over every detail of our last time together. The picnic on the mountain couldn't have been more romantic, and then when you stole a kiss good night after taking me home…

But I'm asking you to be patient. You know how I long to accept your proposal for marriage, but I also have my family to consider. My father's coolness will warm over time, I am sure, once he gets to know you. He only wants the best for me and has always been overprotective of my sister and me. Please understand. My mother will speak to him again, as well, and try to convince him that your intentions are noble. That you care for me as much as I care for you. Just please, please wait for me.

Yours always,
Abigail

Sadie reached for the next letter. Sara had been right. The letters were extremely romantic, making Abigail and Raymond's tragic ending seem even more tragic—like scenes straight from *Romeo and Juliet.*

Hank nudged against her leg again. Sadie eyed the stack of letters waiting for her to read, then noted the time. With few exceptions, she and Hank went for a long walk every morning, giving her time to think and pray. And as often as she could, she repeated the process in the evening.

"You're determined to go, aren't you, boy? There is still time before it gets dark, and I suppose a walk would be good for both of us."

Five minutes later, Sadie started down the long drive outside her house and threw Hank's Frisbee as far as she could, her mind still on the letters waiting for her return to the kitchen. It wasn't the first time she'd read through stacks of old correspondence. She'd frequently discovered personal letters, vintage postcards, and business correspondence while rummaging through estate sales and attics. Sometimes the letters had historical significance for the area. Other times, she'd bought them for their value to stamp collectors. But these letters between Raymond and Abigail had taken on a personal interest.

She watched as Hank chased after the toy, clearly glad to have the run of the yard. The house sat on the border of a hilly wood, allowing for plenty of perfect spots for hiking. The frequent exercise helped her stay trim as long as she didn't indulge too often in sweets like she had today at Priscilla's.

She followed the long, evergreen-lined driveway, taking in the view she never tired of, while she breathed in the late afternoon's crisp mountain air. Almost immediately, she began praying, as was her normal habit while walking with Hank. She prayed for Sara's foot and the challenging teen years; for Priscilla, who had been forced to rekindle memories of her mother; for the cast and crew, who'd possibly been threatened in the light of today's letter.

After saying amen, her mind slipped back to the letters, and—once again—up to the mines. Her decision to work with the documentary team was supposed to have been a simple job to ensure historical accuracy. Determining that the script, props, and costumes were right had added to the details of the story. She hadn't expected the experience to be filled with technical glitches and anonymous warnings.

Which to her still made no sense. It was easy to justify everything that had gone wrong over the last few days. The missing batteries and blown lights, even Sara's injury, could be easily explained. If nothing else, they could blame it on Murphy's Law—*Anything that can go wrong, will go wrong*—which was exactly what had seemed to plague the filming crew. Sabotage seemed far too strong a word.

But the note had changed that.

Murphy's Law, or even simply bad luck, couldn't explain a warning taped to the dressing table. Someone had put that note there with the intent either to scare or for a good laugh. And if their motive *had* been to scare, they'd clearly accomplished what they'd set out to do.

But the question remained, why? If it wasn't a prank, then what motivation was there other than to stop the filming? And what would prompt someone to want to stop it in the first place?

Those were the questions that still had no answers.

Hank ran up to Sadie. She grabbed the Frisbee from his mouth and threw it again as a car pulled into the long driveway in front of her house.

Sadie smiled at the familiar sight of Edwin's car.

Edwin turned off the motor, then stepped out of his vehicle. The passing years had changed him from a lanky young man with blue eyes to someone far more distinguished. Today, he was a solid man with a powerful build. But he still had the same twinkly blue eyes that once again managed to toy with her heart.

Even though Edwin had moved back to the mountains, he still preferred a sweater vest and oxford shirts with flat-front Dockers over the mountain-friendly gear most people wore. Which made her especially pleased with the hiking boots he was now wearing that they'd bought together a few months back. Sadie chuckled inwardly at the thought. Maybe she'd eventually get him to lose that city look after all.

"I was hoping you'd come by tonight," Sadie said as she crossed the graveled drive. "Hank insisted on a walk tonight, but I could brew up a fresh pot of coffee if you'd like."

"How about a walk for starters?"

She smiled at him, thankful he'd decided to stop by. "Hank and I would love that."

He kissed her lightly on the cheek, clearly glad to see her. "I heard you had a difficult day, and I wanted to drop by in person to make sure you were okay."

"This isn't the first time in the past day or two that I've noticed how fast news travels in this small town."

"I called you a couple of times actually, but I never got through."

Sadie patted her pocket where she normally kept her cell phone, trying to remember the last time she'd seen it. "The battery went dead earlier, and it's now in the house charging."

"After my council meeting this afternoon, I ran into Sheriff Slattery. He told me about the warning note that was left on the dressing table up at the mine. Had me worried about you."

"I'm fine, but Nicole, the girl playing the part of Abigail, was quite shaken up, and I have to say, I don't blame her. Even I found it somewhat unnerving. It was signed Abigail."

"The sheriff thinks it's just a prank by one of the cast members," Edwin said. "I understand she'd made some comments about Abigail not wanting them to make the documentary. Someone might think it was funny to play on those fears."

Sadie watched Hank tear down the road after some movement in the bushes. "It's possible, because quite frankly, I can't understand why anyone would want to stop the documentary."

"I still sense some hesitation in your voice. You're not convinced it was a prank?"

"Honestly? I'm not sure. Except for the note, it's easy to dismiss everything that happened as nothing more than a few coincidences. But I can't dismiss the note."

Edwin stopped and looked at her. "Who do you think might want to stop the filming? Raymond Butler disappeared around sixty years ago, and the man rumored to have killed him is also dead."

"I don't know." Sadie was still trying to sort through all the possibilities. "What if Philip didn't kill Raymond? What if someone else did and that someone else is afraid of getting caught? With the advances of DNA testing, it is likely that when the police are finished with the skeleton, they will have found some kind of evidence. It's possible that whoever killed Raymond can be identified."

"It's definitely possible," Edwin agreed. "But that person probably would be pushing eighty by now, and what does that have to do with the documentary?"

"That, I don't know yet."

They started walking again. The sun was rapidly making its descent toward the peaks of the mountains, leaving a soft yellow glow over the trees.

"If that person is alive, I would think it would be a secret they most likely would prefer carrying to their grave," Edwin said.

"Or," Sadie suggested, walking beside Edwin down the road, "it could be someone's child or grandchild. Someone who doesn't want the truth known about someone they cared about. Maybe the murderer confessed the truth. A deathbed confession that no one else was supposed to find out about. But then Greg stumbled across the skeleton and found possible proof of foul play over a missing person people have been talking about for decades."

Rumors had been circulating since she'd been a little girl: everything from people claiming that they'd seen a ghost up in the mine shaft, to sightings of Raymond—still alive—in town. And while Sadie didn't believe in ghosts—or that the man was alive, if someone had murdered him, that meant there was also a murderer. And even if he—or she—wasn't still alive, someone out there didn't want the truth known.

"I went and spoke with Priscilla today, Abigail's daughter."

Edwin reached down, picked up a branch that had fallen across the side of the road, and tossed it aside into the bushes. "What does she think about the documentary?"

"She's been against it from the very beginning. Believes it will end up further tarnishing her mother's name. There have always been people who believed her mother was involved with Raymond's disappearance."

Which was clearly motivation, Sadie thought. Could she have overlooked something simply because she and Priscilla were friends?

"How upset is she?" he asked as he reached out and took her hand, lacing their fingers together.

"If you're asking if she is upset enough to stop the production," Sadie said as Hank tore past them down the gravel road, clearly enjoying himself, "I don't think she's that upset. Plus, I don't see her as the kind of woman who would rush out seeking revenge and try to sabotage the project."

"Any thoughts on who would want to stop the project?"

"Sara and I went to the library today, and I'd like to go talk to Lucile Knight."

"You think she might know something?"

"She was in one of the photos we found from Philip's funeral, and she was clearly upset. Obviously there was some kind of connection between the families. I can't help but wonder if she knows something about what happened back then. If nothing else, she knew the family and might have some insight."

"Maybe she was simply in love with Philip," Edwin threw out.

"Sara and I both thought of that possibility."

"Despite some of the negative issues surrounding Raymond's disappearance," Edwin began, "there are a number of people who believe all of this publicity with the film crew will bring more tourists into both the mine and into town."

"What do you think?" Sadie asked.

"When the network first came to us, I admit, I was skeptical, but I've pretty much changed my mind now. Everywhere I go in town people are talking about the film crew, how Silver Peak is going to be on the map now, and how people love the excitement of having a taste of Hollywood in their town. And the town folks aren't the only ones who seem happy," Edwin continued. "The director, Tom Wilson, seems pretty thrilled his crew's here, as well."

"Why's that?" Sadie asked.

After working with the man the past few days, she'd assumed the director preferred working in the big city with all of its conveniences.

"He mentioned to me, after they first came to the city to get permission to go ahead with the documentary, that filming in a small town meant a whole lot less bureaucracy than the bigger cities. And not only that, but think of how much less their expenses are here in Silver Peak compared to a place like New York. I'm certain they're saving a lot of money on their budget."

"And on the flip side," Sadie said, "they're bringing in business for Silver Peak from housing, food, and all the extras they've needed. Sounds like a win-win situation for everyone."

"It is," Edward agreed. "And even this situation with the warning letter, no matter who is behind it, it's going to end up stirring up even more interest and more publicity with curious onlookers, which is always a good thing."

Sadie thought through Edwin's logic. It was exactly why she loved being around him. He brought out a needed balance in her life. And while she didn't see it as funny, maybe the letter was simply a practical joke meant for a good laugh for a bored crew member.

Sadie stopped at a favorite spot along the road, overlooking the alpine forests of aspens and evergreens that were nestled among some of the highest mountains in Colorado. Hazy mountains peaked in the distance while white clouds floated overhead. She knew how most of city management worked, and she understood the importance of finding innovative ways to ensure Silver Peak survived. It was just like it had been when the town had first been settled.

Sadie turned to Edwin as they started walking again. "Sometimes it's hard to believe that just over a hundred years ago, Silver Peak was a boomtown with the population eight times what it is today. Jobs were plentiful, and because of the mines, many became wealthy overnight. Those people built this town from the ground up, and in the town's heyday, they had visits from Oscar Wilde and Mark Twain."

Edwin nodded. "My grandfather and I used to go camping up here in these mountains in the summertime. We'd sit around the campfire, and I'd listen to him tell stories about his father mining in these very mountains."

Sadie looked at Edwin, her interest piqued. "I wish I could have met him."

"His father emigrated from northern Ireland like hundreds of other men, following the gold rushes across the continent from the time he was sixteen."

"What was he like?"

"Driven, with an extreme love for adventure as well as practical jokes."

Sadie laughed.

"The work in the mines was hard," Edwin continued, "but he wasn't like most of the greenhorns who arrive with unreasonable expectations. He'd listened to stories from his older brother and knew of the dangers and chances of starving, so he didn't travel in the winter, for example. He worked in Colorado, Idaho, and British Columbia, and even panned the sandbars in the Yukon for gold."

"Wow, he was quite the adventurer."

"He started corresponding with a girl he knew from back east, sending letters that took up to two months to arrive, and eventually proposed. She arrived on a ship from Panama. He'd arrange for a preacher so they could be married before they stepped onto the shore."

"What did she do while he worked in the mines?"

"Story is that she made more money selling doughnuts and homemade pies than he made mining."

"So he never made it big?"

"He kept working for another five years until they finally took her earnings and moved back east as far away from the mines as he could get. Ended up raising a passel of children and dying at the ripe old age of ninety-two."

"I wish I could have met him."

Edwin nudged her side with his elbow, sending a spark of electricity through her.

"He would have loved you, Sadie."

"And I would have very much enjoyed knowing him." She paused, enjoying their time together. "Back to our original discussion about the warning note. Do you agree with the sheriff? That the warning note is probably nothing more than someone's idea of a bad prank?"

"There was something else my grandfather told me about in regard to working in the mines. These men were always looking for some sort of amusement to break up the monotony of their jobs. So in their free time, when they weren't playing cards in the local store or involved in other sorts of, well, unscrupulous activities, they were playing jokes on the other miners."

"And in our situation?" Sadie asked.

"Like in the mines, something tells me it more than likely is nothing more than a practical joke."

Sadie was just about to respond when she noticed a car pull over to the side of the road about a hundred feet ahead and come to a stop. Black plumes of smoke poured out of the engine.

"Edwin... I'm not sure whose it is, but that car's on fire."

8

Sadie hurried beside Edwin toward the car with Hank running ahead of them.

"I don't think it's on fire, Sadie, but something's wrong."

Sadie paused a few feet from the car as a young woman stepped out of it.

Nicole?

"Sadie, hi!" Nicole shoved back a strand of hair that had fallen over her eyes as the smoke began to clear, then she pressed her hand against her heart. "I don't think I've ever been so happy to see someone I know."

"What happened?"

Nicole shook her head. "It's all my fault, really. I don't know this area at all, but it's so beautiful, so I thought I'd go for a drive in my rental car. But just now, coming up this hill, the engine started smoking, and now...and now I can't start it."

Edwin stepped up to the car and propped open the hood, careful not to burn himself on the hot engine.

"Nicole, this is Mayor Edwin Marshall." Sadie didn't normally introduce Edwin so formally, but she thought that knowing

Edwin's credentials might comfort Nicole in this nerve-racking moment.

"The mayor. Wow." Nicole flashed Sadie a grin, then shook Edwin's hand. "It's nice to meet you."

Edwin laughed. "Don't look too impressed."

"Well, if you've had anything at all to do with this quaint town, then I am impressed." Nicole's hands settled against her hips. "I'm originally from Blue River, Colorado, population 723—or at least it used to be. I left for New York when I was seventeen, but I still find being in a quaint, small town like Silver Peak feels like being home."

"Small towns seem to have a tendency to hold on and not let you go," Edwin said.

"Kind of like this car." Nicole laughed. "I hate to bother either of you, but you don't happen to know the name of a garage around here, do you?"

"We can call Mickelson's Auto Repair. I know Charlie will be happy to tow your car." Sadie nodded in the direction of her house. "And I live just up the road, not more than half a mile. I've got his number there."

"I would appreciate that, though I do hate to be a bother."

"You're not a bother at all, Nicole."

"I would take a look at your car," Edwin offered, "but with the engine still smoking, I'm pretty sure I wouldn't be much help in finding the problem."

Hank chose that moment to nuzzle up against Nicole.

"Who's this beauty?" Nicole asked, bending down to scratch Hank behind both ears.

"This is Hank," Sadie said.

"Hi, Hank," Nicole said, rubbing Hank's belly. "My parents have an English shepherd named Milly. I miss her when I'm not home."

The three of them started back up the road toward Sadie's house with Hank clearly having just found a new friend.

"Besides the letter you received today," Edwin began, "how has the filming gone?"

"I'm enjoying it. Sadie came up with the most darling costumes. In fact, I've been inspired to add a few things to my own wardrobe. There is something about the whole vintage look I just love."

"You like design?" Sadie asked.

"I actually attended The Art Institute of New York City, but ended up dropping out to take an acting job. My parents keep nudging me to go back and finish, but I'm still hoping I can find my big break."

"Everyone has to start somewhere," Sadie said.

"True, but I've given myself another year, and if nothing happens, I'll be back in school."

Ten minutes later, they'd made their way back down Sadie's long drive to her house. Sadie ushered Edwin and Nicole into the living room where she kept the number for Charlie's Auto Repair.

"Sadie, this room is stunning. Vaulted ceilings, the stone fireplace, and this bookshelf…" Nicole stopped in front of the tall bookshelf where Sadie kept an abundance of books on the history of Colorado, specifically Silver Peak, and pulled out one of the volumes. "Growing up, I couldn't decide between being a librarian, an interior designer, or an actress. Clearly the actress bug took over, but being here with all of these books…" She ran her finger across the cover. "People don't read like they used to."

"No, they don't." Sadie smiled at the young woman's approval. She'd always loved the cozy main room with its high ceilings, particularly because of the two beautiful built-in bookcases lining the fireplace. She'd decorated it in a warm, cozy Colorado style with two deep, leather lounge chairs and a couch in paisley upholstery.

Sadie dug out the phone number of the garage from her address book, then handed it to Edwin. "If you don't mind calling Charlie, I'll go get us something to drink while we wait for the tow truck. Would you like something, Nicole?"

"Do you have any herbal tea? If I drink caffeine this late in the day, I'll be up all night, and I don't think the director will appreciate my falling asleep on the set tomorrow."

"I'm sure you're right about that."

Five minutes later, Sadie carried an antique silver tray with tea for Nicole, coffee for her and Edwin, and a plate of brownies.

"Did you get ahold of Charlie?" Sadie asked, setting the tray down on the coffee table.

Edwin nodded from one of the leather lounge chairs where he now sat across from Nicole. "Charlie said he should be here in about fifteen minutes."

"I love the peace and quiet of the mountains." Nicole's gaze looked toward the window. "And to be honest, it was a nice escape after today's... what shall we call it... excitement. At first anyway."

"I've been telling Sadie, I highly doubt that you have anything to worry about. The sheriff's looking into things. If there's anything to be found, he'll find it."

"There is one thing you can do, Nicole," Sadie began. There was no use passing up an opportunity to find out more information, in this case, information about the cast and crew.

"What is that?" Nicole asked as she spooned some sugar into her tea, stirred it, then took a sip.

Sadie sat down on the paisley couch. "I know the sheriff has already spoken to you, but I'd like to ask you a few questions about what happened before the note appeared. Things were a little chaotic this afternoon up at the mines, and I didn't have a chance to talk much with you."

"Of course." Nicole cupped the tea between her fingers. "But I'm not sure how I will be of any help. I still can't imagine why someone would leave a note like that, even if it was nothing more than a prank."

Sadie added milk to her coffee, along with a couple of spoonfuls of sugar, then leaned back into the couch cushions. "I'm sure the sheriff already asked you, but have you seen anyone strange hanging around the set?"

Nicole pursed her lips slightly. "I can't say that I have. There's the cast and crew, of course. Greg and his wife and their normal employees who work the tour, but I've met most if not all of them as far as I know. And I've never seen any of them hanging around that old house."

Sadie shook her head. "There are also usually a group of spectators watching the filming, but security seems to be doing a good job of making sure the public stays in their designated locations."

"Any bad vibes with any of the crew or cast?"

Nicole shook her head. "No crew is perfect, but honestly, there haven't been any real issues surface on this job…except for that note."

"There has to be a connection somewhere," Edwin said, snatching a brownie from the tray.

Sadie resisted the brownie sitting in front of her, determined not to indulge in anything more tonight, and shifted her focus instead back to Nicole. “There is one other thing I am curious about. When I was first asked to help with this episode, I did my own research into the show and found out that Tom Wilson—the current director—wasn’t the man originally slated to direct this documentary. And that his predecessor, Brad Masters, was a bit...difficult.”

Nicole shook her head. “That’s putting it nicely. The series was originally directed by the ‘legendary’ Brad Masters. He’s done a number of highly rated shows over the past ten years or so for the channel. I met him once, he was screaming at his secretary about something. Obviously he was a bear to work with. Three months ago, the bosses upstairs apparently had enough of his demands and according to rumors, decided not to renew his contract.”

“How did he take the dismissal?” Edwin asked.

“Not surprisingly, he was furious. He even hired a bunch of lawyers to fight the decision. I don’t know all of the legal details, but apparently it was a mess.”

“What are you thinking?” Edwin leaned forward. “That Masters could be the one trying to sabotage the show?”

“It’s definitely worth looking into all of the possibilities.”

Nicole set her teacup back on the coffee table and shook her head. “I didn’t know him beyond his reputation, but my opinion is, if he wanted to sabotage a show, he wouldn’t do it with broken light bulbs and a mysterious letter from a dead woman.”

“How would he do it?”

Nicole laughed. “He’d tell you to your face he was upset. There are plenty of stories circulating through the studio about Brad’s temper. He's thrown things, broken things, even punched someone once. To be honest, I was glad when I found out he wasn't going to be directing our show."

Headlights swept through the living room as Charlie's tow truck pulled into the drive.

"Charlie's here," Edwin said, setting his coffee cup on the table in front of him.

"Thank you both for your help," Nicole said, grabbing her purse from beside her. "I really appreciate it."

Ten minutes later, Edwin helped Sadie finish washing the cups in the kitchen. Charlie had generously offered to drop her at the motel where the crew and cast were staying during the shoot. The young woman's theory made sense. Brad Masters didn't seem the type to play games. When he showed up, no one would be mistaken as to whether he was playing a prank or not.

Something had clicked in Sadie's mind as Nicole spoke. She'd been looking all this time for a connection to Abigail and Raymond's disappearance. But Nicole's insight into the show made her wonder if the strange things that had happened over the last few days were truly connected to a murder in the past, or to something that had happened in the present.

"You're awfully quiet," Edwin said, hanging up the cloth to dry.

"Nicole got me thinking about a few things."

"Such as?"

"I have a couple other ideas I've been toying with, though I'm not sure either will pan out."

"What are they?"

"For starters, I want to talk to Troy Haggarty. He has his morgue file of articles down at the paper and might be able to help me find something from that time period that I missed while going through the microfilm machine at the library."

Edwin nodded in agreement. "He's definitely a good source. Not only is he full of energy, but he always seems eager to help. Who else?"

"I also want to talk to Tom Wilson, the director, to see what else I can get from him about Brad Masters. He's likely to know things Nicole doesn't."

Edwin looked at her with those twinkly steel-blue eyes of his. "I have an idea."

"Another person I need to talk with?"

"No. This has more to do with you and me." Edwin smiled and took her hand. "Forget about Abigail, uncovered skeletons, and warning letters, and even Nicole for the next fifteen minutes, while you and I enjoy the sunset and the beauty of God's creation out on your front porch."

Sadie smiled, knowing Edwin was absolutely right. A moment later, she was settled in beside Edwin on her white wooden porch swing, looking out past the potted asters and geranium plants that dotted the wide plank floor and wooden porch railing to the aspen trees shimmering in the fading pink and gold light of the sunset.

"It doesn't get much more beautiful than this, does it?" Edwin said.

Sadie breathed in a lungful of crisp mountain air. It was a reminder to her that the heavens really did declare the glory of God and His majesty. And a reminder of how much she truly had to be thankful for.

She was thankful for the fact that she lived in a place where she could daily see the beauty that God created. A place where she knew most of her neighbors and the shop owners in town. A place where she could worship with her friends at the old white clapboard church with its antique bell and mountain backdrop.

"What are you thinking about?" Edwin asked.

"How thankful I am for this moment. And for how much I have to be thankful for in general."

He squeezed her hand. "We do have so much to be thankful for."

"Have you ever stopped to think how much has happened across this area over the past century?" she continued. "I can almost imagine this area untouched by buildings—just the mountains and trees. The discovery of silver changed everything for this area, and yet while so much has changed since then, so much has stayed the same. People are still the same. Hardworking and full of life. It's why I love living here."

"I want you to promise me one thing."

"Of course."

Edwin pulled her hand against his chest and caught her gaze. "Promise me you'll be careful up there at the mines. While I still think it's just someone's idea of a crazy hoax, it would be foolish to completely dismiss the possibility that someone wants to stop the documentary. And if the warning *is* true, we have no idea how far they might be willing to go to prevent the truth from being known."

"I know." She caught his gaze and nodded. "And I promise I will be careful."

Sadie looked up at the clock after Edwin left. It was nine thirty, and despite Edwin's attempts to settle her mind, it had shifted once again back to Abigail's story. Was it too late to call Troy Haggerty? She hesitated for a moment, then picked up the phone. Troy answered on the second ring.

"Troy Haggerty?"

"Yes."

"This is Sadie Speers."

"How are you, Sadie?"

"I'm fine, Troy. I hope I'm not calling you too late."

"Not at all. I'm a night owl. More than likely, I'll still be up for hours. What can I do for you?"

"I do need your help, actually. I'm sure you know about the filming going on up in the mine and here in town with the *American Treasure Chest*."

"Of course. The entire town's buzzing about a documentary being filmed in Silver Peak. I'm planning a front-page spread on the story, actually. I've already spoken to the director and some of the actors. As far as I'm concerned, next to last year's Founder's Day picnic, it's the most exciting thing that's happened for some time."

Sadie laughed. "I suppose finding a skeleton is going to cause quite a stir in town, along with the TV crew showing up."

Troy laughed. "So what can I do for you, Sadie?"

"I'd like to stop by in the morning, if you're available, to look through some of the old articles in your morgue file. See if I might be able to dig up something new on Raymond Butler's disappearance."

"Along with who might have written that warning note besides Abigail Chaplin?"

"How did you know about the note?"

Troy laughed. "Word travels fast in this small town."

Sadie clicked her fingers against the kitchen's granite countertops. "True."

"And as a reporter, the story intrigues me. I could see if I can pull some things out from that time period. What exactly are you looking for?"

"I'm not sure specifically, but perhaps letters to the editors for starters. Anything that might give me an idea if there could be someone else who might want to stop the filming of this documentary."

"Got it."

"I'd appreciate that, Troy."

"As for tomorrow, I usually get in to work early and leave late, so feel free to drop by the newspaper whenever it's convenient for you."

Sadie thanked Troy, then hung up the phone, her mind replaying Edwin's words.

If the warning is true, we have no idea how far they might be willing to go to prevent the truth from being known.

And that someone, Sadie worried, was somehow tied to a murder.

9

The next morning, Sadie woke up just before the sun began to peak over the mountains. While she loved her work at the Antique Mine—and despite the concerns they were facing with the documentary—there was something invigorating about feeling needed, especially by the people she loved in this town. And while what happened yesterday had unsettled her, yesterday evening's chat with Nicole had helped to point out to Sadie what she believed to be the real issue. Too often, jealousy and power permeated man's existence—because nothing had really changed since Adam and Eve. The constant desire to have what one didn't have caused divisions between people.

She opened up her Bible and turned to Psalm 112.

Blessed is the man who fears the Lord, who finds great delight in his commands. His children will be mighty in the land; the generation of the upright will be blessed.

Sadie pondered the psalmist's words. Nicole had mentioned that where a person's heart was, there their treasure would be, as well. Fearing the Lord and finding delight in God's commands should be like treasures—treasures not found in a gold or silver mine that could in turn be lost or destroyed, but true treasure that would never be lost.

As she had the evening before, she spent the next few minutes praying for Alice and her grandchildren, that they would continue to pass on their faith down to the next generation and the generation after that. She also prayed for Nicole, that she would grow in her faith and seek true treasures; that she would discover that following God's Word might not take away all of her struggles, but it did bring balance and would help her keep perspective of what was really important in life.

After her regular morning routine was finished, including a short walk with Hank out in the crisp morning air, Sadie was ready to go.

She reached down and rubbed the golden retriever's belly. "We'll try to go out again tonight, Hank."

A minute later, Sadie headed into town to meet with Troy Haggarty, thankful she'd decided to call him the night before. She parked in front of the newspaper offices where Troy, now twenty-five years old, had taken the job as editor of the weekly *Silver Peak Sentinel* fresh out of journalism school. There was no doubt in her mind, or anyone else's in town for that matter, that Troy loved his job. She wouldn't be surprised at all if at some point he was grabbed up by some big newspaper in the city where, like Nicole, the offer might just prove to be too tempting for him to ignore.

A bell jingled as she opened the front door.

"Good morning, Sadie." Troy walked into the small foyer with a grin, then held out his hand. "I thought that might be you."

Sadie shook the young man's hand, matching his smile. "I appreciate your meeting with me so early."

"Early bird gets the worm, as they always say, and I've never been one to waste my morning." Troy nodded toward a back room. "Why don't you come with me to my office."

Sadie followed Troy down a narrow hallway to his desk, which was located in the back corner office. Besides the buzz of a water cooler, and the sound of coffee percolating, the office was quiet.

He started stacking up scattered papers across his desk and moving files out of the way. "Writing editorials and articles might be my strong suit, but cleanliness isn't. So I'm sorry about the mess. I keep telling myself I'll get organized and clean all of this up, but there's always something that has to get done, another deadline, another paper to get out…"

"Don't worry about it on my account. I was friends with the former editor of the *Sentinel* before he retired. Always had ink stains all over his hands and a pencil tucked behind his ear. Of course, he didn't have all of the computers and equipment you have today, but the man knew how to write a captivating story and really brought the *Sentinel* to a whole new level."

Troy offered her a seat, then sat down on the other side of his desk. "I realized when I took the job that I had big footsteps to fill, but I'm determined to raise the level of the *Sentinel* even further. We might be a small town with small town news, but that doesn't mean the paper has to be substandard."

"I agree completely." Sadie smiled at his enthusiasm. She'd definitely come to the right place. "How's your mother, by the way?"

"She's well, thank you." Troy picked up a pencil and tapped it against the desk. "I'll let her know you asked about her. Retirement has done wonders for both her and my father. It's almost as if they are off on a second honeymoon. They travel around in that RV of theirs until they get the urge to move on. And as much as they love Silver Peak, I think they like traveling even more."

"It sounds like the perfect situation for all of you. They don't have to worry about the house while they travel, and you have a place to stay close to where you work." Sadie leaned forward, ready to discuss the reason she'd come by. "I know you have a lot of work to do, so I won't take up any more of your time than I have to."

"Okay, but before we start, I was wondering if you would mind my asking you a few questions at a later date for an article I'm working on regarding the documentary. I'm certain that the national coverage we are going to receive will be great for Silver Peak."

"I think most people agree with you on that. So, of course, I'd be honored."

"Wonderful."

She wasn't surprised that having a TV crew in town was news, though she wasn't sure how far the news would reach beyond Silver Peak—at least until the episode aired. But then again, as Edwin had implied, if having a TV crew brought more tourists into the sleepy mountain town, that would be wonderful. Tourism was essential not only to her business at the Antique Mine, but to all of the bed-and-breakfasts, restaurants, vacation rental properties, and other business owners in town.

"Now…" Troy reached for a folder off the top of one of the stacks. Perhaps the young editor wasn't as unorganized as he appeared. "Your questions on the phone intrigued me, actually, so I hope you don't mind, but I did some digging last night in the morgue file after you called. I found something I think you will be interested in."

"Wonderful," Sadie said, knowing that any information he'd already found would save her time this morning. "What did you find?"

"You said you were looking for someone who could have a motivation for stopping the documentary up in the mines. So I looked through the dates you gave me, and found a number of Dear Editor letters by a man by the name of Gus Fergusson. He was upset about how the mining was affecting the area in connection with the environment."

Troy reached for a stack of papers he'd placed in the file and handed them to Sadie with a grin. "There's logic to my filing system, believe it or not. I rarely lose things."

"I can see that." Sadie chuckled as she flipped open the file and skimmed the first letter Troy had copied for her. "I do know that there was a trend back in the fifties to find uranium deposits in the gold and silver mines, which many opposed."

"You're right, and Gus was one of them." Troy tapped his fingers against his desk. "If you read through those letters, you'll see that he was an environmentalist who was very vocal in his protests against the mining process."

"I remember my father talking some about the issues," Sadie said, flipping to the next page. "Unless adequate ventilation systems are installed, there were problems with the ore emitting radon gas. Those who worked in the mines often had health problems. The same was true for uranium mining, with higher reports of lung cancer and tuberculosis."

"That's all true, and why, more recently, the state has ordered the clean-up of several idle uranium mining sites in the state." Troy leaned back in his chair. "While it was never proven, Gus believed that his brother died from working in the mine."

"That certainly gave him motivation to stop any further mining," Sadie said. "Is Gus still involved in environmental issues?"

Troy checked something on his computer. "I looked up a watchdog group that works with companies that are noncompliant. They help ensure they follow the state law that requires uranium mines to be reclaimed and closed a maximum of ten years after mining ceases."

"Is Gus's name there?"

"He was back in the fifties and sixties, though his name isn't listed anywhere on their site today. But while he's never made a secret of what he thinks, he doesn't seem to be active like he was in the past. Of course, the man has to be pushing eighty by now."

"Did you find out anything else about him?"

"He's lived in Silver Peak most of his life." Troy glanced back at the computer. "He was arrested twice for protesting, but since the late seventies, there doesn't seem to be any record of a clash with the law, or even another editorial that I could find, in regard to the mining. Oh, and there was one other arrest, but all charges ended up being dropped. The police reported a fight between Fergusson and a man from out of town that didn't look to be related to the issues up in the mines."

"Do you have a date on that?"

"Yeah...June 15, 1955."

Sadie leaned forward. Raymond had disappeared just days later. "Any other details about that fight?"

"Probably...just give me a minute."

Sadie's mind churned as she waited for Troy to look up the information on his computer.

"Here we go," Troy finally said. "It says that police arrested two men for fighting. Gus Fergusson of Silver Peak and... Raymond Butler."

10

"RAYMOND BUTLER?" SADIE SAID, HER EYES WIDENING AS SHE took in the information. "So Gus knew Raymond."

"Looks like it."

Sadie worked to put everything together. "So Raymond and Gus got in a fight, then Raymond disappeared four days later. Interesting how everyone knows the story about the fight between Raymond and Abigail's brother, but now we have proof of a second man who had an issue with him, for some reason."

Troy shook his head. "The connection is definitely there, but the man's pushing eighty. It's hard to imagine him trying to sabotage the film."

"According to the sheriff, without the identity of the body that was found, we're still only guessing that it really was Raymond Butler in that mine until the DNA results come back from the lab."

Troy nodded his head, as Sadie continued.

"What we do know is that not only did Gus know Raymond, but he had a bone to pick with the man. Of course, clearly Gus wasn't the only one at odds with Raymond."

"Very true on both accounts. It does seem, though, that even if Gus isn't involved in the sabotaging of the documentary—if that is indeed what is going on—he might know of someone else with something to hide."

Troy leaned forward and rested his arms against the desk. "So do you think any of this ties in with the disappearance and possible murder of Raymond Butler? A cover-up maybe?"

"It's possible."

"What if he was the one who killed Raymond?"

"Stranger things have happened," Troy admitted.

"Do you have an address for him?"

"Yes..." Troy searched the top of his desk. "He has a house just outside of town and a daughter who lives nearby."

"You've done a fair amount of research, Troy. I hope you realize how much I appreciate it." Sadie glanced at her watch. "But for now, you'll have to excuse me. I'm going to be late if I don't hurry, and the director doesn't go for tardiness."

Three hours later, Sadie grabbed a needle and thread off the supply table in order to sew up a small rip she'd discovered in one of Nicole's costumes, while Mary freshened up the young actress's makeup for the next shoot. Given the tight schedule the director had set, it was the first time she'd been able to speak to Nicole all morning.

Sadie slipped into the empty chair beside the young actress, squinted, then threaded the needle. "Were you able to get your car sorted out, Nicole?"

"Thankfully, Charlie turned out to be a big help. His place is definitely..." Nicole seemed to search for a word.

"Old-fashioned?" Sadie offered.

Nicole laughed. "I was going to say charming, but yes. You're right. Anyway, he called me this morning to report he'd found an electrical malfunction, which is why smoke started coming out of the vents. Can you imagine what might have happened to me if the car had caught on fire?"

"It's frightening." Mary caught Nicole's gaze in the lighted mirror and shook her head. "When you rent a car, you don't expect problems with the vehicle."

"I know, and let me tell you, after yesterday the last thing I need is more excitement," Nicole said. "*And* it's almost a brand-new car! You're right, Mary, things like that aren't supposed to happen."

"What about the rental company?" Sadie asked.

"They've promised to get me another car by the end of today, though I'm not sure it matters anymore at this point. I don't think I'll do any more driving up in the mountains."

Sadie caught Mary's deepening frown in the mirror, and she knew what the women were thinking.

"You don't think the breakdown has anything to do with that warning letter, do you?"

"Mary and I have been talking about that very thing." Nicole's voice lowered as if she didn't want anyone to hear what she was saying. "I've never been superstitious, mind you, but I have to admit, I can't help but feel jumpy. Like something terrible is about to happen. Someone did warn us to stop filming."

Either way, Sadie needed to let the sheriff know what had happened with Nicole's car so he could look into the incident. She tried to put the other women at ease despite her own questions as she tied the knot on the string and started sewing up the rip. "The truth is that a terrible thing happened fifty-plus years ago, but no one has been able to find a connection to any of the recent incidents. More than likely the sheriff is correct and someone thought it would be funny to scare you, Nicole. I've seen the crew. They're always teasing you."

"Teasing me. Not trying to scare me. There's a big difference."

Sadie held up the black-and-white retro dress with the full skirt she'd picked out for Nicole, inspected the fixed seam, then proceeded to hang it back up on the rack. "Your dress is ready for the next shoot."

"Thank you, Sadie."

"You're welcome." Sadie turned back to the woman. She had one more thing she needed to do during the break. "Have you seen the director?"

Mary brushed off some powder from Nicole's shoulder, then nodded toward the front door. "I think he went off to make another phone call. He's been arguing with someone all day."

"Any idea who he's talking to?" Sadie asked Nicole, wondering if the conflict had anything to do with Brad Masters.

"Your guess is as good as mine," Nicole said.

Nicole had dredged up the possibility that the note and other signs of "sabotage" were, in fact, tied to the show itself, and *not* Silver Peak's past, a question she'd yet to fully answer. Either way, Nicole and the rest of the crew were clearly anxious, but the electrical issues with the car could once again be nothing more than a coincidence. And while she was sure that Sheriff Slattery had covered all the bases with his own investigation, he had encouraged her to keep her eyes and ears open, which was exactly what she planned to do. Asking a few additional questions to the director couldn't hurt either.

"If you'll both excuse me, I'm going to try to find the director."

With fifteen minutes before the next rehearsal, Sadie found Tom, a cell phone pressed against his ear with one hand and holding a large cup of coffee in the other. He stood at the top of the ridge overlooking the valley, but he was clearly not taking in the beauty of the Rocky Mountains surrounding him. If the man wasn't watching a rehearsal or shooting a scene, she'd noticed he spent most of his time on his cell phone. She waited, just in his line of sight, until he ended the call, ready to snag him.

While Tom was at least half her age, the man seemed completely in his element behind the camera and had proven himself as a capable director. Her only critique was that he was clearly out of place in the small town. He was much more of a city slicker in his gray suit, blue plaid collared shirt, and shiny leather shoes. No doubt he preferred Denver or other big cities to the quaint mountain town of Silver Peak. But to his credit, she'd never heard him complain about their small town ways.

A minute later, after a few animated gestures, he hung up, a deep scowl on his face.

Sadie stepped forward. "Tom, is everything all right?"

"Yes, it's just something…personal I had to deal with." He waved his hand as if dismissing the person he'd been talking to.

Sadie decided not to let his demeanor deter her from jumping into the conversation she needed to have with him. "I was wondering if I could have a few minutes of your time."

He started walking back toward the house. "A couple minutes is all I have. I need to go over the script with Darren again. I'm not particularly thrilled with his interpretation of Raymond in that last scene."

"How so?" Sadie's brow rose as she hurried to keep up with him. She thought he was doing a fine job.

While she'd noticed Darren's acting to be a little stiff at times, he definitely looked the part of Raymond Butler. Tall, dark, and incredibly distinguished. Sadie could imagine how a man like that could have swept Abigail off her feet.

Tom's scowl only seemed to deepen. "Which is why you're the historical consultant, and I'm the director."

"True," Sadie said, firmly put back in her place.

Tom stopped, letting the majestic Rocky Mountains frame his stature. Not that the man would listen to any advice she gave him, but if he were to ask her, he needed a monthlong vacation up in these mountains where all he did was hike and rest. It had always been amazing to her how a few days, or even hours, in God's creation could put perspective on life again.

"What is it you wanted to speak to me about?" he asked.

"First I just wanted to tell you how much I appreciate your letting my granddaughter fill in as one of the extras. She really enjoyed it."

"I was sorry she couldn't stay longer." His features softened slightly, surprising Sadie. She'd heard he had a couple of kids. "Thankfully, I believe I was able to get the footage I needed to splice her into the scenes."

While Sadie wasn't sure she wanted to see her granddaughter caught up in the trappings of Hollywood, it had given Sara a boost in confidence and even more importantly, something fun for

Sadie to do with her granddaughter—which was exactly what she had hoped for.

"Was there anything else?" Tom pressed, any moment of connection clearly over. If she was going to get anything out of him, she was going to have to get to the point quickly.

"There is, actually. I didn't really come to talk about Sara. I need to ask you a couple of questions about the note Nicole found."

"The note?" Tom took a sip of his coffee and started walking again. "You sound like Sheriff Slattery. I met with him yesterday, trying to help him come up with who might want to shut down the show. He seems to agree with me that the note was a prank."

"He's just looking at all the possibilities, I'm sure," Sadie said. "But I take it you don't agree that the note was a prank."

As far as Sadie was concerned, the verdict was still out on that one. "I'm not sure, but if it isn't, I'm worried about the threat. I'm also worried that someone else might get hurt like Sara did. Or the possibility that Nicole's car breaking down wasn't an accident."

"Like I said, I'm of the mind that it's just some silly prank by someone wanting to scare Nicole and the rest of the crew." The director seemed to only want to brush Sadie's concerns away. "I'm not planning to take it seriously at all."

"You might be right, but if you're not…" That was what had her concerned. There were threats in the note that someone else would get hurt. Someone clearly didn't want anyone digging around into the past. Which meant someone else in the present could get hurt. Or if someone like Brad Masters was angry about being replaced, as Nicole had suggested, then they had another possible motive behind the note.

"I'm not sure what you are implying." Tom set his hands against his hips. "Do you think we should just shut the whole thing down and walk away?"

"Not at all." And from his expression, clearly the director wouldn't agree with that conclusion either. "But neither do I think we can simply dismiss some of the odd things that have been happening lately."

"Wait a minute." Tom shook his head as if he'd just figured out a funny joke. "Oh, I get it. The sheriff told me you'd been helpful in solving a few mysteries related to this town's rough-and-tumble past."

Sadie tried to ignore the irritation in his tone. "Silver Peak has been my home my entire life. I care about the people here and what happens to them. Nothing more. If there is any chance that someone else could get hurt, well, I simply believe it's worth looking into."

"Like I said, Sadie, I respect you, and so far you've done an admirable job helping our cast look authentic for their parts. But as far as I'm concerned, your role ends there. Let the sheriff poke around if that's what he wants, but I'd advise you to stay out of it."

The director hurried toward the house, forcing Sadie to hurry to keep up with him. Maybe it was time to throw out another angle.

"What if that note was directed to you personally?"

The director stopped suddenly, then turned to face her. "What do you mean . . . to me personally?"

Sadie chose her words carefully, knowing that this would more than likely be her only chance to have the man's complete attention. If she'd learned anything about him, she knew he wasn't going to play around with small talk and petty issues. "I understand that you recently took over for the original director for this project. The man who originally came up with the idea, in fact, for this series."

"I see you've done your research," Tom said. "Brad Masters was fired, but Masters was a jerk and he deserved it. Yes, he had a few good ideas, but lately those were few and far between. The *American Treasure Chest* series was originally his baby, but the man's creatively dried up."

"Do you think he'd attempt to sabotage the show?" She threw out the question and waited for the director's reaction.

Tom laughed, then started walking again. "If Brad wanted to get back at me over being fired, he wouldn't steal a bunch of batteries, leave a note on a piece of flowery paper and sign it with Abigail's name, trust me. He'd show up here, in my face, and demand that this job was still his."

Which was what Nicole had said. But still...

"Did he ever threaten you?" Sadie asked. The attention span of the director was about to run out, but she wasn't quite finished.

"Threaten me?" Tom laughed. "Brad threatened everyone. If you made him angry, he'd threaten to fire you—and if he was really angry, he might follow through. I'm sure he went through a dozen assistants in the past two years. Forget his coffee or leave out a spoonful of sugar and you'd find yourself on the street the next day without a job."

"But this time, *he* lost his job. Did he threaten anyone?"

"He screamed and cursed all the way to the front door." Tom held up his hands, then caught Sadie's gaze. "Listen, Sadie, I'll admit that Brad has a temper, but that's not a secret. I'll admit he threatened the producers of this show and even me personally. But do I take him seriously? No. For the most part, Brad Masters is simply good at venting and whining, which was one of the underlying reasons he was let go in the first place. But I can't see him doing anything... illegal."

Sadie slowed down her steps as they approached the wood-framed house, but she wasn't completely convinced of Brad's innocence. She still had one last question. "Where is Brad right now?"

"Last I heard, he was in Florida. Took off a few weeks ago to hang out on the beach and drown his sorrows in a string of pretty women and margaritas." Tom shook his head. "I do appreciate your concern, but I really feel as if you're barking up the wrong tree."

"What about the person you were just arguing with?"

Tom's expression darkened. "Like I said, that was personal."

"So Brad hasn't tried to contact you?"

"No."

"But something's wrong," she pressed.

The director's frown deepened. "Yes, something is wrong, but it has nothing to do with Brad or anything related to the show for that matter. It's... personal."

"I'm sorry then. I know how tough it can be balancing your professional life when there are other things you are having to deal with."

Sadie caught a flicker of pain in his eyes.

He hesitated, then let out a sigh. "I was speaking to my wife on the phone... or shall I say, my soon-to-be ex-wife. Two weeks ago her lawyer served me divorce papers. No heads-up. No warning.

So now I'm in the middle of a divorce, and she's insisting on no visitation with my kids. But even when life is falling apart around you, the show must go on."

"I'm so sorry," Sadie said, wishing now she hadn't pushed so hard for answers.

"Yeah, so am I."

A look of sadness washed over him, and he glanced back at Sadie.

"And just in case you're wondering," he continued, "no, my wife isn't the kind of woman who would sabotage one of my projects with frilly warning notes and missing batteries just to take revenge. She's more like Brad in that way, no games. She'd simply shoot me while I was sleeping."

Tom shot her a sardonic smile, then turned and walked away.

Whether or not what he'd said about Brad not being involved was true, she was going to talk to the sheriff, and at the least have him verify the man's alibi. Because until she had the answer to that, she couldn't shake the lingering question. *Was someone trying to cover up secrets from the past, or something very real from the present?*

11

At three in the afternoon, with the cast getting ready to rehearse, the director told Sadie that unless she wanted to stay and watch, she wouldn't be needed on the set until the next morning. An offer, she'd decided, that was fine with her.

While there had been no more incidents over the course of the day to suggest that someone was trying to sabotage the set, she still had questions she wanted answered. She'd considered dropping by to visit Frances's on her way into town, but a phone call had confirmed that Frances was spending the afternoon with her sister and wasn't planning to return until later in the evening.

Which was why Sadie found herself in the back room of the Antique Mine, working to restore an old trunk with Alice. Even when there weren't customers in the shop, there was always plenty of work to be done: from pricing and stocking new inventory, to repairing items so they were ready to go out onto the floor, to the more mundane things like keeping up with the accounts.

Today, she decided to take the extra time to work in the back room on an antique, wooden steamer trunk she was restoring for a buyer. She'd already removed most of the leather strips and hardware. Anything that was reusable, she kept in a ziplock bag.

Once that was done, she would start the process of sanding down the entire wooden surface of the trunk with sandpaper. By the time she stained it and put it back together, the stunning chest would be ready for its new owner.

Sadie hummed along with the country tune playing in the background as she brushed off the surface of the trunk with a scrub brush to get rid of all the loose debris. On the other side of the trunk, Alice used a pair of pliers to remove a stubborn nail.

"Any more strange happenings up at the mine today?" Alice asked, still tugging on the nail.

"Thankfully, everything went smoothly." Sadie moved on to a new section with her scrub brush.

"That has to be a relief."

"I still have questions, but perhaps it's proving the theory that at least Edwin, the director, and the sheriff seem to share."

"That the letter was a prank?" Alice asked.

Sadie scrubbed harder on a section of embedded dirt on the top of the trunk. "I made sure the sheriff knew about Nicole's car and the fact that the previous director had been fired. He promised to look into both situations, but I think he's still convinced it was a prank."

"And all of the other strange incidents?"

"Coincidences," Sadie said.

"He could be right, you know."

Sadie nodded. "I realize that covering up a murder from so many years ago seems almost... silly. But I just can't quite connect the dots. And until I do..."

"You'll keep asking questions," Alice said with a smile. "Sara's convinced it's a publicity stunt put on by the TV channel."

Sadie laughed. "She must be bored."

Alice nodded her head as she finally yanked the stubborn nail out. "Finally! I can't imagine what you did as a parent to keep me busy in the summer without the Internet and video games. Or at least that's what my kids seem to think. And now Sara's moaning because she's not up there at that set with all the actors."

Sadie looked up from her brush. "Let's see... I remember bikes, swimming lessons, books, lemonade stands... Shall I continue?"

"At least the swelling's down on her ankle so she can get around better now."

Sadie looked up as the front bell jingled. While she'd thoroughly enjoyed working on the documentary set, she'd also discovered that she missed the day-to-day interaction back at the Antique Mine with the tourists, as well as the locals who regularly stopped by the shop.

"I can finish up in here if you'd like to take that customer," Alice offered.

Sadie quickly washed her hands, then went to meet Marilee Welch, a local, who had just walked into the shop, wearing a red polka-dot dress and lace collar. The woman had a style all her own and had never been afraid to show it.

Sadie reached up to grab a wooden box off the shelf where she'd stashed the doorknobs she'd saved for her. "I've been hoping you'd drop by, Marilee."

Marilee's smile was brighter than a kid in a candy shop. "I came as soon as I could after getting your message."

Sadie set the collection of draw pulls and accent knobs she'd set aside onto the counter, then stepped back to watch Marilee's reaction. Marilee's broad smile widened as she took a closer look. A year ago, she'd decided to begin work on restoring some antiques, and she often came by the shop to learn techniques from Sadie as well as pick up new items for her house.

"Do you like them?" Sadie asked.

"I do. They're absolutely beautiful. Where did you get these?"

"I bought them at an estate auction in Colorado Springs last week and thought of you and your furniture restoration projects."

"These"—Marilee picked up two of the knobs—"will be perfect for the dresser I'm restoring, and for several other projects I'd like to get to before I retire."

Sadie's grin broadened. Marilee still had at least two decades left before retirement, and enough projects to fill her free time until then, she was sure.

Alice joined them from the back room, brushing off a smudge of dirt from the sleeve of her shirt. "Marilee, it's good to see you."

"Your mother has done it once again," Marilee said.

"She thought you might like them."

"Like them? I love them. Who were the sellers?" Marilee asked, looking through the box at the different knobs and pulls. "They clearly had quite a collection."

"Yes, they did. I met with the son of the couple, Franklin Peterson. He was organizing their estate for them, which, let me tell you, was no easy task. The house they just sold sits on five acres with at least four large sheds. They're planning to move into a condo, which means they had to downsize drastically."

"That has to be difficult," Marilee said, continuing to look through the knobs, this time perhaps in a different light. "That's going to be quite a change for them."

"I agree," Sadie said. "But their son took photos of things they couldn't keep and was making them into a scrapbook. According to him, they'd both decided that after sixty years of collecting, they were ready to simplify."

Sadie knew there would come a time when she'd have to do the same thing. She and her first husband had been the fourth generation to live in the family's house. T.R. had remodeled the kitchen only a year before his death, and before that, they'd done dozens of projects to fix up the spacious farmhouse.

When that time came, however, it was the memories she planned to hold on to—growing up in the house, moving there as a new bride, raising her daughter, and more recently her grandchildren. After all of those years—and all of those memories—she was endlessly grateful she was still able to live in such a beautiful home. And she was also grateful for the new memories she was making with Edwin.

"These glass ones are particularly stunning," Marilee said, holding up the pair.

Sadie shifted her mind back to the present and nodded in agreement. "Back when the United States joined World War I, glass knobs became popular because metal was previously used for doorknobs then had to go to manufacturing airplanes and other war items. I'm always on the lookout for cobalt, red, and Vaseline glass knobs, but if you ask me, these are just as beautiful."

"Well, if you ever do find any of those other colors, let me know, but for now, I'm thrilled with everything you have right here."

"And I have one more thing to show you that wasn't on your list, but I heard you mention it a while back."

Marilee rested her hands against the counter and leaned forward, as if she couldn't imagine her day getting any better than it already was. Finding her customers the perfect piece was part of the reason Sadie enjoyed her job so much. And without even showing Marilee what she'd found, she knew she'd done just that.

"We picked these up at the same auction." Sadie reached under the counter where she'd set them aside. "They're black cast-iron door handles with levers."

"You do know me far too well, Sadie. They're perfect for the bathroom I'm finally redoing on the second floor."

Last winter, Marilee had proudly shown Sadie her first stages of remodeling the old Victorian home she owned on Main Street. The downstairs bathroom had just been completed with a claw bathtub, pink wallpaper, moldings, and ornamental wall scones.

"There is one other thing before you ring all of this up for me," Marilee said, glancing around the room. "I heard you're using that dressing table I've been eying for the documentary being shot up at the mine."

"I'll have it back at the end of the week as soon as filming is finished," Sadie said.

"Have you seen the new one my mom just picked up?" Alice showed Marilee the mahogany dressing table Sadie had found at the same auction. Marilee's smile told Sadie she'd just made another sale.

Marilee held up her hands. "I'm going to have to leave before I end up taking half the store home with me. Which is my problem. I have more projects than budget."

As soon as Marilee had left twenty minutes later, with the knobs, door handles, and dressing table in tow, the bell on the front door of the Antique Mine chimed again. With only fifteen minutes left until closing, Alice offered to finish cleaning up the back room while Sadie helped the last customer.

Sadie leaned backward to stretch her back muscles and decided that holding down two jobs was definitely something that should be left to the younger generation. And she still needed to try to see if she could catch Frances Knight, the woman Sara had discovered a photo of crying at Philip's funeral, at home later this evening and ask her a few questions.

Evelyn Winston slipped through the front door, carrying what appeared to be two large paintings. The woman often brought in items, primarily things passed down from her mother-in-law, either to ask Sadie's opinion on the price, or to sell on consignment.

"Hi, Evelyn." Sadie cleared off the counter beside the old-style brass cash register to give her room to set the paintings down. "I didn't expect to see you again today."

"I've been meaning to drop these by for weeks now—in fact, they've just been sitting in my car—but with Greg's discovery of that skeleton, the documentary people, and now all of the strange things happening at the mine, I've been a bit... distracted."

Evelyn certainly wasn't the only one, Sadie thought. "I can completely understand how you feel."

"Anyway, Greg sent me into town to pick up something at Putnam & Sons, and when I saw these sitting in the backseat, I decided I needed to stop in and see you before another week goes by." Evelyn set the paintings onto the counter, sounding slightly out of breath. "So what do you think?"

Sadie pulled back the felt separator covering the fronts of them to reveal two oil paintings of Mount Princeton, one of Colorado's "collegiate peaks." "These are beautiful, Evelyn. Are you sure you want to sell them?"

"They belonged to my mother-in-law, and I'm hoping they might fetch a good price to an interested buyer. They've hung on one of my bedroom walls, but to be honest, they never were my taste."

"I'd need to do further research on the pair, but they are in quite good condition." Sadie turned them over to study the gilded frames. "The work is signed."

"I saw the name, Ben Roberts, but I don't know who he is," Evelyn said.

"He's a local artist who lived in the area around the turn of the twentieth century, but his work has been showing up lately for sale in art galleries across the state." Sadie dug up everything she could in her memory regarding older paintings, and Ben Roberts in particular. "It's from the early nineteen hundreds, and appears to be in rather good condition. If we can find the right buyer, I believe it could bring in a fair amount."

"How much?"

Sadie carefully considered her response. "You have to understand that there are numerous factors involved in antiques. Any price I quote you is simply my opinion of how much the piece is worth, not how much a buyer will be willing to pay."

Evelyn leaned forward as she waited for the answer.

"There has been quite a gain in the value of prices for many quality nineteenth-century pieces of art. I'm guessing that the paintings could be auctioned off for...one, maybe two thousand dollars."

Evelyn beamed at the answer. But for Sadie the monetary value of something wasn't the only thing she looked at. She found the historical background of a piece just as fascinating, if not more so.

Last month, she'd attended an estate sale forty miles north of Silver Peak. Three daughters were selling their parents' home after they both had passed away. It had been a difficult process, but the girls had spent as much time as they could with each of the buyers, telling the stories they knew about each item. For Sadie, it was never just a stack of tea towels she was able to get for a bargain. It was the fact that a young bride had spent hours delicately embroidering each stitch.

"Do you really think they will fetch that much?" Evelyn asked.

"To the right buyer, perhaps a collector of Robert's works, it is definitely possible. I could put them on display for commission for you."

"Well, that is good news." Evelyn shoved back a lock of her dark hair behind her ear and let out a sigh. "I loved my mother-in-law while she was alive, but the clutter she left behind, well, let's just say I feel as if I'm continually going through and getting rid of things."

"I've been told I should do that, as well," Sadie said with a smile, handing the woman a form and a pen. "You've filled out the commission form before."

"Of course." Evelyn took the offered pen from Sadie and started filling in her information. "I did want to ask you about Sara before I left. Greg and I haven't been able to stop talking about what's been happening at the mine with all the strange events, but we feel awful that she was injured. We pride ourselves in keeping visitors safe."

"It seems to me that incident was Sara's fault completely," Sadie said. "She knew the rules going there, and I can't imagine what she was thinking going off like that. But still, Sara is better, thank you."

"And what do you think about the note and all of the strange things that have been happening?"

"I still have a number of unanswered questions like we all do, I suppose," Sadie said.

"I know I do. And Nicole is still shaken up." Evelyn tapped her pen against the form and caught Sadie's gaze. "If I believed in ghosts, which I don't, of course, I just might believe that Abigail *was* the one trying to stop the documentary."

"Except we both know that's ridiculous." Sadie walked around the counter and found a place to display the paintings near the front of the store where they were out of any direct sunlight. "Trust me, when this is all over, there will be a perfectly logical explanation for everything that has happened, though I do agree with you on one point. It certainly has been disconcerting."

"So what do you think about the documentary, Sadie?" Evelyn followed her to the front of the store and handed Sadie the form and the pen. "I told Greg maybe we should simply tell the TV crew to leave, but he assured me it was just a prank."

Sadie reached up to straighten one of the paintings. "He's probably right. That's what the sheriff thinks anyway."

"Prank or not, I hope nothing else happens while they're here."

Sadie switched the sign to Closed, then opened the front door for Evelyn. "I agree completely."

"I'll see you tomorrow up at the mine then." Evelyn asked.

Sadie said good-bye to Evelyn, then shut and locked the door as Alice came back into the room. "Everything in the back is cleaned up, Mom."

"Thank you so much, Alice. We should be able to finish up that trunk by the beginning of next week." Sadie started for the back of the room, then paused at the window display. "Alice, there were three perfume bottles sitting in the window display. The ones we got from the sale last week. Now there are only two. Did you sell one of them today?"

"No." Alice shook her head. "I noticed one was gone, but I assumed you'd decided to use it as one of the props."

"I already have one there for Abigail's dressing table, where she sits and reads the letters, but it wasn't one of these."

Alice shrugged. "Strange, but I'm sure it will show up."

"Maybe." Sadie frowned. She'd seen enough strange incidences for the week. A missing perfume bottle seemed insignificant. "Why don't you go home, Alice? I can finish up here and lock everything up."

Alice grabbed her purse. "Are you sure?"

"Of course," Sadie said, following her daughter to the front door.

Alice grabbed the door handle, then stopped. "Sara told me about the photograph she found at the library. Do you really think you should get involved, Mom?"

"Probably not," Sadie said.

But it was too late for that. She still had more questions than answers and she was hoping Frances would be able to give her some of those answers.

12

Halfway down Main Street, Sadie started to wonder if she should have taken Alice up on her offer for dinner. Because while she normally didn't mind eating alone, she was beginning to realize that eating alone wasn't what she wanted to do tonight. What she needed was someone with whom she could bounce off her thoughts while trying to sort through the facts. Because Priscilla's plea for her to find out the truth behind Raymond Butler's disappearance had not stopped nagging at her over the past forty-eight hours.

Edwin had a meeting tonight that was supposed to go late with the city council, which meant calling him was not an option. She started to turn the car around and head back toward her daughter's house, then thought about Roz. Roz was always up for dinner, especially when Roscoe was out of town, which he was tonight. And after dinner, they could even swing by and visit Frances, who should be home by then.

Sadie pulled over onto the side of the road next to Centennial Park and called Roz's cell phone.

"Sadie. I was just about to call you," Roz chirped on the other end of the line. "I was wondering how your day went up at the mine on that fancy Hollywood set."

Sadie laughed. "It's not exactly Hollywood, or fancy for that matter, considering the setting."

"True, which is why I would have insisted on meeting somewhere a little more scenic than an old, rustic mine for a backdrop if I were Abigail."

"It's the view *outside* the mine from that mountaintop that is spectacular. The mine is simply where it is believed Raymond was murdered."

"That is true," Roz said. "So how did it go? Any more warning notes?"

Sadie had been right. Roz was the perfect person for her to be around tonight. Make it any night for that matter. "No warning notes, but there's been a slew of technical problems."

"Sabotage."

Sadie laughed at her friend's comment. "I still don't know if this is simply a normal part of the process, but the director's clearly frustrated. And add to that, the lead playing Raymond kept forgetting his lines."

"So he's not exactly Cary Grant?"

"No, though he does look the part. You can almost understand how Raymond managed to sweep Abigail off her feet and convince her to run away with him. He was clearly something of a Casanova."

"Have you had supper?" Roz asked. "Roscoe went fishing with a couple of his buddies, and I've yet to decide what I want to eat."

"How about meeting me at Sophia's, if pizza sounds good. I could use a sounding board tonight."

"I can manage that. How much time do you need?"

"I'm in town and on my way there now. I'll get us a table and wait for you."

Most of the folks of Silver Peak, Sadie included, thought Sophia's served some of the best calzones and pizza in the west. The owner and head chef had transformed the older house into a typical Italian restaurant, complete with low lights; old, empty bottles of wine with candles; and a giant wood-burning oven where the chefs baked the pies. The back of the house had been taken over by a wide marble-topped table cluttered with flour dust, mounds of rising dough, fresh ricotta, mozzarella, and parmesan cheeses, basil plants, and various pizza toppings like garlic and red peppers.

Sadie had already settled at one of the handcrafted wood tables in the corner of the cozy room and was watching the chef toss the dough when Roz arrived five minutes later. Their waitress, Emily, brought them each a menu and a glass of water, then assured them she'd be back to take their order.

Sadie thanked Emily, then took in Roz's new, multicolored ethnic print skirt paired with a bright red top and leather sandals. "I take it your shopping trip while in Phoenix with your daughter-in-law went well."

"You should have come with me." Roz took a sip of her water. "You probably would have saved me money, but I saw this outfit and couldn't resist."

"I have to say I like it. It's fun, colorful, and exactly what I'd expect you to be wearing."

"I thought so, and even Roscoe likes it. I found this fantastic store he thought he'd never get me out of, but I was just getting back at him for dragging me through the hardware store for an hour and a half."

Sadie laughed as the waitress returned with a plate of two large bread sticks, sprinkled with Parmesan cheese and sauce.

"They're complimentary this week," Emily said with a smile as she placed them on the table between them. She then asked if they were ready to have their orders taken. Sadie asked the waitress to thank the owner for the bread sticks, then ordered a mozzarella and basil pizza, while Roz decided to try the special of the day, a spinach calzone.

"These look fantastic," Roz dunked one of the bread sticks into the sauce and took a bite. "Have you heard the latest from the *Chatterbox*?"

"News or gossip?" Sadie asked with a raised brow as she tried one of the bread sticks.

The *Chatterbox* reported on social events in Silver Peak like weddings, births, and funerals. But while Sadie appreciated the blog for its news and a chance to keep up with people, including former residents, every once in a while the blog author—who to this day was still anonymous—tended to cross the line from news to gossip, which had more than once caused problems around town.

"Definitely news," Roz said. "And good news at that."

Sadie waved a hand in the air. "I tell you, forget my trying to figure out what might have happened to Raymond Butler sixty-odd years ago. I want to find out who's the author of that blog."

Roz laughed. "Good luck. But you'll like today's post. It was news about Josh."

Sadie leaned forward. "What kind of news?"

"He just got a huge order for Adirondack chairs from a company in Grand Junction."

"That's fantastic," Sadie said.

"The post also mentioned at the end some of the troubles up in the mine. So now it's your turn. Tell me everything, starting with how Sara is doing."

"Her ankle is already feeling better, and I'm hoping she learned an important lesson. I took her with me yesterday to visit Priscilla Chaplin to ask her a few questions about her mother."

"Was she open to talking?" Roz asked.

Don Sweeting, pastor and founder of Campfire Chapel, walked past their table with his wife, Jeanne, and greeted her and Roz with a warm smile and a hello. A former rodeo star and retired Denver police captain, he went into the ministry after an injury ended his roping career and he had to retire from the force. Since his arrival in Silver Peak, he and his wife had been a blessing with their obvious compassion for the community. Even the children loved him as he always carried around cherry licorice sticks to dole out to them.

Sadie turned back to Roz as the Sweetings settled into their table on the other side of the room. "Priscilla has always been reluctant to talk about her mother's past. I assumed it was because her mother had never been willing to share the entire truth, which left open lots of speculation. What I do know is that their relationship was troubled, though in the end I believe they made peace."

"I never understood why some people blamed Abigail for what happened," Roz said, sipping her water. "I always saw her as the victim."

"Philip was an up-and-coming lawyer, and many believe her behavior tarnished the Chaplin name, which eventually led to Philip's drinking, and then the fatal car wreck he was killed in."

Roz frowned. "Isn't that how it often happens. The woman gets blamed and the man walks away scot-free. Think about the woman the Pharisees brought to Jesus that had been caught in adultery. I've always wanted to know where the man was."

"You do have a point, except this time, Raymond—or Philip—for that matter, didn't walk away scot-free," Sadie said.

Sadie shuddered. Instead, Raymond had been presumably murdered.

"Priscilla did give me something that had belonged to her mother," Sadie said.

"Really? What?" Roz asked.

Sadie grabbed her purse she'd slung over the back of her chair and pulled out the stack of letters between Abigail and Raymond. "These are letters written over fifty years ago between Abigail and Raymond."

Roz picked them up, then started reading the first letter on the top. "So are there any clues in them as to what happened?"

"No, and I've read them all. Twice. Though, according to Sara, they're better than any romance novel she's ever read."

Roz's brow rose slightly. "Well, the director needs to see them."

Sadie shook her head. "Priscilla asked me to keep them confidential."

"I can understand that, but if you ask me, quotes from these letters would make the story even more authentic and a whole lot more romantic for that matter."

"You're right, but I can't go against Priscilla's wishes. It's a touchy situation, and I have to respect her privacy."

Sadie waited to continue while their waitress set down their order. Her mouth watered at the savory smells of basil and cheese, making her glad she'd opted to come here rather than settle for whatever was leftover in her fridge. "Looks delicious."

Sadie closed her eyes and offered a prayer before they started eating.

"I probably shouldn't have finished off that bread stick, but their food is so delicious." Roz picked up her fork and knife and started into her calzone.

For the next few minutes, they ate in silence, enjoying the food, until Roz asked another question.

"So do you think Raymond's disappearance really is connected to what's been happening up at the mine?"

Sadie had already written down her theories—theories for the moment, anyway—in the journal she always kept in her purse. "I have two . . . really, three theories."

"Which are?" Roz prodded before dipping another bite of her calzone into the sauce and eating it.

"One," Sadie began. "The letter was nothing more than a joke meant to spook Nicole."

"Which it did, no matter what the motive."

"Exactly. Two, someone knows what happened the night of Raymond's disappearance because either they were there, someone confessed to them, or I suppose it's possible that they *are* the murderer and don't want anyone to find out the truth. Probably more likely they're associated with the murderer, since this happened so long ago. The documentary, even if it doesn't discover the truth, could still be the catalyst for someone's secret to be uncovered."

"And murder is a very nasty secret," Roz said.

"I still have a few people I'd like to talk to who might know something about that night. Troy from the paper helped me this morning. We discovered that Philip wasn't the only man who got into a fight with Raymond."

Roz rested her fork against the side of her plate. "Really? Who else?"

"Gus Fergusson."

"Gus Fergusson...I know that name. I think Roscoe knows him."

"I'd like to talk with him, though I haven't been able to get ahold of him yet. But the bottom line is that he's somehow connected to Raymond Butler," Sadie said. "And Philip wasn't the only person who held a grudge against the man."

"Do you think Priscilla knows more than she's telling you?"

"I wish I knew. Clearly Priscilla has more motivation than anyone else I know, but she hardly seems like the type to traipse up to the mine and leave anonymous warning notes. What would really be the point?"

"Which is what makes this entire situation so odd." Roz took a sip of water with the lemon floating on top and shook her head. "Raymond Butler disappeared over fifty, almost sixty, years ago, which means that anyone alive who knew them back then has to be close to eighty."

"And your third theory?"

"I've been looking into the possibility of someone who wants to stop the filming because of issues with the director and network, not the story of Abigail and Raymond specifically." Sadie took another bite of her pizza. "There were issues, for example, between the current director who took over for one who was fired."

"Sounds like motive to me. How many times is jealousy the true motive?"

"Sara also came across a photo of Frances Knight at Philip Chaplin's funeral, clearly distraught over his death."

"That's interesting."

"I'd like to stop by and see her after dinner, but again, it's hard to imagine Frances involved any more than it is Priscilla. The woman is as healthy as an ox, but after all of these years... what would be the point?"

"Unless she—or whoever left the note—really does have something to hide."

"Such as?" Sadie asked.

Roz smiled. "I'll leave that to you to figure out."

"So far that is easier said than done," Sadie said, finishing up her last bite of pizza. "And let's face it. No one really knows what happened up there that night except for Abigail, Raymond, and presumably Philip, and all of them have long since died. Even Priscilla said her mother would never talk about it."

The waitress stopped by their tables and asked them if they wanted any dessert. "We have something new on the menu."

"That isn't fair." Sadie smiled up at the waitress. "Saying no to a great dessert is almost impossible for me. What is it?"

"It's an Italian trifle with chocolate, custard, espresso coffee, and sponge cake."

"Is it good?" Sadie asked.

"Fantastic."

"We'll split one," Roz said decisively. "You need something to get your mind off of the drama up at the mines, and I saw this on the menu last week when I was here with Roscoe and was tempted to try it then."

"I'll get it out to you in a jiffy." The waitress spun around and headed to the kitchen.

"I know you're tired of talking about this, but what if I came with you to the set tomorrow?"

Sadie shot her best friend a grin. "Do I hear a hint of giddiness in your voice? You sound like Sara did when she first asked to come. What happened to what I normally hear from you about the evils of reality shows taking advantage of people?"

"Well, *American Treasure Chest* isn't really a reality show, and I'm intrigued by the idea of Abigail's story and the possibility that someone is out to stop the filming of her story. And now that there have been warnings against continuing to film, well, I'm even more intrigued to know who might be behind this."

Sadie leaned forward and winked. "It could be dangerous."

Roz rolled her eyes. "I tend to think it's nothing more than a silly hoax. But even so, what do you think? With Sara unable to come, you never know when you might need an extra hand."

Sadie smiled, happy to have her friend on board. "Looks like I have myself a sidekick again. And that's not all. After we finish our dessert, I believe it's time to pay Frances Knight a visit."

13

THIRTY MINUTES LATER, SADIE PULLED INTO THE CIRCULAR DRIVE on the edge of town in front of Frances Knight's modest one-story home. Frances was working out in her garden amid a colorful mixture of white and yellow alpine asters and blue columbine flowers. Her flower beds were ablaze with color, with everything from larkspurs to Iceland poppies and a number of plants Sadie wasn't sure she would be able to identify if pressed with the question.

Sadie spoke as she and Roz crossed the lawn to where Frances knelt on her plastic kneeler, weeding the flower beds. "Your garden is lovely, Frances."

Frances looked up, then used her hand to block the setting sun. "Can I help you?"

"It's Sadie Speers. I called and asked if I could come by and talk with you for a few minutes."

"Of course. I remember now." Frances pressed her hand against her thighs, then stood and peeled off her garden gloves. "I love working out here, but every time I get up or down, I'm reminded that I'm not twenty-something anymore."

Sadie laughed. "I know what you mean. I have those same reminders every day."

Frances dropped the gloves onto the ground beside where she was working. "Believe it or not, my grandmother planted these columbines and poppies back in the sixties. My mother expanded the beds some, but they have been thriving ever since."

"They're beautiful," Roz said.

"I'm waiting for my blue sapphire flax to come in. Have to find plants hardy enough to survive the altitude, you know."

"Well, it certainly seems as if you know what you're doing," Roz said with a laugh. "The closest I'll get to having a garden like this is if I hire a team full-time, and I don't see that happening any time soon."

"You don't mind if I sit down, do you?"

"Of course not," Sadie said.

"I'd invite you inside, but I'm behind on my housework." Frances sat down on a wooden yard bench that had been set in front of a row of Colorado spruce and rested her hands beside her on the seat. "I have to say, I never appreciated my grandmother and mother's work until recently. After years of working inside the library, and cooped up in the wintertime, I'm enjoying spending so much time outside, though I'll admit I pay a man to do most of the work for me."

Most of the town had bought into the rumors that the retired librarian was a bit crazy, an old spinster who stayed to herself. But in their few encounters over the years, Sadie had always found the woman to be quite pleasant, albeit eccentric.

"We just want to ask you a few questions," Sadie said. "You remember Roz Putnam, don't you?"

Frances nodded as she brushed off the front of her khaki-colored apron. "Of course. You're married to Roscoe Putnam."

"Almost forty-five years," Roz responded.

Frances's expression softened. "He came by with a couple of friends this past winter. Saw that my rain gutter had fallen on the front of my house and offered to fix it. Didn't want any money. Settled for a cup of hot chocolate and a plate of store-bought cookies."

Sadie wasn't surprised at all at Frances's confession. Roscoe was one of the most generous men Sadie knew, always willing to lend a hand to a friend, or a stranger for that matter. Growing up poor on a farm in Kansas as the oldest of eight children had taught him how to work hard. He even quit school at sixteen to work for the railroad so he could help provide for the family, but despite his lack of a high school diploma, Roscoe could easily hold his own in a debate and was an avid reader. "Roscoe didn't mention that to me, but he has a tendency of going around and helping people out," Roz said.

"He invited me to church at…"

"Campfire Chapel?" Sadie offered.

"Yes. That was it."

"We'd love to have you."

"It's one of those things I keep meaning to do, but I don't get out much anymore other than to work in my garden, spend time with my sister and her family, and fetch a few supplies now and then in town."

Sadie decided to jump straight into her questions. "You probably know by now that TV show, *American Treasure Chest*, is doing a documentary up in the mines about the skeleton Greg Winston found."

The smile on Frances's face faded. "I read about it in the paper. Can't imagine finding something like that myself. My grandmother once found some bones in the garden patch out back. Nearly thought she was going to have a heart attack, until she insisted on taking them down to the police station in order to solve a crime. She was eventually assured they were the bones of the neighbor's dog and *not* her missing neighbor, who, it turned out, had gone off on an extended vacation to Florida that winter without telling anyone."

"I think that would give me quite a fright, as well," Sadie said with a chuckle.

"She was always cautious after that and insisted that Grandfather till the garden." Frances's gaze narrowed. "Did you tell me what you needed to speak with me about?"

"On the phone earlier today . . . " Sadie looked to Roz, hoping the woman's long-term memory was better than her short-term memory. "As I mentioned, I'm working as a consultant for the documentary. The producers were looking for someone to provide a touch of authenticity and help with props and costumes, and they wanted someone from this area who knew Silver Peak."

"I'm not sure how I could help with that," Frances began.

Sadie smiled. "Thanks, Frances, but we're not looking for help in that area specifically. We're curious about your connection to the Chaplin family."

"The Chaplins? There isn't much to tell, really. Why do you ask?"

"We saw a photo of you at Philip Chaplin's funeral in one of the old Silver Peak newspapers."

From the expression on Frances's face, Philip's name clearly struck a chord.

"Philip... That was over fifty years ago." Frances's fingers gripped the edges of her apron and twisted it. "A lot of time has passed since then."

"I realize that, but there have been some warnings made about the documentary. As if someone didn't want the filming to continue. Since most of the people involved in that incident aren't alive, we're looking for anyone who might know what happened the night Philip disappeared. To see if someone might be trying to cover up what happened back then."

"I can't imagine who would care after all these years about the story being told," Frances said.

"What do you know about what happened back then, Frances? What happened between Philip and Raymond?"

"Philip was a good man. He was smart, considerate, kind..." Frances looked past them. "He and his sisters were close. He was always looking after them, but Abigail..."

"What about Abigail?" Sadie prompted.

"I hate to say it, but...she was selfish. She was caught up in the money and thought she was better than everyone else. I think that's why she fell for Raymond. He offered her a way out of Silver Peak. Philip was different, though. He didn't care about who I was or where I was from. He just liked...me."

Maybe their assumptions had been right, Sadie thought. "You were in love with him?"

Frances looked up and Sadie caught a sense of sadness in her gaze. "We'd always been good friends, until one day—I don't know what happened—but I realized that I felt different toward him. Yes, I was in love with him."

"Did he feel the same way?" Roz asked.

"Family was important to Philip. The Chaplins were wealthy, and there were certain expectations for Abigail and Philip. Philip was supposed to follow in his father's footsteps at the bank, and he took those expectations seriously. He was also expected to marry a girl with money and prestige."

"Did you ever tell him you loved him?"

"Of course not." Frances's laugh rang hollow. "Good girls didn't do things like that back then, though today… If I could go back today and tell him what I felt, I would. I'd tell him that money shouldn't be a factor when it comes to love. But it's far too late for that."

"I'm sorry. It all must have been hard for you."

"It was. The family picked out a young woman from Denver for Philip. Her name was Helen Miller. Apparently after the fiasco with Abigail, Philip's father decided he wasn't going to take any chances." Frances drew in a deep breath and let her gaze sweep the garden as she seemed to be—once again—lost in the past. "The funny thing is that at first, I didn't see what was happening. We'd always been friends—close friends—I somehow thought he, too, was beginning to feel different about me. I decided it didn't matter what his father said. But as the months and weeks passed, I noticed that he was busy. I thought he was simply trying to stay caught up at work, but then I found out he'd asked her to marry him, and I… I realized I'd lost him."

"I'm sorry, Frances," Sadie said. "I truly am."

Knowing what she did now, made it easier for Sadie to understand Frances. She'd been in love with a man she couldn't have. And all these years later one could still see the hurt in her eyes.

"I don't think he really ever loved Helen. He'd come by the library, and we'd talk every now and then. And while he never expressed his feelings toward me, it was always implied. But while Abigail had been willing to go against her parents' wishes, Philip wasn't. And then, two months before the wedding, Philip was killed in a car crash. According to the police, he'd been drinking."

"What about Abigail's engagement to Raymond Butler?" Sadie asked, shifting the direction of the conversation back to Abigail.

"She was always the life of the party. The girl everyone wanted to be friends with. Her father was wealthy, and she dressed like a city girl with beautiful store-bought clothes from Denver. Most of my friends back then wore clothes suitable to the mountains or handmade dresses our mothers sewed from Simplicity patterns."

"So you weren't friends?"

"I might chat with her at school or run into her at the Depot or the library, but that was about it. But everything changed after Raymond disappeared."

"What do you mean?"

"Folks in town started spreading rumors. Rumors that Philip had killed Raymond in a rage. Others said that Abigail had killed him and Philip disposed of the body in the mine. Whatever the truth, Abigail ended up going away, and Philip died that next summer."

Sadie saw the sadness in Frances's eyes, but she needed to know the truth. "Do you know what happened that night up at the mines?"

The older woman glanced out across the flower gardens again. "I know the rumors like you do, but I wasn't there, if that's what you mean. I don't care what people say, or what the documentary ends up saying. There is no way that Philip could have killed Raymond."

"We're just looking for answers," Sadie said.

"You're not the only one still looking for answers, but I don't know who—beyond myself—would really care after all of these years. Raymond and Philip are dead. Abigail is gone. What does it really matter anymore? The public will watch the story and see two star-crossed lovers, a *Romeo and Juliet* story where there is no happy ending."

Just like Frances's own romantic story, Sadie thought sadly.

"I just wish things had been different," Frances said. "I wish that Philip would have followed his heart instead of his father, but the truth of what happened that night—all of it—is buried in the past."

Frances stood up slowly, her knees cracking with the movement. "If you'll excuse me, I've said far too much. The past is a place I try not to visit very often. Hearing about the documentary only brings up unwanted reminders of what happened all those years ago."

Sadie looked at Roz, taking her cue that it was time for them to leave. "Thank you for talking with us, Frances. I know it hasn't been easy. We just want to find out the truth and ensure no one gets hurt."

"What do you think?" Sadie asked Roz a few moments later after they'd slipped into the car and started down the road.

"Honestly, I think the whole situation is sad," Roz said. "It's a tragedy full of broken hearts and lost love where no one seemed to find true happiness in the end. But I also think she knows something she's not telling us."

"I think so too," Sadie said, heading back toward Main Street. "But what?"

"I don't know her. There seemed to be anger toward Abigail, but do you think she was the selfish woman Frances painted her out to be?"

"I don't know. Priscilla doesn't talk about her that way, and really, the letters I read through don't either. Falling in love can be tricky. It's not an excuse, but when one follows one's heart, it can lead to problems, which is exactly what seemed to have happened to Abigail."

"So what now?" Roz asked. "Do you think Frances had anything to do with the threats to stop the filming?"

Sadie shook her head as she headed down the narrow road back toward town. The only thing she really knew was that Frances clearly longed to salvage Philip's tarnished name.

"Honestly, like with Priscilla, I don't believe Frances is capable of trying to stop the documentary. What would be the point all these years later?"

"I have to agree. And you can understand to a degree why she went through the rest of her life feeling jilted and dejected."

Sadie pulled in behind Roz's car, where they'd left it parked by the restaurant, and shifted into park. "Frances's only real crime, it seems, was to fall in love with a man who didn't love her back."

14

Sadie's mind was still going over her conversation with Frances from the night before when the director yelled "Take five!" before storming over to have a talk with the three lead actors.

"You were right about the director getting frustrated." Roz tugged on Sadie's sleeve, pulling her away from her thoughts. "But it's still exciting, isn't it?"

"It's definitely not your typical day in Silver Peak," Sadie responded.

But even with the stunning backdrop of the Rocky Mountains for that day's shoot, the "glamour" of TV production had worn off as far as Sadie was concerned. Not that she hadn't enjoyed an insider's view behind the filming—because she had. But not only was it far less glamorous than she'd imagined, the tension stemming from the past few days' events had put a damper on the day.

"I love the costumes you came up with, Sadie. Everything seems so nostalgic," Roz continued. "Makes me long for the days when neighbors sat on their back porches instead of glued to their cell phones, and when kids were free to ride their bikes into town without their parents living in fear."

"Life has changed, hasn't it?" Sadie agreed. "Changes not only in technology, but in family and faith."

"Forget the fifties then, can you imagine living in the late eighteen hundreds?" Roz asked. "Married to a miner who took off across the country in search of a fortune he might never find?"

Edwin had made her think about the same thing. A century ago, Silver Peak was in its prime, bustling with over fifty thousand people in search of that same fortune. Maybe it was no different from people buying lottery tickets today, knowing their chances of winning were slim to none.

"You're distracted today," Roz said.

"I'm sorry." Sadie tried to shake off the feeling of melancholy that had settled over her. "I'm finding it hard to focus for some reason this morning."

"Did you watch that last scene they're rehearsing between Abigail and Raymond?" Roz pressed her hands against her heart and sighed. "It was so romantic, so tragic. I know we don't know exactly how things played out, but still . . . "

Sadie smiled. The woman was a true romantic. "I'm not sure I see it in a romantic light, because every time I think about the story, I keep seeing how tragic the situation really was. Lives were lost because of whatever happened that night."

"I know you're right," Roz admitted. "There's just something about the costumes and the backdrop with the mountains that makes it so . . . There really isn't another word but *romantic*."

Roz stopped to take a deep breath, completely starstruck.

Sadie smiled, deciding that she was the one who needed to shake off her somber mood. "I'm just glad you're enjoying yourself."

"They could be filming a group of snails, and I'd still be having fun."

Sadie glanced at Roz and realized that her eyes were wide with interest as she watched the director talk to the lead characters. "You remind me of Sara when she met the director and was convinced she was about to be discovered and become the next Hollywood starlet."

Roz laughed at Sadie's comment. "Trust me, I don't have *those* kinds of aspirations, because clearly that will never happen. But still, I love all the lights, cameras, costumes, and action."

"You're right that it feels nostalgic."

For Sadie, though, that feeling came from the fact that they were filming in her town. A charming, historic mining town perched high in the majestic Rocky Mountains she was proud of and happy to show off to the world.

"And, by the way, there are still quite a few 'over sixty' actresses who still know how to steal the spotlight." Roz's brow narrowed. "Though they do a much better job of hiding their wrinkles and age marks than I do."

Sadie laughed again as Mary approached them with a questioning look on her face.

"Everything okay, Mary?" Sadie asked.

"I just need your opinion," Mary began. "I've been watching the scene, and I think Nicole's outfit needs something. I'm just not sure what."

Sadie studied Nicole's dress from across the set. For this scene they'd chosen a white dress with a circular skirt and a halter-style top. The only color was a red belt and a red flower on one of the shoulder straps.

"Maybe it does need a little more color," she finally concluded.

"I think so too," said Mary.

"There was a pair of earrings I noticed up at the house," Roz began. "Those red crystal dangly ones. Those earrings would add a pop of color, and they would sparkle in the light."

Mary's hands settled against her hips. "Roz, you're a genius. I think it's perfect. And I think I'll pull her hair up for the next scene to show them off a little and since it's being filmed outside, I won't have to worry about the wind."

Sadie nodded toward the wood-framed house. "I'll go grab them."

Halfway up the slight hill, Sadie encountered the production assistant coming toward her, slightly out of breath. She'd had little if any interaction with him over the last few days, as he seemed to be constantly running.

"Rob? You okay?"

The young man shot her an awkward, clumsy smile, as he combed his hands through his curly hair, slightly out of breath. "Yes, yes . . . Sadie, hi. I'm okay. Just trying to find something for the director." He shoved his hands into his pockets. "The director hates it when I'm late—or when I can't find something—and according to him, I'm always late and never can find anything."

Sadie had noticed. She'd also noticed that the man seemed completely out of his element on the set. To be honest, Sadie wasn't sure what experience was actually required for the job of production assistant, but Rob's main task seemed to be exactly what he'd just said—running. Sadie had seen him do everything from fetching espressos, to picking up provisions in town, to ensuring there were always replacements ready for things like light bulbs and batteries. Maybe the problem was simply that this was his first job, but it did seem that no matter how hard he tried, he wasn't able to keep up with the pressures.

Sadie started back up the hill as Rob pulled his hands out of his pockets. She noticed a cut on his hand, red and raw. "Rob?"

The young man stopped. "Yes."

"I couldn't help but notice your hand. Did you cut it?"

Rob glanced at his injured hand before slipping it back into his pocket. "It's nothing."

Sadie reached out and touched his arm. "Let me look. Please."

He held out his hand and pulled up the sleeve that had partially hidden the end of a nasty cut.

"I wouldn't say that's nothing. It looks infected. How did you cut it?"

Rob shook his head, clearly not wanting to talk about it. "Really, it's okay. It's just a scratch. It's nothing."

"You sound like my grandchildren trying to avoid a question. There's a first-aid kit up at the house. If you'll just give me two minutes, I'll have it rebandaged."

"You really don't have to do that." Rob's eyes shifted toward the bottom of the hill where the day's filming was taking place. "Like I said... it's fine."

"Nonsense. All it needs is a good wash and some antibacterial cream and it will heal up in a few days. If you don't take care of it, though, it's going to get infected."

Sadie followed Rob up to the house, nodded to a chair on the front porch, then quickly found the first-aid kit. Rob Tannehill was clearly a single boy who could use someone to help take care of him. She balanced the kit on the porch rail, then rummaged for the disinfectant and antibacterial cream.

Sadie turned back to Rob, then peeled off the makeshift bandage he'd put together that more than likely hadn't been changed since the original cut. Clearly, if he didn't take care of it now, he'd end up having to pay a visit to Doc. "Does it hurt?" she asked.

"A bit." Rob frowned. He seemed more worried about getting yelled at by the director than the cut on his hand.

"So I'd guess you're living on your own now?" she asked, trying to draw him into conversation.

Rob winced as she dabbed the cut with some disinfectant. "Yeah, I . . . I finished school in May, then managed to get this job. I'm living in a small studio apartment in Denver."

"Do you know how to cook?"

"Cook? Only if you call mac and cheese and instant ramen noodles cooking."

Sadie laughed. "I remember my first job. I was teaching business and history at the high school in town, but no one told me how little I would make. My husband and I lived on macaroni and cheese and cans of beans the first couple of years."

Sadie smiled at the memory. They might have been poor, but today she looked back on those days and only remembered the good things. In the end, it had taught them to be thankful for what they did have. Too many kids had everything handed to them on a silver platter these days. There was nothing wrong with a little hard work and missing a meal or two to help you be more thankful for what you did have.

"If you cut it on something metal," Sadie said, still concerned about the wound, "you might need a tetanus shot. There are all kinds of potential hazards around here, and you can't be too careful."

"It wasn't metal, it was just..." Rob's gaze shifted as if he was trying to decide which lie would be the most believable. "I cut it on a light bulb."

"A lightbulb?" Sadie asked, surprised at his confession. "On that broken light bulb a few days back?"

"You won't tell the director, will you? I really need this job, but to be honest, I'm not...I'm not exactly qualified. Not that anything they have me do is rocket science. A friend owed me a favor, and I needed work, so he pulled a few strings and got me this job. I didn't think it would be that challenging. I mean, essentially I'm a gofer, but the director has me running from sunup to sundown."

Sadie dropped the rest of the supplies back into the medicine kit. "What did you major in, Rob?"

"Computers."

"You're kind of out of your comfort zone."

The young man nodded. "I'm still looking for a job in my field, but you know how hard it is to find jobs right now. Besides, I thought working on a TV set with a crew and actors would be exciting."

Sadie laughed. "You're not the only one."

"I'm not saying I don't like the work or the people. There are even days when I think I'd like to stay in the business. I remind myself that this could be the door to something in Hollywood. I mean, everyone has to get experience on the grunt jobs before they make it to a big budget production. I guess my expectations were just off, though. Completely off. Funny how I thought making movies would be more glamorous, and I end up working in a damp mine tunnel with a director who hates me."

"I'm sure he doesn't hate you. All you need is some confidence and experience." Sadie shut the lid to the first-aid kit. "Keep it clean and use some of this ointment a couple of times a day and you'll be fine."

Rob shot her a grateful smile. "Thank you, Sadie."

"You're welcome, Rob."

Sadie picked up the first-aid kit to return, reminding herself she still needed to grab the crystal earrings, then hesitated.

"Rob... I was just wondering about something. You said you'd cut your hand on the light." Sadie tried to sort through the pieces of the puzzle in her mind. "There have been a number of technical issues and missing items over the past few days."

"Like the missing batteries... I know." Rob ducked his head and frowned.

"Like I said, I can be kind of a klutz. But if the director finds out I'm the one responsible... "

If Rob was the one responsible for the technical issues and missing items, then they weren't dealing with someone trying to sabotage the show. But if not a saboteur, then who? Someone *had* left a note and made threats.

"Sadie?"

Sadie glanced up. "I'm sorry, I was just thinking. Listen, don't worry about the director right now. I appreciate your clearing things up. Now I'm just curious about the warning note that was left... " Sadie left the sentence hanging, unsure of how to go about asking. "Most people think it was a joke, but others... well, there are others who believe it was just a joke to scare Nicole. Do you know who left it?"

"No, I..." Rob's gaze narrowed. "Wait. Do you think I left that note?"

"At this point, no one knows who left it."

Rob shook his head. "No way. I promise, I had nothing to do with that warning. I might be clumsy and even kind of scatter-brained, but I would never threaten or try to scare someone. And what would be the point anyway? Like I said, I need this job. It might only be until I can get something in the computer field, but to be honest, it beats sitting at home filling out job applications, or flipping burgers."

She studied his expression. "I believe you, Rob."

"Thank you. And the director?"

"It might not be a bad idea to tell him the truth."

"I'll lose my job," Rob countered.

"And if he finds out the truth himself? I'd think he'd be far less reasonable at that point."

"Maybe."

Sadie ducked inside the house to grab the earrings. So the technical issues plaguing the film hadn't been sabotage, but instead an unqualified assistant. But Rob's confession still didn't explain the warnings that had been left. With the earrings in her hand, she headed back out of the house just in time to see Roz coming up the stairs.

"Sadie?"

Sadie held up the earrings. "Sorry, I was just patching up Rob's hand. He's the production assistant, and he has a pretty badly infected cut."

"Is he all right?"

"Yes, but I found out something rather interesting while talking to him. We've been assuming that whoever left the note might also be trying to sabotage the film, and that maybe the other strange things that have happened on set were related."

"And you don't think they are?"

"Rob confessed to the mishaps on the set, but insisted he had nothing to do with the warning note. Or any knowledge that it was a joke."

"Do you think he's telling the truth?"

"I could be wrong, but I think so. For one, I don't see what motivation he has to actually sabotage the set, and besides, I've seen him work. I think he's trying, but he's clumsy and forgetful."

"Excuse me. Sadie?"

Sadie looked past Roz to a man walking toward them, wondering why security had let the man through. And how he knew her name. "Yes?"

"Are you Sadie Speers?"

"Yes."

"Could I have a second of your time? My name is Landon Marx. I'm a reporter from the *Denver Post* and am interested in not only the filming going on, but on finding out what really happened to Raymond Butler."

"You're from Denver?" Sadie's curiosity rose as she studied the man in front of her. He was in his late forties to early fifties, wearing jeans, a sports jacket, and a broad smile. Apparently Troy wasn't the only person interested in the story. "I'd love to help you, but I need to deliver these earrings to the set. Besides, I assume speaking to the director might be better."

"I intend to. But I understand you're a resident of Silver Peak."

"Yes—"

"Go ahead and talk to him," Roz said, taking the earrings from Sadie. "I'll take care of these."

Sadie nodded her thanks to Roz, then turned back to the reporter. "I'm surprised this is stirring up interest in Denver."

"Are you kidding? This is a great human-interest story. Not only do you have the tragic love story, but the angle of someone wanting to sabotage the making of the documentary."

"Who told you that?" Sadie asked.

"I'm a reporter," Landon said. "Our readers eat this stuff up."

While she still wasn't sure where he'd gotten his information, no doubt Edwin and even Greg for that matter would be thrilled to hear that their small town was making the news beyond the *Silver Peak Sentinel*. But there was still the chance that the letter was nothing more than a prank. Which would seem there really wasn't much of a story.

"The sheriff has looked into the warning note, but he isn't sure at this point if the letter was simply someone's idea of a prank, or, as you said, sabotage," Sadie explained.

"Even if it is a prank, stories like this are good for publicity," Landon said, still smiling. Apparently, the man was desperate for a juicy human-interest story.

"Good publicity for your paper or the town of Silver Peak?" Sadie wasn't sure she wanted someone twisting the story into something juicy that would sell papers instead of the truth.

"Both—including especially the Silver Peak Mine where it all happened—which makes it a win-win situation for everyone." Landon grabbed a pen from his jacket pocket along with a small pad of paper, then slipped on a pair of reading glasses. "So would you mind if I asked you a few questions for my article?"

Sadie hesitated, unsure of what the man was looking for. "If you want answers for the case, I think the sheriff is the one you need to talk to."

"I plan to, but like I said, this is more human interest, and I think my readers will be extremely interested in your story. I looked into your background and discovered that you've assisted the sheriff a few times in the past with your knowledge of the area." Landon tapped his pen against the pad of paper, still grinning. "The antique wedding gown hidden in the attic, for example, found in perfect condition except for the bullet hole in the bodice, and the mysterious visitor who arrived wanting the gown at any cost. And then there were the threats to you and your family over a safe found sealed within the opera house wall."

Landon stopped to take a breath, giving Sadie the chance to respond.

"I guess you have been doing your research, but the truth is, I'm simply a retired schoolteacher with a love of people—and antiques—who believes it's always important to discover the truth."

Landon jotted down some more notes. "Have you always had an interest in history and antiques?"

"I started out as a history teacher. That was probably because my parents exposed me to lot of opportunities as well as traveling when we could, which helped broaden my world. I've always loved how the past is often entangled with the present."

"That's what I'm talking about. That's a fantastic quote." Landon kept scribbling, sounding out of breath as if he was struggling to keep up. "And what do you think really happened to Raymond Butler? Do you think he was murdered in these mines?"

Sadie looked down the hill toward the clearing outside the mine where rehearsals had started up again, hoping the man understood that anything she said was simply speculation.

"I think it's possible," she began, "though clearly we won't know for sure until the DNA comes back from the police."

"Do you think someone is trying to cover up his murder?"

"Again, it's not possible to know at this point. Most of the people involved in the situation have already passed away."

Someone shouted from the other side of the set near the opening of the mine.

"What's going on?" Landon asked, his attention drawn to the commotion below.

"I'm not sure."

Sadie hurried down the hill beside the newspaper reporter to where people were gathering just inside the tunnel.

Sadie spotted Roz in the crowd and grabbed her arm. "What happened?"

"I don't know exactly. Evelyn just said another warning was left."

A spotlight shone on the tunnel wall. Sadie shivered beside her friend as she read the message on the cave wall.

You were warned to stop. A

15

SADIE'S FINGERS SQUEEZED TIGHTER AROUND ROZ'S ARM AS SHE stared at the writing on the wall.

"Sadie!" Roz started. "My arm."

"Sorry." Sadie let go of Roz's arm as the reporter started snapping photos. "You still think this is a prank?"

"I don't know, but even I'll admit it's pretty creepy," Roz said. "Let's get out of here."

"Everyone back to work," the director shouted as he headed out of the tunnel behind them. "Because this has gone on long enough. And mark my words, I will ensure that whoever is behind this—prank or not—will be prosecuted. But in the meantime, we have a film to shoot and I'm not letting some... prankster... stop me."

"What if it isn't a prank?" someone called out.

Sadie turned around in the bright sunlight outside the cave. Nicole stood in the doorway of the tunnel, her face almost as white as her dress, arms stiffened at her side, and a look of panic across her face.

The director shook his head. "The sheriff couldn't find any evidence that anything is at play here other a stupid prank."

"Maybe that's true, but like I said, what if it isn't? I'm not going back on that set. Not until I know what's going on. Too many strange things have happened, and if you want to take a chance, that's fine. But not me. These warnings…my car…You can call me once you find out what's going on."

"Nicole, you can't leave," the director ordered.

"Sorry, but yes, I can."

"Nicole!" the director shouted as she started for the parking lot. "Someone stop her."

"Nicole?" Sadie said.

Nicole brushed past Sadie. "Sorry, Sadie. But I've had enough of this."

Nicole ran across the grass, slid into her new rental car, and sped off down the mountain while Sadie and the others looked on.

"This is just great." The director pulled out his cell phone and punched in a number.

"What happens now?" Roz asked.

The rest of the cast and crew milled around the entrance of the mine, no one seeming to know exactly what they should be doing.

Sadie turned to Roz. "I think it's time to call the sheriff again."

With filming officially canceled for the rest of the afternoon, Sadie found herself back at the Antique Mine with Alice and Sara, trying to figure out what her next move should be. Roz had gone home to fix lunch for Roscoe, but had promised to come by the shop later to discuss the situation. Sadie had turned down Roz's lunch invitation to join them as her normally healthy appetite had vanished for the moment.

With Theo at his afternoon honors class, Sara sat on one of two matching cushioned French armchairs near the back of the store with a book in her hands, while Alice peppered Sadie with questions as to what had happened up at the mine. Sadie had gone into detail, starting with the discovery by Evelyn Watson of the warning left in the mine and ending with the sheriff's questioning of the crew and cast. Thankfully, she'd been one of the first to be allowed to leave.

"I almost wish I'd been up there this morning," Alice said as she finished dusting an antique mahogany desk next to the counter. "That warning clearly caused quite a stir."

"That it did," Sadie said.

Alice joined Sadie at the counter, where she was finishing tallying up the receipts.

"Did the sheriff really close down the set?" Alice asked.

"Not technically. With Nicole refusing to go ahead with the filming until the sheriff gives them some answers, there's not much anyone can do. She was already shaken by that last note and the car. I tried to talk with her and several people called her, but she's adamant and, of course, the director is furious. With only one more day of shooting left, he's worried about not finishing on time."

"There is one positive element in all of this," Alice said.

"I can't imagine what that is at this point."

"Thanks to the documentary and the drama surrounding it, there is definitely an upsurge of tourists coming through our fair town. There are twice as many receipts already today as we typically have, and it's just after lunch."

"You might be right," Sadie said.

"The last couple of days there has been a steady stream of customers. I was talking to Luz and she told me that business next door has been brisk the past few days too, though I told her it could also be due to the new almond custard Danish pastry recipe she tried out."

Sadie laughed at Alice's response, helping to ease the tension she was feeling. What she did know was that for her, the city of Silver Peak managed to give her a balance of the simplicity of the past with the conveniences of the present. Running the Antique Mine, along with her civic duties, like her current role on the historic preservation council, was enough to keep her both busy and fulfilled—which was something she was thankful for.

"Whatever the reason, I can't complain about the upsweep in business," Sadie admitted. Sadie finished tallying up the receipts, then filed them away. "But I've still decided that I'm ready for the filming to be over and my schedule to go back to normal."

"I've enjoyed the extra hours working in the shop."

"You also need to enjoy your summer vacation with some real time off. I remember how quickly they go by," Sadie said.

"You know I enjoy working here, especially after a long year of teaching. While I love my students, there are days when I love summer vacation even more. I can only stay home doing nothing for so long before I start getting antsy."

"And you don't mind the extra time to read, I'm sure." Sadie nodded at her daughter's book still lying on the counter that she'd been reading between customers. "What are your plans for the rest of the day?"

"At some point, I need to run over to Putnam and Sons to drop off my lawn mower. Theo's planning to mow the yard as soon as I can get it fixed, but after that, I don't mind staying the rest of the day if you have something to do."

"Are you sure? Because if you don't mind, I thought I'd offer to take Sara with me. I have a few visits I'd like to make this afternoon."

"I'm not sure I want Sara involved, Mom. That warning was pretty specific."

"All I'm planning to do is stop by the land office records and ask a few questions. Maybe stop by Priscilla's and ask her a few additional questions. I finally got hold of Gus Fergusson and would like to visit him, but Edwin is insisting on going with me, so I'll have to do that later this evening."

"That's probably a good idea," Alice said, the concern back in her eyes. "A man was murdered, which means there could be a murderer out there who was never caught."

"Who's pushing eighty if they're even alive," Sadie said. "Besides, even if Gus Fergusson isn't a murderer, I hope he might be able to shed some light on what happened back then."

Sadie wanted to shake off her daughter's concern, though she realized there was some truth in what Alice was saying. But like she'd said, more than likely the murderer wasn't even alive.

"As long as you stay in town and don't take any chances, I'm sure Sara would enjoy going out with you."

Sadie glanced at Sara. She hadn't turned a page in the past five minutes. Sadie walked to the back of the store and sat down next to her granddaughter.

"You've been awfully quiet this afternoon, Sara," Sadie began.

Sara shrugged.

Sadie leaned forward, not missing the look of irritation in her granddaughter's eyes. "Sara? If you feel like walking around town with me—"

"I think I'd rather just read. My ankle's sore this afternoon."

"Okay…are you sure that's all that's wrong?"

"Yeah." Sara let out a sharp sigh and dropped her gaze. "I'm fine."

"You don't seem fine," Sadie said.

"It's nothing. Really."

Sadie sat back, wondering if she should press the question or chalk up Sara's response to teenage moodiness.

"You do look pale." Alice bustled up beside her and pressed her hand against Sara's forehead. "Do you have a fever? Maybe we should take you back to Doc."

Sara snapped her book shut. "I'm not sick."

"Sara? There's no need raise your voice."

Sara started to rise, but at Alice's raised brow, she sank back into the chair. "I'm sorry."

"What's going on?" Alice asked.

After raising a teenage girl and teaching high school for twenty-five years, Sadie knew something about the moods of teenage girls, but for Sara this seemed…different from normal.

Sara pulled the book to her chest, her jaw set tight as she continued staring at the floor.

"Sara?" Sadie prompted.

"I'd rather not talk about it."

"I think it's too late for that," Alice countered.

"Fine… I guess I have a confession to make." Sara's gaze stayed fixated on the floor.

"A confession?" Sadie leaned forward. The girl looked miserable. "What kind of confession?"

Sara drew in a deep breath. "You're not going to be happy about it."

"Sara... what's going on?" Her mother slipped into the chair across from them.

"I know what happened to the missing perfume bottle."

"The perfume bottle?" Sadie shook her head. She'd completely forgotten about the missing perfume bottle, because in the light of everything, its disappearance seemed insignificant. But maybe she'd been wrong.

"I'm not sure I understand," Sadie said. "How would you know what happened to that bottle? I didn't think you were even in the shop the past few days."

"I wasn't." Sara fiddled with her hands in her lap. "Two nights ago I went up to the mines with... with some friends."

"You did what?" Alice's voice rose. "Sara Marie Macomb... I don't even know what to say. I specifically told you *not* to go up there, and you went without my permission with a bunch of friends?"

Sara pulled her knees to her chest. "I know what you told me, but after I hurt my foot, everyone wanted to know what happened. I told a few of my friends about the skeleton, and about Abigail, and the whole story about how I was one of the extras."

"Sara—"

"Let's let her finish," Sadie suggested gently. The girl was confessing. The least they could do was listen to her. "Please. Tell us exactly what happened."

Sara pressed her lips together as if debating whether or not she wanted to go on. "Like I said. After I hurt my foot up at the mine, some of my friends came over to see if I was okay. I started telling them about the skeleton and the mystery up at the mine. They started teasing me and told me they didn't believe I'd actually hurt my foot up there. That I'd probably just tripped on the sidewalk."

Sara paused, but this time, neither Alice nor Sadie said anything. "I told them if they took me up there, I'd show them where it all happened and tell them the story of Abigail and Raymond."

"How did you get up there, let alone get into the mine after dark?" Alice asked. "They keep that site locked up at night for safety reasons."

"Greg and Evelyn Winston's son Craig drove us up there. He has access to the keys."

"You were supposed to be at Mia's house."

"I know, but they kept bugging me, so I finally gave in. Mia doesn't know what I did."

Sadie tugged on the bottom of her shirt, vacillating between anger over the decision she'd made and feeling sorry for the struggle Sara had faced. She might be way past her youth, but that didn't mean she didn't remember how difficult peer pressure could be. "What did you do up there?"

"Nothing much. I thought it was creepy up there during the day, but let me tell you, it's ten times creepier at night. There were weird marks on the wall, things that looked like—I don't know—bones, and strange noises. I'm sure there were rats in there too. Ben made a video of us inside the tunnel, then I showed them the costumes up at the house.

"At one point Craig accidentally knocked over the perfume bottle and it broke. I panicked and told Craig that he had to take one up there from the shop to replace it, because I was afraid you'd notice. You've been working so hard to make sure everything was exact, but the only perfume bottles I could find were the three in the window. I know that going up there was stupid—and even dangerous. And I knew you'd eventually find out. Especially since Ben put the video he shot online."

"He put the video online?" Alice asked.

"The whole thing was stupid, and I'm really, really sorry. Honest, Mom."

Sadie rubbed the back of her neck with her fingers. "I think this is at least partly my fault."

"Your fault?" Alice's cheeks reddened. "I'm not sure how you think that. I'm still counting how many rules were broken in this excursion. Sneaking out without permission, driving in another teen's car who may or may not have had a proper license. Going back to the mines when you were specifically told they were too dangerous, possibly breaking and entering… Shall I continue, Sara?"

"No."

"Can we talk for a moment, Alice? In private?" Sadie hesitated a moment later in the back room. "I know this isn't my business, and neither am I trying to offer an excuse, but I think I know—to an extent anyway—how Sara feels. She told me how Theo's the one who loves to help with the sleuthing. He's the one the girls like. The one who is taking honors classes this summer. And while Sara made a mistake, sometimes being a fourteen-year-old girl is tough."

"Maybe you could talk to her first then, while I clear my mind and pray."

"Are you sure?"

"You raised me, Mom, and you did a pretty good job."

Sadie smiled. "I remember that raising a teenager isn't always easy."

A moment later, Sadie sat down across from Sara. "Can we talk? Your mom will be back in a minute."

Sara clutched her book in her lap, clearly unsure if she'd just been given a reprieve, or if things were about to get a whole lot worse.

"Go ahead and flip the sign to closed," Sadie suggested to Alice. "I'm sure the tourists can wait a bit."

Sadie sent up a prayer for wisdom as Alice slipped out the front door. Sara was a good girl who rarely gave her mother problems, but peer pressure could be strong and making the right choices wasn't always easy.

"Would you like some tea?" Normally, Sadie preferred coffee, but there were certain occasions when a cup of tea seemed more appropriate. "I've also got a few brownies Julie brought in."

"Sure." Sara shrugged. "But we both know this isn't your fault."

"I'll be back in a second."

Sadie went to the back room to put on the teakettle. She dropped two tea bags into cups, then opened up the antique basket tin containing half a dozen brownies. As far as Sadie was concerned, this was an emergency. She set two brownies on a small plate and put them on the counter while she waited for the tea to boil. It seemed like Sara—at least on the surface—was willing to take responsibility for what she'd done, which was definitely a good sign. Sadie worked in silence, organizing the tea tray she'd picked up at an auction in Denver. She'd ended up liking it so much, she'd decided not to sell it. The kettle's whistle started blowing. Sadie poured the hot water into two cups, then took the tray back into the store.

Someone stopped in front of the large front window of the shop and pressed their face against the glass. Sadie squinted slightly, but she couldn't tell who it was.

"Grandma?"

"Sorry." She looked back at the window again for a second, but whoever it was had already vanished. Sadie set the tray down on a small table, then sat down, focused once again on her granddaughter. "I remember one Friday night years ago, when I suppose I was about your age. A few friends of mine decided they were going to go joyriding through town and they dared me to come with them."

"And you went along?"

Sadie set one of the teacups in front of Sara and nodded. "I knew that my friends would make fun of me if I didn't go, and I'd be in a heap of trouble with my parents if they ever found out, but I still decided to take the risk and go with them."

"I totally get that." Sara shook her head. "Did your parents find out?"

"I'm still not sure how, but my father found out a few days later, and let me tell you, I didn't think I'd ever hear the end of it. I spent the next two months mucking stalls at the Henderson Ranch, until I thought I never wanted to see another horse again."

"I'm sorry. I really am. I never set out to disobey, things just got out of control, and I didn't know what to do."

Sadie took a sip of her tea, then set it down, deciding to wait a few minutes until it had cooled off. "The next Friday night, my friends went out again, but this time I was stuck at home with my parents."

"It must have been awful."

"It was, but that night, their car crashed into a tree."

Sara drew in a sharp breath. "Was anyone hurt?"

"There were a few broken bones, but over all they were very, very lucky. Someone easily could have been killed. I learned an important lesson that night that I've never forgotten. I realized that while it was hard to obey my parents sometimes, they usually knew what they were talking about."

"I know. It's kind of like Abigail and Raymond's story," Sara said, taking a sip of her tea. "Maybe it would have ended differently if she'd listened to her parents, or at the least, if she'd just heard their concerns and talked to them about what was going on. It seems like a lot of her relationship with Raymond was based on lies and secrets."

Sadie nodded. "She thought Raymond could bring her a happily-ever-after ending, but you're right. In the end she lost so much. I'm sure it took her a long time to build back the trust she'd once had, especially with her parents."

"I don't want that." Sara's eyes filled with tears. "I don't want Mom to lose her trust in me. I...I wasn't thinking, except I wanted my friends to believe me and they kept teasing me, which I know isn't an excuse, but sometimes...sometimes it's so hard."

"You're right. It's not an excuse, but I do remember what it is like trying to fit in, and I have a feeling that it's a whole lot harder today than it was when I was fourteen." Sadie chose her words carefully. "The thing you have to realize is that relationships and friendships based on lies and secrets almost always manage to get you into trouble and let you down."

"I can see that."

"I'm not saying they're bad kids, but true friends are going to support you, not try to make you do things you're not comfortable with."

"So are you going to punish me?" Sara asked.

"That decision is up to your mother, though there is the perfume bottle to pay for. A couple of hours working here at the shop should take care of that." Sadie set down her teacup. "There is one other thing. I would like to see that video."

"I filmed it for a few minutes on my phone." Sara pulled her phone out from her back pocket, switched it to video, and pushed play. "It's mainly just the four of us being stupid. At one point, they went back down that tunnel where I was injured. Craig insisted it wasn't dangerous."

"And you believed him?" Sadie's heart skipped a beat as she watched the kids goofing off and making faces at the camera, the weathered walls of the mine behind them. "Mines are not a place where *anyone* needs to be messing around. People have died up there taking a wrong step."

"I promise I didn't go with them, and I told them not to, but they didn't listen. Later, they recorded me telling the story of Abigail and Raymond. I watched it last night and planned to erase it."

"Stop." Sadie waited for Sara to pause the video, then pointed to the edge of the screen. "What's that?"

Sara frowned. "I don't know. I thought it looked like a bone or something. They showed it to me, then got all freaked out. We left after that."

"I would be tempted to think so too, but that tunnel isn't where they found the skeleton. If it is a bone, it could just be from an animal."

"Either way it's gross." Sara shivered, then leaned over and hugged Sadie. "As awful as it was, I feel better now that I've confessed."

"It's true when they say that confession is good for the soul." Sadie looked up at her granddaughter. "You know this isn't over, though. You've still got to deal with your mother."

The bell on the front door rang as Alice entered the store.

Sara stood up and nodded at Sadie. "I'm ready."

16

At half past four, the bell on the front door of the Antique Mine jingled as Sadie pulled the door shut and locked it with the key. Apparently, Alice's observations had been correct as she'd been busy with customers—most of them from out of town—all afternoon. When the last customer left ten minutes before, she'd decided to go ahead and close the shop early. She'd called Roz, who had agreed to go with her to the motel where the cast and crew were staying so they could check on Nicole. Abigail's story was weighing heavily on Sadie's mind, along with Sara and Nicole's, as well.

Thankfully, Alice had called an hour ago and told her that she and Sara had had a good talk. While there would be a punishment involved, and time to build back Alice's trust, from Sadie's point of view, the two were on their way in the right direction again.

"Sorry I'm late," Roz said, getting out of the car. "Roscoe needed me to watch the hardware store for a few minutes while he ran an errand. Bill—who normally waits on customers—is home sick with the flu."

"No problem. Do you mind if we walk?" Sadie asked as Roz stepped onto the curb.

"Not at all. A brisk walk would do me good. Especially after last night's dessert," Roz teased.

"I definitely agree."

Sadie dropped her keys into her purse, then started down Main Street, the town's only shopping area, toward the Crestview Motel, which was located on the edge of town, where the cast and crew were staying during the shoot. Most of the buildings on Main Street, including the Antique Mine, were brick, lending to the charm of the town. Except for the need to drive to one of the nearby larger towns for the occasional supply, Sadie found that Silver Peak offered almost everything she needed.

"So you haven't heard from Nicole?" Roz asked.

Sadie shook her head. "I've called a number of times, but she's just not answering. I hope she's calmed down by now and has decided not to hold up the filming any longer. I don't know how an actor's contract works, but it seems as if her refusing to work could put her job—and possibly even future jobs—in jeopardy."

"Maybe I can understand why she might be spooked," Roz said. "She's the one who found the first note, then she had the car issues... That along with an emotional role has to play into her reaction."

Sadie and Roz continued down Main Street, until the Silver Peak Opera House loomed in front of her in all its grandeur—an imposing edifice of brick, stone, and Colorado history. After months of gathering donations, applying for grants, and dealing with safety and preservation issues, the town had finally restored the historical opera house to its former glory, which had thrilled Sadie. Today, it boasted an arched entryway, an open lobby with maple floors and detailed murals, along with the grand auditorium with a raised stage and five hundred plush red seats.

"Every time I go by the opera house, I can't help but imagine all of the performers who graced this town and this very stage. Just think, Roz. Oscar Wilde appeared on this very stage along with John Philip Sousa, and Houdini, who amazed the people of this town with his cleverly crafted escape acts. Operas with celebrated artists and singers straight from Broadway and Europe performed with elaborate scenery and fancy costumes. Sometimes I wish I had lived back then."

Sadie let out a deep sigh. Unfortunately, all that had changed after the turn of the century. For a short time, the opera house had been used as a motion picture theater until the final curtain call had fallen and the historic building was turned into three stories of steam-heated apartments.

Something caught Sadie's eye. She turned to see someone slipping into the shadows of the opera house as they passed. Her heart sped up. It was probably just a tourist looking for a good spot to take a photo. Apparently Nicole's paranoia was beginning to rub off on her. But jumping at the sight of her own shadow—or whatever she'd seen out there—wasn't her. In her experience, one almost always eventually found a perfectly logical explanation to strange events. Someone—namely Rob—had broken the light bulb and lost the replacement batteries. Nicole's car trouble could be explained away by a faulty wire. And the warning notes had to have had a flesh-and-blood author.

So if all of this was true, why was she turning the deepening shadows formed by the late afternoon sun into ghosts out to get her?

She shoved the eerie sensation aside. Besides, why would someone want to follow her?

Doc was just coming out of his office a few moments later, his normal smile in place. Even though he was nearing seventy, she wasn't sure the old man was ever planning to retire.

"Why Sadie...Roz...twice in one week. This is a treat."

"And much better," Sadie admitted, "considering I'm not running into you in your office with a crisis."

The doctor laughed as he slipped his hands into his jacket pocket. "How's that granddaughter of yours doing, Sadie?"

"She's much better, thank you. Barely a limp at this point. I believe that in another few days she'll be completely back to normal."

"I'm thrilled to hear that. She's lucky it wasn't worse than a light sprain, but she'll back on her feet in no time. I heard another warning note was left up at the mine," Doc said.

Apparently Edwin had been right in that the entire town was abuzz with what was happening up there. "The entire situation has left me puzzled."

"I have no doubt that if anyone can get to the bottom of this, you can," Doc assured her.

"Well, I do appreciate your confidence, Doctor."

Doc slipped into his car while Sadie and Roz continued down the street. She paused, looking out of the corner of her eye, certain once again she'd seen something—or someone—move in the shadows behind them. Sadie slowed her steps.

"Are you all right, Sadie?"

"I don't know. When I was speaking to Sara earlier, someone was standing outside the shop looking in. I'm sure it's nothing, but after all the strange things that have been going on..."

"You think we're being followed?" Roz said.

Sadie grabbed her friend's arm. "I thought I saw someone when we were passing the opera house, but they're still behind us. I'm certain of it."

"Maybe you're right, but why in the world would someone want to follow us? There are lots of people out here enjoying the beautiful summer evening the same as we are."

"Just look back casually. It's a woman wearing dark trousers and a beige tunic."

A minute later Roz nodded. "I think you're right, but still, why would someone be following you?"

"I have no idea. But I have been poking around and asking questions. Maybe I'm on the right track. Maybe one of the people I've spoken to doesn't like it, or maybe someone wants me to stop before I uncover their secret."

Sadie frowned. Her explanation seemed almost silly. Roz was right. Why *would* someone be following her? All she'd done so far was ask a few questions about something that had happened decades before.

The truth was that she hadn't slept particularly well the night before, and she must be tired. Considering how much had happened this week, some fatigue was to be expected. Paranoia, however, was not.

Which was exactly what she was feeling at the moment.

"Whatever the reason"—Roz linked her arm with Sadie's—"I saw someone out of the corner of my eye. Hanging in the shadows as if she doesn't want to be seen, but definitely keeping up with us. And now she's just turned the corner."

So she really hadn't been imagining things.

"And maybe it isn't such a stretch," Roz continued. "I mean, the warning was clear. Stop filming or someone will get hurt."

Sadie frowned. "You're not helping, you know. You're supposed to convince me that the thought of someone following me is silly, not back up my suspicions."

She felt a shiver zip down her spine. Silly or not, she knew she'd seen someone. She pulled Roz into the recessed doorway of one of the shops and held her breath. She wasn't in the mood to play games. If someone was following her, she was going to put a stop to it right here and now.

"I think we should turn the tables."

She counted to ten, then stepped out onto the sidewalk.

Frances Knight bumped into her.

"Frances?"

Sadie let out a sigh of relief. Whether she'd been following them or not, Frances was hardly a threat. But while Frances wasn't who Sadie had been expecting, the woman clearly looked guilty.

"You've been following us?" Sadie asked.

Frances shook her head, but the fear on her wrinkled face was clear. "Why would I follow you?"

"I don't know. Did you need to speak with me?"

"I..." Frances hesitated. "I might have a few questions for you."

"If you do, you could have just called or stopped by the shop."

"I did stop by the shop, but you were closed." Frances leaned closer to Sadie. "Can we keep walking? The park is up ahead, and I'd like to sit down."

Sadie glanced at Roz, then nodded. Centennial Park was public land, located on the west edge of Silver Peak. It was landscaped with lots of trees and a huge grass lawn. There was even a bandstand that was often used for concerts and other performances. The younger crowd loved it for the jogging trail that encircled the park. She'd been known to take a few walks herself around the trail in the cooler days of summer when the sun wasn't too intense.

Frances said nothing until they'd sat down on a bench, side by side, piquing Sadie's curiosity even further.

"I came by your shop, but you'd already closed. I've been thinking about the conversation we had yesterday."

Sadie frowned. She must have just missed her. "And?" she prompted.

"There's another reason someone might want to stop the filming of the documentary. One that few people beyond myself know about."

Sadie leaned forward. "Why is that?"

"Abigail had a baby."

Sadie wasn't sure where Frances was going with this line of thought. "You mean Priscilla."

"Of course not." Frances frowned. "That's not a secret."

"What do you mean then?"

Frances drew in a deep breath before answering. "Abigail was pregnant with Raymond's child. She was planning to tell him the night she met him up at the mines."

17

"Abigail was pregnant with Raymond's child?" Sadie asked at Frances's revelation.

Sadie tried to process the information. How could Abigail have been pregnant without anyone knowing?

"Why do you think Philip was so angry when he found out?" Frances said.

Angry enough for murder? Sadie thought.

"The Chaplin family was a pillar in this community, and while nowadays having a baby out of wedlock doesn't carry the same stigma, back then, things were different. When girls got pregnant, most of them disappeared for a while, then gave up the babies for adoption, never telling anyone."

"That's sad," Roz said.

Frances nodded. "Many of them, like Abigail, didn't have a choice. She simply did what her father told her to do."

"How do you know about the baby?"

"Philip told me. Abigail believed Raymond loved her, which was why, without her family's approval of the marriage, she'd decided to elope. But something happened when she met Raymond that night."

Frances's story made sense. Everyone had been told that Abigail was going away to visit friends, presumably to heal. Instead she'd gone away to have a baby.

"What happened up there that night, Frances?"

"Philip would never tell me, but whatever did happen ended up destroying him. That was when he started drinking, when he started pulling away from people."

And a year later he'd died in a wreck after drinking and driving.

"It sounds as if he was trying to protect his sister."

"Her and the family name. A lot of pressure was put on Philip. He was being groomed to take over for his father. He was forced into an engagement to a woman he didn't want to marry. People whispered behind their backs, but there were rumors going around that Raymond wasn't the man he claimed to be."

"What do you mean?"

Frances leaned back and started rubbing the knuckles of her left hand. "Raymond Butler swept into town full of charm and charisma. I remember meeting him several times. He was handsome, and when he spoke to you, you felt as if you were the only person in the room. I understand how Abigail fell for him. But Philip told me once that he believed he was a con man out to steal the family fortune."

"Why did he think that?"

"Raymond came to Silver Peak looking for people to invest. I don't know any of the details except that there were promises of great profit with virtually no risk."

"And the baby? Did anyone else know?"

"I'm not sure anyone did beyond the Chaplin family and myself. I'm not even sure Priscilla knows. It was a quiet adoption. When Abigail returned home, everyone assumed she had been traveling around Europe after a broken engagement."

"Do you know what happened to the baby?"

"No."

"Thank you for telling me the truth, Frances."

Frances's frown deepened. "So many people were affected by what happened."

Including Frances, Sadie thought. "I do have one other question. Do you know Gus Fergusson?"

"Of course. He lives a few miles east of town on Highway 65. He was one of the people who claimed he'd lost money with Raymond's get-rich scheme."

"Do you think he could have motivation to stop the documentary?"

"I don't know. But what I do know is that there were a lot of things that happened back then that people don't want coming to light. Like Abigail's baby. I've never—in fifty years—told anyone else about it, but for some reason… It's been nagging at me since you came to visit. Seems that the truth has been buried far too long."

"I agree," Sadie said.

Sadie leaned back against the bench and breathed in the scent of the freshly mowed lawn as Frances walked away. "She's spent her whole life carrying around that secret."

"Why tell us now?"

"Haven't you ever kept a secret that weighed heavily on your heart? Maybe it was time."

"And definitely an interesting twist to the story."

"One I'm sure the director wished he knew. Because it definitely ups the motivation for Philip to murder Raymond."

Roz shook her head. "We still might never find out the truth."

"But someone left those notes. Someone who's still alive."

"What is next on your to-do list?"

Sadie glanced at her watch. "I still would like to see Nicole, but I think we need to talk to Priscilla first."

Fifteen minutes later, Sadie stopped on the sidewalk beside Roz, trying to formulate what she needed to say to Priscilla. The sun was hiding behind a string of clouds sweeping across the sky, leaving shadows across the landscaped lawn. Sadie breathed in slowly. There was always the possibility that Priscilla had never been told about her mother's pregnancy, or that she didn't want Sadie—or anyone else—to know.

And there was a strong possibility that Sadie should simply walk away because it really wasn't any of her business.

"Sadie? Are you okay?" Roz asked.

"I don't know." She caught Roz's gaze. "Do you think we're doing the right thing, visiting Priscilla again?"

"I'm not sure I understand why you are asking that. She, clearly above everyone you've talked to so far, has the motive to stop the documentary. Between the reporters and the director, it seems likely that someone else will find out the truth before all of this is over. You did. And at least you're a friend."

"I know part of the truth, anyway." They began walking up the landscaped drive of the Victorian home. "But I'm still not convinced I'm doing the right thing. Sometimes I feel like this case has done nothing more than dredge up situations that might be better left forgotten. Abigail is dead. Raymond and Philip are dead. And even if everything that Frances told us is true, does it really matter at this point that there was a baby involved? What if it only causes more hurt in the end?"

"I don't know." From the look on Roz's face, she didn't agree. "Have you forgotten the warnings up at the mine? Or that whatever is going on could affect you and others if those warnings are real? Someone is unhappy about the filming. No matter what your heart is telling you right now, you can't overlook that."

Sadie let out a deep sigh. This was exactly why she'd wanted Roz to come with her. She needed a levelheaded response, not just one based on emotions.

"Like I've accused the *Chatterbox* more than once of crossing the line from news to gossip, I don't want to be guilty of the same thing. It's something I've been praying about a lot lately. I don't want to be accused of simply chasing a juicy story. Which is why part of me wants to simply walk away from all of this."

But walking away wasn't going to help them find the truth. Instead, Sadie took Roz's advice and knocked on the door, praying again she was doing the right thing.

Someone called out "Just a minute" from inside. A moment later, Priscilla opened the door, balancing a sealed cardboard box against her hip.

"Sadie... I didn't expect to see you back so soon. Roz." Priscilla nodded. "Did you find out anything?"

"Not about what happenedup at the mines that night, but there was another warning note left at the mine this morning."

"Another note? That's crazy."

"The sheriff is doing everything he can to find out who is responsible, but it does seem that someone wants the filming to stop."

"You'll have to excuse me," Priscilla said, carrying the box toward the formal living room. "You can come in, but I need to finish packing up these boxes. I've got someone coming by in about thirty minutes to pick them up. You wouldn't believe how much stuff we've accumulated over the years."

Roz glanced at Sadie and grinned. "Oh, I'm sure I can imagine."

"Clothes, bedding, kitchenware, small appliances... " Priscilla shook her head, then motioned for them to sit on the floral couch beneath a large picture window. "The new owners are buying most of the furniture, but we still have to go through all of our personal things."

The living room of the Painted Daisy was warm and cozy and filled with beautiful pieces of solid wood furniture and country antiques. The walls were painted a soft yellow contrasted by gold and red throw pillows on the couch and matching wing chairs. Many of the items Priscilla had used to decorate the space had been bought at the Antique Mine over the years.

"So I take it that the sale of the house went through?" Sadie asked as she took a seat next to Roz on the couch.

Priscilla nodded as she started putting miscellaneous items from the hutch into another box. "The couple contacted our Realtor this morning and gave us an offer. We accepted it."

"That's fantastic," Roz said.

Priscilla let out a sharp sigh. "We're excited, but they want to be in the house by the end of the month, which means things are moving fast now, and we still have so many things to go through."

"I'm sure there are people at church who would be more than willing to help," Sadie suggested.

Priscilla wrapped a glass bowl in newspaper, added it to the box, then sealed up the box with packing tape. "My husband called Don Sweeting this morning at the Campfire Chapel, and he offered to put together a moving team the day we have to load the moving van."

"That's wonderful," Sadie said. "Have you found a house near your daughter yet?"

"Honestly, we haven't even looked, but our daughter has offered to have us stay with her and her family until we find something." Priscilla added the closed box to the pile near the doorway. "You mentioned another warning note was left."

"Yes, the sheriff is trying to discover who is behind the warnings." Sadie hesitated, her mind shifting back to Abigail.

"There's something else, isn't there?" Priscilla stopped in the middle of the room. "About my mother…"

Sadie decided not to beat around the bush and just tell Priscilla what she'd discovered. "I found out that she and Raymond had a child together."

Priscilla's frown deepened. "Who told you that?"

Sadie looked at Roz before continuing. "Frances Knight."

"Frances?" Priscilla shook her head. "My mother told me once that she was in love with my uncle Philip and thought he was in love with her."

"Was he?"

"I don't know if he loved her, but I do know he was fond of her." Priscilla walked back over to the hutch, picked up another box, then dropped it back on the floor, her shoulders stooped. "I guess I was foolish to think I could ask you to find out the truth about what happened to Raymond without your discovering her secret. My mother...she was young and impressionable. She dreamed of seeing the world beyond Silver Peak, and Raymond offered it to her. He was suave and sophisticated and knew exactly what to say to her."

Priscilla sat down on one of the chairs, thoughts of packing for the moment seemingly forgotten. "Maybe she should have run in the other direction, but she loved the attention. Her father had high expectations of her, but when my mother met Raymond, she was able to see—for the first time—a glimpse of a world she thought could be hers."

Sadie chose her words carefully. "I'm not here to question the character of your mother. I knew her in her later years as a God-fearing woman, who apparently had put her past behind her."

"And that is what I want people to remember. Not the mistakes she made as a young woman."

"Like I said, I'm not interested in exposing your mother's secrets," Sadie sought to reassure her. "Right now, I'm interested in finding out what's going on up in the mines, because I believe that the warnings have to be somehow connected to your mother and what happened half a century ago."

"I told you the truth. I had nothing to do with those warnings, and why would I? I certainly don't want to draw attention to my mother's story. I told you before, I'm not happy about the fact that they are telling the story in the first place."

Sadie leaned forward, nodding. Suddenly the doorbell rang, interrupting their conversation.

"I'm sorry," Priscilla said, standing up, "but that's the scheduled pickup for these boxes."

Sadie and Roz rose to leave.

"I'll be praying for you, Priscilla," Sadie said.

Priscilla nodded her thanks as she walked them to the door. A minute later, Sadie and Roz were back on the sidewalk, walking back toward town.

"What do you think?" Roz asked, interrupting Sadie's thoughts.

"I'm reminded how the consequences of our decisions can be so far-reaching and affect so many people. But nothing that was said gives us an answer as to what happened that night, or to the warnings that were left up at the mine."

"I believe she's telling the truth."

"So do I. She has no desire for people to know the truth about her mother. Leaving warning notes has done nothing but garner publicity, which is definitely not what she wants." Sadie paused in front of the Market, her mind still trying to put the pieces of the puzzle together. "What if there's someone else out there, though, who *does* want publicity?"

Dr. Ben Armstead—Silver Peak's local veterinarian—and his daughter, Lacie, walked out of the store with a couple of bags of groceries. She greeted them with a smile, but her mind couldn't let go of the thought.

"What do you mean?" Roz asked.

They started walking again toward the Antique Mine where Roz had parked her car. Sadie remained quiet, continuing to mull the puzzle over in her mind. What if this had nothing to do with sabotage, but everything to do with publicity? The story had hit the front page of the *Silver Peak Sentinel.* A reporter had showed up from Denver, planning to write a feature article, which could very quickly turn into national exposure. And according to the *Chatterbox*, everyone was talking about the story, a story that was clearly adding to the rise of tourism in the town.

But who needed that kind of publicity?

"If publicity is what someone wanted, then publicity is definitely what they are getting," Sadie began finally. "People in Hollywood seem to do it all of the time. Their philosophy seems to be that no publicity is bad publicity. You've got an unidentified skeleton combined with a half-century-old tragic love story—not to mention the discovery of a love child."

"So perhaps the show itself then would be the logical place to look," Roz offered.

"I agree. I've already spoken to the director, and I know there have been issues between him and the previous director he took over for. But while he seemed candid enough, he could certainly be hiding things."

"So what do you think we should do now?"

Sadie stopped alongside Roz's car. "I think we need to consider this entire situation from a different angle, and start asking new questions. Like who has the most to gain from all of this publicity."

18

By the time Edwin stopped by the Antique Mine to pick up Sadie so they could visit Gus Fergusson, she'd eaten a tuna sandwich on rye from Arbuckle's Coffee next door, and she had been able to briefly speak to Nicole. Nicole had told her that she was planning to go ahead with the filming tomorrow, but if anything else happened on the set, she was going to walk out again…and this time she was planning to walk out for good.

Sitting in one of the French armchairs where Sara had been reading earlier, Sadie swallowed the last of her coffee, then smiled as Edwin settled in across from her.

"Long day?" Edwin asked.

"More interesting than long," she admitted. "Funny how I'd looked forward to the new challenge of working with antiques and costumes on a TV set. Instead I find myself caught up in a decades-old murder and wondering why someone might want to stop the filming."

"Tell me what you know about Gus Fergusson so far," Edwin said.

"He was actively involved in trying to shut down the mines back in the fifties, and was arrested a couple of times throughout the years for protesting. Even more interesting, though, is the fact that he was arrested for getting into a fight with Raymond Butler, just a few days before the man disappeared."

"*Hmm.*" By the look in Edwin's eye, he was clearly intrigued. "You think he had something to do with the warning notes?"

"I don't know, but if nothing else, maybe he knows who was involved. I'm hoping we find out something from him."

"His motivation?" Edwin asked.

"I read all of the stuff Troy at the paper gathered for me. Greg's brother died of lung cancer, and he blames it on an inadequate ventilation system in the mine."

"Any foundation to his claims?"

"There are definitely higher reports of illnesses like lung cancer and tuberculosis for miners."

"He sounds like someone to look into."

"You know you don't have to go with me, though, Edwin. I'm sure I'm not the only one who's had a long day."

Edwin stood up and pulled his keys from his pocket. "You know I'll feel better if I go along with you."

"The man has to be at least seventy...maybe seventy-five. I don't think there's anything to worry about."

Edwin squeezed her hand. "Maybe not, but humor me. Besides that, I enjoy your company."

She smiled up at him, a feeling of contentment radiating through her as she realized—not for the first time—just how thankful she was he was back in her life. "Me too, and thank you."

He smiled back. "Anytime."

Ten minutes later, Edwin pulled up in front of Gus Fergusson's house on the outskirts of Silver Peak, located off of Highway 65 at the end of a narrow, winding road. The one-story, ranch-style house sat back from the street with two cars parked in the driveway.

Sadie knocked on the front door, which was opened by a woman in her forties with long red hair. "I'm looking for Gus Fergusson. He knows we're dropping by."

"He told me you were coming, but wait a minute." The woman pressed her lips together as if she were thinking. "I've visited your shop in town, the..."

"The Antique Mine," Sadie offered.

"Of course. I love your shop."

"Why, thank you."

"In fact, I was just talking to one of my girlfriends in Denver. I told her the selection and the prices were better here. I'm Katie, by the way," she said, her hand outstretched.

"And I'm Sadie Speers," Sadie said, shaking the woman's hand, "and this is Edwin Marshall. I do recognize you from the shop, and I definitely appreciate the business."

"Well, I'll definitely be back."

"Is Gus Fergusson here?" Sadie asked.

"Yeah, we're just making up a batch of strawberry ice cream." Katie turned and yelled into the house, "Dad? Sadie Speers is here to see you."

Gus joined his daughter in the doorway, and Sadie recognized him immediately from the photos Troy had shown her from the newspaper. Today, though, his full head of dark hair had thinned to a narrow fringe of gray around his balding scalp. His shoulders were slightly hunched, and his bearded face was now clean-shaven and marked with age spots and wrinkles. Life had continued since the man's arrest nearly six decades ago.

"Mayor?" Surprise crossed Gus's face as he reached out to shake Edwin's hand, recognition sparkling in his eyes. "Never thought the day would come when the mayor of our fine town would decide to pay me a visit. I'm proud to say I voted for you."

Edwin beamed beside her. "That's always good to hear, Gus. I appreciate it."

"And I appreciate how you seem to realize that your decisions actually affect people's lives. Too many politicians forget that there are real people behind the voters."

"Well, I truly want to make a difference to the people of this community, which is why that is something I don't ever want to forget."

"You do that and I'll keep voting for you, Mayor."

Apparently Gus's interest in politics hadn't faded over the years.

"You'll have to excuse my father's enthusiasm," Katie said. "He's always been kind of outspoken on politics, especially environmental issues."

"Something I've never regretted," Gus countered with a grin. "Now, if I recall correctly, you said you needed to speak to me about something regarding the mines." The older man glanced at Sadie. "You don't mind sitting outside, do you? My daughter and grandsons are over for the afternoon and evening."

"We'll be fine, Pops." Katie reached up and kissed her father on the forehead. "I'll finish up the ice cream and get it into the freezer."

Sadie and Edwin sat down on one of the wooden rocking chairs next to Gus and took in the view of the mountains in the distance.

"I'm blessed that my daughter and grandsons live close by. Can't imagine what I'd do with myself if they didn't. They come by at least once a week, as well as every Sunday afternoon. Bring me lunch or we go into town and eat."

"I understand how you feel," Sadie said. "I hadn't realized how much I missed my daughter and grandchildren until they moved here from Denver a few years back."

"So how can I help you?" Gus asked.

Sadie nodded. "Have you been following the news of what's been going on up at the Silver Peak Mine?"

Gus frowned. "Heard they found a body up there that might belong to ol' Raymond Butler. And something about some TV show coming in and filming the story. Always hated those reality shows. Bunch of garbage that numbs the mind, if you ask me."

Sadie chuckled inwardly, certain the older man wasn't the only one with that opinion. "The show is the *American Treasure Chest*, and it's a documentary series. Currently they're featuring American treasures and mysteries across the country, specifically in the mines."

Gus rocked back in his chair. "If you ask me, the only good thing that came out of those mines was the fact that they closed down. I did everything back in the day to stop the mining, because it seemed to me that the money to be made was always far more important than following any safety regulations."

"I know you lost your brother, Gus, and that you believe he died because of his work in the mines."

"He certainly did." Gus leaned forward. "I was told over and over that there was no connection. They gave me a bunch of numbers and statistics, but it was just a bunch of garbage to me. Eventually, the mines did close down, but by then it was too late. At least for my brother."

Sadie glanced briefly at Edwin. "We are sorry for your loss, Gus."

"Jake was only nineteen years old." The older man shook his head. "I'll admit to both of you that I was sort of a hothead and did a lot of things in my youth that I shouldn't have. But if I am to be honest, while my methods weren't always the best, I don't regret my motivation. Someone had to stand up and try to stop what happened to my brother from happening to someone else."

Sadie chose her words carefully, hoping to move the conversation forward without dismissing the man's feelings. "I can understand then why you were arrested several times when you were younger, mainly for your stance on environmental issues."

"I'm not sure I understand your need to dredge all of this up again." There was a tinge of agitation in the older man's voice. "Those arrests were years ago."

"I understand that, and I'm certainly not accusing you of anything. We're just looking for information. Some strange things have happened up at the mine. To be more specific," Sadie explained, "there have been warnings to stop filming. We believe it could have something to do with Raymond Butler and what happened back then. And I believe there is a chance that you might have information that would point us in the right direction."

"I still don't understand what that has to do with me. I haven't been up to those mines in years."

"Can you tell us about your relationship with Raymond?" Edwin asked.

"I'm sure it's all public record." Gus leaned back again. "I lost my temper with the man and punched him."

"Doesn't sound as if there was very much love lost between the two of you."

"Hardly. Raymond Butler wasn't the man everyone thought he was."

"In what way?" Sadie asked.

"You've probably heard the story—or at least one version of it—especially if you're working with that documentary. I suppose I should have known better, but Raymond swept into town convincing everyone he could offer higher returns than other investments. Turned out, it was nothing but a Ponzi scheme—a fraudulent investment opportunity that pays investors from existing capital instead of profit earned."

"Did you or any of the others taken in go to the police?"

"I didn't." Gus stood up and turned to face the mountains as if contemplating just how much he wanted to disclose. "I was too embarrassed to admit that I'd fallen for one of Raymond's Ponzi schemes to go to the police. And then just a few days after our fight, Raymond disappeared."

"Surely the police could have done something."

"Looking back, I know I should have gone to the police." Gus shook his head as he sat back down in the rocker. "He made me believe that I was going to triple my money for little risk, and somehow... somehow I was stupid enough to believe him. When the rumors started flying around that he was dead, I figured he'd gotten what he deserved. Plus I figured if I went to the police, they might realize that I had motivation to kill him, so I wasn't exactly keen to call attention to myself."

"I'm sure you weren't the only one taken in by Raymond," Sadie said. "Do you know of anyone who might have something to cover up? Someone who doesn't want the true story of what happened that night coming to light?"

"There were a dozen or more people who lost money, but as to the possibility of one of them killing Raymond? I honestly don't know. Most of them probably thought the same as I do, that they were thankful when he disappeared. He was a con man who'd taken in many people—including myself—for hundreds of dollars. As for Abigail, I have no doubt he wanted to marry her for her family fortune, not for love. He was charming and charismatic, and she fell for all of his lies. And so did I."

"Did Abigail ever find out the truth?"

Gus leaned against the back of the chair. "Her father had tried to tell her, but she wouldn't listen. Abigail's father paid me to convince Abigail of the truth about Raymond. I could earn back the money I'd lost, and she'd be convinced to break things off before she married the guy. I met her in town one afternoon. We had coffee in the back corner of the diner and I told her everything. At first she didn't believe me, but I had enough proof that what I had to say was compelling."

"What was her reaction?"

"She was devastated, and I hope, grateful she hadn't married him. It was hard to gauge her reaction. Then, while we were talking, Raymond came in and saw us sitting together."

"Is that what started the fight?" Edwin asked.

Gus nodded. "That night Raymond disappeared. Two weeks later Abigail left town. I heard she went to Europe to stay with some distant relatives. I figured she had to be better off without him."

"One last question, Gus, and we'll let you get back to your daughter and grandchildren. Do you know what happened the night Raymond disappeared? Did Philip really show up that night and shoot Raymond, or did he simply disappear, knowing he'd been caught?"

Gus took a moment to ponder the question. "Your guess is as good as mine, Sadie. You know, if you would have asked me that question back then, I could have named a dozen people who wanted that man dead, but today? I don't know. Most of those on my list are dead or too old to remember what happened. All I can say is that if it really is Raymond Butler who was murdered up in that mine, if you ask me, he got what he deserved."

"What now?" Edwin asked a few minutes later as they pulled out of Gus Fergusson's driveway.

Sadie leaned back against the passenger seat, as a wave of fatigue washed over her. "Maybe Gus is right. Maybe what happened back then really doesn't matter."

It wasn't that she didn't believe that justice shouldn't play out, but so much time had passed, and there was a good chance that finding out the truth wasn't even possible.

"But that doesn't explain who's leaving the warning notes," Edwin said. "So what are you thinking? Do you believe him? Or do you think he did more than just get in a fistfight that day with Raymond?"

"I think so. I think he was a man taken in by a con man, but is he a murderer? I could be wrong, but I don't think so. And besides, from what I've learned, there were plenty of other people who wanted Raymond dead."

"I tend to think you're right. I don't know the man, but while his passion gives him a strong motive with the death of his brother, that doesn't seem to be a reason for leaving warning notes."

"I agree."

"Why don't we take the long drive home?" Edwin suggested. "A few slow miles through the mountains before it gets dark."

"I'd like that." Sadie smiled. Edwin's company easily ranked up there along with the incomparable Rocky Mountain sunsets.

"Have you made a decision about the wood floors in your house?" she asked, thankful for the chance to talk about something beside the issues up in the mine.

"I think I mentioned to you that I spoke to Roscoe after church on Sunday," Edwin answered. "He says it's a good investment that will add to the price of the home if I ever decide to sell."

"I would think that they would be a major draw for a buyer," she said, though she couldn't see him actually selling the house.

When Edwin moved back to Silver Peak, he'd moved into his parents' old house and was always working on some kind of home improvement project. For the last few weeks, he'd been debating on whether or not he should replace some of the old carpet throughout the house with wood flooring.

Sadie could feel herself begin to relax. The wonder of God's creation always managed to calm her spirit. From the surrounding snowcapped mountains peaking at well above ten thousand feet to the colorful layers of clouds marking that night's sunset, the setting was the perfect backdrop to their conversation. They talked about his daughter, Noelle, and his five-year-old grandson,

Sam, whom he was hoping to visit again soon in Atlanta. Then Sadie brought up Sara's growing pains, and Pastor Sweeting's sermon on Sunday, which had appropriately been on the importance of storing up treasures in heaven.

Sadie's phone rang, interrupting their conversation as the colors of the sunset began to fade in the background. She was about to ignore the call, when she noticed it was the sheriff.

"Sheriff Slattery," Sadie said. "How are you this evening?"

"Fine, though I apologize for calling so late. This is the first chance I've had all day to contact you. I was hoping to get some information."

"Of course." Sadie felt her pulse quicken as she waited for the sheriff to continue.

"Perhaps this doesn't come as a surprise, but the lab was able to confirm that the body Greg Winston found in the mine was definitely Raymond Butler. And he was murdered," the sheriff said. "Forensics proved he was shot in the chest."

"Is there any way to find out who shot him?" Sadie asked.

"Possibly. That's why I need your help. I understand Philip Chaplin had an antique gun. Do you know anything about that?"

Sadie glanced at Edwin, then nodded. "I do, actually." Her father had been a gun collector and taught her everything she knew about antique firearms. "It's been a few years, but I helped the relative who inherited it find a dealer to sell them."

"Do you remember the kind of gun?"

Sadie searched her memory for the details. "It was a 1903 Springfield."

"I was hoping to hear that. We'll need to do some further testing, of course, but I think we finally found Raymond Butler's killer."

19

INSIDE SADIE'S SPACIOUS FARMHOUSE, AFTER DARKNESS HAD settled over the mountains, Sadie stopped in front of the built-in bookcase that sat beside the fireplace. That was where she kept all of the books she'd collected on the history of Colorado and Silver Peak. She ran her finger across the books that had been her father's, searching through the familiar titles for a specific book her father had left her on mining in Colorado.

One of her father's hobbies had been reading every history book he could get his hands on, especially ones on Colorado mines, mining camps, and today's ghost towns. She pulled out a worn edition of the book she'd been searching for, then sat down on one of the leather lounge chairs. Hank slept curled up in front of the fireplace.

She wasn't certain exactly what she was looking for, but after talking to the sheriff, she and Edwin had continued driving through the mountains as she tried to settle her mind. Instead, her thoughts continued to shift from Sara's confession of sneaking up to the mine, to Nicole's refusal to work, to Frances and Priscilla's revelations, to Gus's declaration that Raymond had been a con man, and finally to the sheriff's suggestion, by asking about his gun, that Philip *had* killed Raymond.

If Raymond's murderer *was* dead—which seemed likely—what connection did his story have to the threats up at the mine? Sadie started flipping through the black-and-white photographs in the book she'd chosen, most of them taken around the time of the boom back in the 1800s. Back then, most of the excavation of the mines would have been done by hand, using tools like shovels and picks. Ore at the surface could often be extracted by water- or steam-powered machinery, but either way, drilling was a dangerous and difficult profession. Still, that had never stopped men from trying to find their fortune.

When the first veins of silver were discovered, the population of Silver Peak exploded. Prospectors set up makeshift towns of cabins and tents. Hundreds of thousands of dollars' worth of gold and silver was discovered, much of it using sluice and pan. Stores were built, along with hotels and boardinghouses. And on the shadier side, there were dozens of dance halls and saloons that went up practically overnight.

By the 1950s—when Raymond and Abigail had fallen in love—everything had changed. Towns like Silver Peak had diminished in size over the years as the hunt for riches died out and the prospectors moved on. Young girls now read *Vogue* magazine and watched Marilyn Monroe on the silver screen, leaving some like Abigail to dream about life beyond their hometowns. Life had changed drastically and would continue to change over the coming decades.

Sadie's thoughts shifted once again to Sara's comments at the Antique Mine, as she set the book on the coffee table and headed upstairs to her room for bed. It was probably nothing. Sara had been inside the tunnel of a mine, in the dark without permission. Of course, she'd seen strange things on the wall and heard strange noises—Sadie had seen them, as well, on the video and would probably have felt uneasy herself being there. But even so, she couldn't help but ask the question, why had there been drill marks—drill marks that looked as if they'd been made with modern tools—on a tunnel wall that had been marked unsafe?

By the time Sadie had finished cleaning up the kitchen the next morning, Hank was at her side, anxious to start the day with a morning walk. Despite her turbulent thoughts, she stuck to her typical morning routine, which included sitting at the kitchen table where she read through her Bible reading for the day, then taking Hank on a walk while she prayed for wisdom and discernment. In Psalm 116 where she'd read today, King David prayed for God to guide him as he sought out the Lord's wisdom. That was exactly what Sadie was praying for today.

"I love You, Lord, because You hear and answer my prayers." Sadie repeated the verses she'd read that morning from the Psalms out loud as she started the engine. "Because You bend down and listen, I will pray as long as I have breath."

She drove her Chevy Tahoe a half mile from her house to her nearest neighbor, Milo Henderson—a true mountain man, with black hair, beard, a mustache, and friendly blue eyes—who owned a prosperous horse ranch and boarded horses, four of which belonged to Sadie, Alice, and her grandchildren.

Today, though, Sadie wasn't going to the ranch to take her horse, Scout, for a ride. She was hoping to find Sara.

Sara was exactly where she expected her to be, brushing Daisy, her three-year-old light bay filly inside the paddock. Sadie slipped out of the car, locked it, then crossed the gravel driveway, mentally noting that as soon as the filming of the documentary was over, she was going to come back out and do some riding. Scout was a five-year-old chestnut gelding that had given her not only the opportunity to do something she loved to do, but something she could do with her daughter and grandchildren.

Sara, wearing a pair of leggings with a striped top and jean jacket, glanced up at Sadie and smiled. "Grandma, I didn't expect to see you this morning."

"I thought you might be here."

"I was planning to go for a ride today, but after yesterday... Well, I won't be going riding for a while."

"Daisy looks beautiful." Sadie ran her hand down the horse's mane. "How did things go with your mom last night?"

Sara's gaze dropped as she moved down the side of the filly with the brush. "I received the expected lecture and am officially grounded for the next month from my phone and pretty much everything else. And it's now my responsibility to brush the horses down and muck out the stalls."

Sara wrinkled her nose in disgust as Sadie chuckled inwardly. Despite the fact that they both knew she deserved the punishment, she still felt sorry for her granddaughter.

"I'm sorry," Sadie offered.

"It's okay. I know I deserved it. I shouldn't have gone up to that mine. I just... I wish I didn't care if I felt like the oddball."

"Growing up can be a tough balance between becoming your own person and fitting in with others."

Sara frowned. "Tell me about it."

"Maybe when your punishment is up, we can go on a trail ride. I haven't been for a while, and I know that Scout needs to be ridden more often."

"I'd like that." Sara's frown morphed into a slight smile. "Are you heading up to the mine now?"

Sadie nodded. "Today is the last day of filming, and I have to say that I'm relieved."

"I hope you don't run across any more of those warning messages." Sara shuddered. "The whole thing still creeps me out."

"I think it's set a lot of people on edge."

"Do you have any idea yet who might have left the notes?"

Sadie shook her head. Sharing the information the sheriff had given her last night would need to wait for the moment, as well.

"I wish I could come watch the rest of the filming," Sara continued. "At least I got in some shots as an extra."

"We'll plan to throw a big party when the show is aired," Sadie suggested.

Sara moved to the other side of the horse, her limp barely detectable, then went back to brushing the horse. "With my luck this past week, they'll probably cut the scene."

"I doubt that," Sadie said. "Is your foot still bothering you?"

"Just a little bit."

"Have you been back to Doc?"

"Mom's been watching it like he said. The swelling's gone done, and it's just a little sore now."

"Good." Sadie stroked Daisy's shoulder and let her nuzzle up against her. "I wanted to see how you were doing, but there was one other reason I stopped by. I was wondering if I could see those photos you took and the video again."

The niggling questions about what Sara had seen in the tunnel hadn't gone away.

"Sure. My phone's in Mom's purse, though. She went up to the house to talk to Milo." Sara looked up toward the ranch house that sat on the edge of the property. "There she is."

Sadie met her daughter halfway up the path that connected the house to the stables.

"Mom, I didn't expect to see you until later today. You're not planning to go riding, are you?"

"Not today. I dropped by hoping I could catch Sara," Sadie said as they headed back toward the paddock together. "I was hoping the two of you were doing okay."

"I told you we had a good talk last night, but it's the trust thing that bothers me the most."

"Don't be too hard on her, Alice."

"Don't be too hard on her?" Alice frowned. "The girl snuck out of the house and went up to the mines."

"I know. I also remember not only how tough it is to be a teen, but also how tough it is raising a teen."

Alice caught her mom's gaze and winked. "I don't remember causing you any trouble."

Sadie laughed. "You had your moments."

Alice rested her hands against the railing. "It's just hard being on the parent end—as you know."

"Yes, but she's growing up, learning to make her own decisions. Be glad that so far the consequences of her actions haven't been life-altering so far. And if that day comes, God will give you the strength to deal with it."

"Makes me think about Abigail," Sadie said as she opened the gate. "She wasn't much older than Sara when all of that happened. And the choices she made... well, they clearly affected her for the rest of her life."

"You are right. You about done, Sara?" Alice asked.

"I'm ready, but Grandma wanted to look at the video I took up at the mine," Sara said, walking toward the two of them.

Alice frowned at the reminder as she rummaged through her purse. "Then I guess it's a good thing I didn't erase it yet."

Sadie took the phone from Alice, then handed it to Sara. "Could you find the video your friends took while up at the mine?"

"Sure."

"What are you looking for?" Alice asked.

"I'm not sure." Sadie waited for Sara to find the video. "It's probably nothing, but I was looking at photos taken up in the mines from back in the late eighteen hundreds. When I looked at the video, the marks on the walls were more precise—as if they'd been drilled recently."

"But why would anyone be drilling in an unsafe tunnel?" Alice asked.

"That's one of my questions," Sadie said.

Sadie studied the screen Sara held out in front of her and again watched the kids fooling around inside the mine. "Rewind it fifteen seconds and play it again."

Sara started it over.

"Freeze the video right there. You mentioned seeing strange marks on the wall. Is this what you saw?"

"Yes." They looked like drill marks. "Can you e-mail me the file?"

"Done," Sara said a few seconds later.

Sadie said good-bye, then headed for the mine, ready for the last day of filming. With more questions than answers, Sadie decided that as soon as filming was over that day, she was going to pay a visit to Ol' Sam at the American Mining Museum in town, to see if she could find any answers.

20

At four o'clock, the director shouted "cut" for the final time, and Sadie breathed out a sigh of relief. The filming for the *American Treasure Chest* episode at Silver Peak Mine was officially over. On the last day of filming, there had been no threats or warnings of injuries. No major technical issues or lost props. Nothing but beautiful blue skies and the majestic Rocky Mountains as a backdrop.

Nicole caught up with Sadie as she headed up the hill to the wood-framed house to pack up the rest of the props and costumes.

"Are you glad you came back to work?" Sadie asked the young actress.

"Yes, but call me emotional or overreacting if you'd like, but I'm glad it's over." Relief echoed in Nicole's eyes, as well.

"I'm just thankful that there was nothing to the threats."

Perhaps she was right. The threats that had been made had been simply that. Threats with no real plans to follow through on them.

"We're heading into town to the Depot to celebrate," Nicole said, twisting the silver flower ring on her finger. "Would you like to join us?"

Sadie hesitated with her response. Both Edwin and Roz had told her that she should simply forget everything that had happened over the past few days now that the filming was over. All they could do was chalk it up to an immature action by one of the members of the cast or crew. The sheriff hadn't found even a hint of proof that the warning notes pointed to anything other than someone's bad idea of a practical joke. But for some reason, Sadie had been unable to shake the feeling that they'd missed something.

She smiled at Nicole, thankful the young woman was feeling better. "I need to return all of the props and costumes, but I'll definitely try to stop by."

"Just in case I don't see you again, I wanted to let you know that I'm not going to forget what we talked about the other night at your house." Nicole rested her hand on Sadie's arm. "I realized, even with all the problems on the set, that I'm not ready to give up acting, but neither do I want to forget that it's time I started laying up treasures in heaven."

Sadie hugged the young woman good-bye. "I'll look forward to seeing you on the *American Treasure Chest*, and maybe one day on the silver screen."

Moments later, Sadie made her way up the short drive of the Winston home, carrying the box of props Evelyn had donated. The large dwelling had once served as the residence for the owners of the mine back in the late 1800s. Over the past century, the house had been added to and renovated, but it had never lost its historical charm.

Sadie set the box against one hip and knocked on the front door. "Evelyn?"

"Why, Sadie!" Evelyn opened the door, all dressed up in a pair of slacks, a white buttoned-up blouse, and a yellow sweater. "You just caught me. I was getting ready to head down to the Depot to celebrate with the cast. I can't believe the filming is over. It's been so much fun, and the publicity over the show has been fantastic."

"I'm glad to hear that," Sadie said, then nodded at the box she held. "I'm just bringing back the things I borrowed from you for the set."

"Would you mind bringing it into the living room for me?" Evelyn said, holding up her hands. "I've just done my nails."

"Of course."

"I'm glad you came by, actually, Sadie, because I needed to talk to you about something."

Sadie followed Evelyn down a short hallway toward the living room, wondering if the *something* had anything to do with her son, Craig, letting a group of teens in the mine at night. Alice had said she planned to speak to the woman and tell her what had happened.

Evelyn turned around in the doorway, her fingers at her sides. "I just want you to know that I've spoken to Alice about the kids' unauthorized visit to the mine. You can be assured that Craig has been punished, and I don't think he will ever do anything like that again. He, of all people, should understand the dangers of a place like that."

Sadie nodded. "I hope you're right. No one was injured this time, but a mine can be an extremely dangerous place."

"The entire week has been wild," Evelyn continued. "I can't believe all of the filming is over, and thankfully without another incident there either, or any more warning notes. I found the entire situation unsettling."

"You certainly weren't the only one who felt that way."

Sadie stepped into the Winston living room. The last time she'd been in the house was after Evelyn's mother-in-law had passed away. With all of the things Evelyn was always bringing in and asking her to sell, she was surprised at how simply decorated the house was. She'd expected a whole lot more clutter.

"I've been talking to Greg about doing a screening at the opera house when the documentary is released," Evelyn said. "Something simple, but it would be great publicity for the town, especially those like you and me who have businesses in the area. I can see people coming in from all over to attend."

Sadie set the box down in the corner. "I think it's a wonderful idea."

"I was thinking of involving as many people in town as possible. Jeanne Sweeting, for example, used to be an event planner at a large hotel in Denver. She might be perfect to help me arrange the party. I could get Troy from the *Silver Peak Sentinel* to run a big story on the show. And, of course, I could ensure that the *Chatterbox* does a big write-up, as well. We could have Arbuckle's cater some treats—nothing fancy, mind you. Or even better, I could have our fabulous pastry chef from the Market make something for us. She was a pastry chef in New York City before coming here, you know, and I'm sure she wouldn't mind."

Evelyn paused to take a breath.

Sadie chuckled. "I'm sure attendance would be high."

"I'm glad you think so, Sadie. Greg thinks the idea's a little over the top, but I asked him how often it was that Silver Peak had a TV show filmed in its city limits."

"Be sure to let me know your plans," Sadie said. "I'd be happy to help out."

"Wonderful. If we do it right, it might turn out to be as booked as Silver Peak's annual Founder's Day picnic."

Sadie started back toward the door of the living room. "You must have gotten rid of most of your mother's things by now. I was expecting to see an eclectic collection of things on your walls and shelves."

Evelyn shook her head. "She was the hoarder, not me. I've tried to slowly get rid of most of it, though the back room, the one I keep closed, is still full. It's funny. She always told me that all of her *stuff* was worth a fortune, but you know I've never found anything worth more than that pair of paintings I brought you the other day."

"One never knows how much a buyer is willing to pay. I hope you'll do well with those paintings."

Evelyn opened up the screen door and walked out onto the porch with Sadie. "That would be wonderful, but for now, I'm just thankful the filming is over. And that whoever was making those threats didn't follow through."

"I certainly agree with you on that, Evelyn. Thanks again for letting me borrow the props."

Sadie walked back to her car after saying good-bye. She did want to stop by the Depot to celebrate with the crew, but before she did that, there was at least one more thing she needed to do.

The American Mining Museum was located in a grand brick building that had formerly been a deserted Victorian schoolhouse on the edge of town. Thanks to some donations from local businesses, the museum had been completely refurbished a few years back. Ol' Sam was a volunteer at the museum, and he had known Sadie for a good thirty-some years. A mountain man at heart, he was semiretired, meaning he still took people on guided tours, and did some prospecting himself up in the mountains from what she'd heard.

As a benefactor of the mining museum, Sadie was able to visit as many times as she wanted throughout the year and was given a sticker from the young cashier with "Your Support Is More Valuable Than Gold" printed on it.

After pressing the sticker onto her blouse, she asked where she might find Ol' Sam, and was directed to the Gold Rush Room in the back of the museum.

The museum had always been one of those places that fascinated Sadie. It was yet another part of the history of Silver Peak. She often wandered through the museum with her grandchildren—who'd never quite appreciated its history as she did—or simply on her own whenever she had some free time. But while she'd done a lot of research on her own, Ol' Sam would be able to fill in the blanks.

She carried with her the box of props Ol' Sam had allowed her to borrow for the documentary, thankful again for the museum's generosity.

Sadie found Ol' Sam where she'd been told he'd be, answering a question about Silver Peak to an older couple she didn't recognize. Waiting her turn, she browsed the small room that was filled with various specimens and artifacts connected to the state's gold rush back in the 1800s.

A minute later, he crossed the room to greet her. "Miss Sadie Speers. It's good to see you."

Sadie set the box down on an empty table set up in the corner of the room. "How are you doing?"

"Except for a bit of pain in my joints, I can't complain."

"I can sympathize with you, Ol' Sam. I've got a few of my own achy joints, as well." Sadie chuckled, before steering the conversation to the reason she'd come. "I wondered if I could ask you a few questions about the Silver Peak Mine."

The old man smiled. "You know there's not much I'd rather talk about, so go ahead, Sadie. Ask away."

Sadie nodded, pleased by the man's reaction. "For starters, some strange things happened this week up at the mine."

"I heard a few people talking about that. Some kind of warning to stop the filming? Never did quite understand what was going on. Is everyone okay?"

Sadie wasn't surprised. In a town as small as Silver Peak, it didn't usually take long for rumors to make the rounds. "Filming just finished, so more than likely the notes were simply someone's idea of a prank, but I still have a few questions."

"All right."

Sadie grabbed Sara's phone out of her purse. "First, I wondered if you could take a look at this video. It's of a tunnel that's not used anymore because it's not safe, but these marks look new."

Ol' Sam studied the video footage, then nodded. "I'd say you're right, Sadie. Back then people used hand tools mostly like a hand drill or sometimes dynamite, but technology has changed tremendously over the past hundred, even two hundred years. Today miners have access to bulldozers and mechanized drills, and even computerized devices. These things, in turn, reduce the stress on manual digging and allow for miners to access places that were formerly impossible."

Sadie took in Ol' Sam's answer while processing her own thoughts. "Here's the bottom line. Do you think it's possible that there is still silver up there, or even gold?"

Ol' Sam leaned back against the table and folded his arms across his chest. "I can tell you that I haven't stopped looking. I believe that while the prospectors back in the late eighteen hundreds depleted the majority of the better places, they have barely scratched the surface. In fact, even though there might be those who don't agree with me, I believe that hundreds of gold deposits were overlooked. Where there was once gold, there might still be gold, silver, and even diamonds. In my opinion, many times the amount that was mined in the past."

"Wow." Sadie was surprised at his answer. "Diamonds? I know there have been some found in other parts of the state, but do you really think there might be some right here in our county?"

Ol' Sam nodded. "I believe it's possible that thousands of diamonds were mined with the gold and rejected with quartz in the mine tailings because the prospectors had no idea what the diamonds were back then."

"So what happened to them?"

"Back then, quartz was rejected with the mine tailings because the old prospectors didn't know what to look for."

"So they really were thrown away."

"Exactly. Silver today isn't worth much, at least compared to gold, but when I take people out as a guide and they're panning for gold, I remind them just how valuable gemstones can be. Gold is valuable today, but some pink and red diamonds have sold for as much as a million dollars per carat. A carat is tiny compared to an ounce of gold, and some of these diamonds have sold for many thousands of times the value of an equivalent weight in gold."

Sadie started sorting through the questions she still couldn't ignore. What if someone believed they had discovered something and didn't want anyone to know? What if they were afraid that someone involved with the documentary might ask too many questions and find out what they'd discovered? But if that was true, then who? Could it have been Greg? Or someone else?

Sadie had one last question for the old miner.

"What would be the reason for keeping a find like that a secret?"

Ol' Sam shrugged. "The first thing that comes to mind is who actually owns the rights to the mine. Disputes are common. In fact, many men have been killed over the past couple hundred years for that very reason."

Sadie glanced at her watch a few minutes later as she left the American Mining Museum, replaying Ol' Sam's words over and over. And that was why there was one more place she needed to stop before she could celebrate with the crew.

Sadie went over the facts—along with questions they invoked—as she walked to the library, basing her questions on the assumptions that the warning letters had not been a prank.

First, they knew for now that someone—possibly Philip—had shot and killed Raymond Butler and left his body in the mine.

Second, Abigail had carried the secret of her pregnancy and adoption with her to her deathbed, never even attempting to make contact with her child.

Were either of these secrets enough to motivate someone more than a half century later to ensure that no one found out the truth?

Third, had the warnings been given as a publicity stunt by someone working with the documentary?

Fourth, was someone trying to cover up something in the mine itself?

Or, Sadie thought as she walked into the library, to put it simply, had the warnings been given to cover up a secret from the past or something from the present?

"Hi, Sadie." Kimama greeted Sadie from behind the front counter with a smile. "Still working on that TV show up at the mine?"

"Finished up the last day of filming this afternoon."

"So how can I help you? Are you looking for a good book to read now that you're finished?"

"That does sound tempting, but right now I need to do a search online to find out information about who owns a deeded property. Unfortunately, my laptop's at home."

"That shouldn't be a problem. Many counties, including ours, offer an online, searchable database where you can search for information about land records and deeds. All you need to know is the party name, the type of document you are looking for, and an address or date. In fact, I can look it up for you right here."

"That would be wonderful. I'm interested in the history of the sale for the Silver Peak Mine."

"That shouldn't be a problem. Just give me a second..." Kimama adjusted her glasses, then started typing on the computer keyboard in front of her. "Starting with this year, it looks like... yes, the sale of the mine is almost final."

"The sale of the mine?"

Sadie hadn't expected that. Had someone else discovered there was still something of value inside the mine and talked Greg into selling?

"Before that, it was owned by Greg's father, and before that, Nigel Chaplin."

"Wait a minute." Sadie blinked. "Greg Winston is selling the mine?"

"Greg? No. According to this, he's not selling the mine, he's buying out his brother's share."

Sadie drew in a long breath. "I'd forgotten Greg had a brother."

"According to the record, their father left both of them the mine in his will, but as far as I know, Greg is the only one who has ever done anything with it."

"If I remember correctly, Greg's brother lives in Amsterdam. Works with some kind of software developer." Sadie searched her memory for details. "He married a woman from Holland and joined her father's company. From what I hear, they've done quite well for themselves, and I'm pretty sure they haven't been back to Silver Peak for at least five or six years."

But surely Greg wasn't the person behind the warning notes. She'd known the man for years. He and his family attended Campfire Chapel. It simply didn't make sense.

"They're half brothers, Greg and Cecil," Kimama said. "And I don't think they get along too well."

Sadie nodded. She'd heard the same thing. "What is the selling price?"

Kimama scanned the computer screen. "Looks like two and a half million."

"That's a lot of money."

"That price includes full ownership of the hundred and fifty acres, mineral rights, patented mine claims, and the ore, along with the existing permits to work and water rights to the river that runs through the property. Of course, I'm not sure what kind of investment it is. I mean, the mine isn't earning a cash flow beyond the tours that they do. And even if Greg had a considerable amount of capital to get everything ready for production, it could still take years to get it running."

"How in the world would Greg come up with that kind of cash?" Sadie asked.

"That I'm not sure about. Investors would be a possibility. Maybe a bank loan. Others sometimes sell the property, but stay on to manage and work for the new owner. Sadie? You all right?" Kimama asked.

Sadie looked up, pulled from her thoughts, as she worked to clarify a new theory. "Yes, I'm fine. In fact, you've helped me tremendously."

"You think the sale of the mine is tied in to the warnings they have been receiving up there?"

"I'm not sure, but that's what I intend to find out."

Sadie headed outside, still processing what she'd discovered. She could be wrong, but if she put all of the pieces together, there was only one thing that really made sense.

21

SADIE PULLED UP TO THE CURB IN FRONT OF THE MAYOR'S OFFICE in her red Chevy Tahoe, hoping she'd catch Edwin before he left to go home. Calling him on his cell phone had only given her the option of leaving a message, but she needed some of his wisdom along with another point of view looking into the situation.

She stepped into the mayor's office a moment later and was greeted by one of the secretaries who waved Sadie back to Edwin's office. Sadie managed a friendly hello but was barely able to take in her surroundings, her mind was so focused on the questions lying heavy on her heart.

She headed down the narrow hallway to Edwin's office and then knocked on his open door.

"Sadie, what a nice surprise." He smiled as he glanced up, making her heart skip a beat. "I just got off the phone and was getting ready to call you."

He crossed the room and brushed a kiss across her cheek. She felt her nerves settle slightly, reminding her once again of how thankful she was to have him in her life. She'd definitely made the right decision in coming to talk to him.

He leaned back against his desk and focused his attention on her. "My meeting for this evening was canceled, so I thought we could go out for dinner."

"I'd love that, but..." Sadie hesitated, unsure what he would think about what she'd found out. And she was unsure herself if she was digging into something she should simply let go.

"But...," he prompted.

"I need your help."

Edwin's brow furrowed slightly. "Is this about what's been going on up at the mine with the documentary?"

She nodded.

Edwin folded his arms across his chest. "I spoke briefly to the sheriff today. He's convinced that the messages left up at the mine were nothing more than someone's idea of a prank."

"You're probably right, but...," Sadie said, "I still think something's off."

"Well, like I said, I'm done here for the day and could use some coffee. How about I buy you a cup at Arbuckle's?"

Sadie smiled. "I'd like that."

A few minutes later, they were sitting in a pair of comfy chairs across from each other. Sadie breathed in the delicious aroma of coffee mingling with the smell of cinnamon and sugar and felt herself beginning to relax.

Edwin ordered two cups of coffee and two fresh chocolate chip cookies. She thanked him for the pick-me-up. She'd worry about walking off the extra calories with Hank when she got home.

"Tell me what's going on," Edwin said, once he'd added sugar and cream to his coffee.

Sadie had already filled him in on her visit with Priscilla the night before, so she started with her talk with Sara that morning, along with meeting Ol' Sam at the American Mining Museum and what she'd discovered at the library about the Silver Peak Mine.

"Wow." Edwin dumped a second packet of sugar in his coffee and started stirring. "You've been busy."

"Yes, but up to this point, we've all been assuming that the warning notes could be connected to Abigail's story."

"And now? I have a feeling you're looking at another direction."

"Yes." Sadie blew across the top of the coffee to cool it off. "What if we've been looking at all of this wrong?"

"How?"

"What if this isn't about a murder that took place half a century ago?"

"Then what's it about? The mine itself?"

Sadie nodded. "Walk through this with me. Maybe together we can make sense out of all of this."

"Okay."

"I think Greg found something up there. Ol' Sam told me that while many believe that prospectors depleted most of the ore, he believes they have barely scratched the surface."

"So that old, presumed defunct mine could be worth a lot more than just the revenue from the tourists who tour it." Edwin took a sip of his coffee, then leaned forward, clearly trying to work through all of Sadie's findings. "Here's my question. If Greg did find something, why keep it a secret? Greg is always working on publicity for the mine. Surely finding gold would be incredible publicity."

"Yes, but according to the land records, Greg doesn't own all the shares of the mine."

Edwin's brow furrowed. "So Greg doesn't just discover a skeleton. Instead he finds not just a streak of silver—which really isn't worth much on today's market, and doesn't seem worth covering up—but instead something of far greater value, and he decides he wants it for himself."

"That's my current theory." Sadie leaned forward. "The stakes could be very high. For example, there was a group of treasure hunters a few years ago in Alaska. Their team found those small, jagged flakes of gold in a group of streams, started searching, and found a large lode deposit worth seventy billion dollars in gold."

Edwin let out a low whistle, then glanced around the coffee shop, but no one seemed to be paying any attention to them.

"The same thing happened in Wyoming," Sadie continued. "A group found hundreds of garnets and other gemstones that had eroded from diamond pipes upstream. And according to what I read, many believe that it was just the tip of the iceberg. And pink and red diamonds are even more valuable than the equivalent weight in gold."

"What else?" Edwin asked.

Sadie took a sip of her coffee, then set it back down on the table between them. Talking through things with Edwin had further clarified in her mind what she believed had happened.

"I think that Greg was drilling in the mine, convinced he'd stumbled onto a huge payoff. But that wasn't the only thing he found. He found Raymond Butler's body. And that put him in a bind when the *American Treasure Chest* contacted him. He needed the money, plus the documentary would bring him publicity essential for the business, which had been in a slump. But he didn't want his brother—or the world, at this point—to know what he'd found."

"And the warning notes?" Edwin asked.

"I'm not sure, but it has to be connected somehow."

Edwin cupped his coffee mug between his fingers. "So what do you propose we do? Straight-out ask the man?"

"I'd like to look around a bit."

"In the mines?"

Sadie nodded. "Yes."

"I don't know, Sadie. I'm not sure that is a good idea. Besides, what do you expect to find?"

"Before I go to the sheriff with a handful of accusations, I need to have some kind of proof that Greg has started mining again. I want to see the marks on the wall that Sara saw."

Edwin didn't look convinced. "Sadie, it's dangerous up there, and you know it. Sara was already hurt. And the warnings that were left..."

"The crew is probably still packing up, and no one would question my presence there. I suspect that those tunnels really are safe, and the warning signs are nothing more than to keep curious tourists—like myself—away. At least that's what Craig told his friends."

"And if you're wrong?" Edwin asked. "If they really are dangerous?"

"We'll take it slow and be careful."

Edwin shook his head. "You know I'm going to regret saying yes, but you've piqued my curiosity."

The familiar saying "curiosity killed the cat" ran through Sadie's mind, but she pushed the thought away. This wasn't simply her being curious over what Greg was up to—if he really was up to anything. This was a chance to find out the truth.

Edwin ate the last of his cookie, a tinge of concern in his eyes. "Let's just hope neither of us regrets this in the end."

Five minutes later, Sadie sat beside Edwin in silence as he drove up the winding mountain road toward the mine, praying that their concerns would turn out to be false. That the letters had been pranks, and that now that the filming was over, the joke was over. But if she was right, it was time to find out the truth.

Up at the mines, the actors had already left while the TV crew was finishing packing up the equipment. Sadie walked toward the mine opening with Edwin following right beside her. There was no sign of Greg or any of his workers around.

"You're sure about this?" Edwin asked.

Sadie nodded as she fished for her flashlight in her purse. The solar lights cast yellow shadows against the tunnel walls, but she wasn't going to take any chances of them going out this time.

They stepped into the tunnel and Sadie felt the drop in temperature.

"I haven't been up here in years," Edwin said, watching his step. "I've forgotten how cold it is inside."

Sadie shivered as she flipped her flashlight on.

"How in the world did they film anything in here?" Edwin asked. "It doesn't seem light enough."

"The film crew brought their own lighting," Sadie explained.

"You sure couldn't have worked here if you were claustrophobic. Hard to imagine what those miners went through."

They moved slowly past the warning sign in silence. Sadie walked carefully, watching each step, then stopped as her flashlight picked up something.

"Look at this, Edwin," Sadie said. "I think Sara was right. It looks like bone."

"But what does it prove? That the body was moved?"

"Maybe." Sadie reached out, touched the opposite side of the wall, and ran her fingers across the drill marks. "Shine the light here, Edwin. What do you think?"

"That your crazy idea that Greg is somehow involved in this might be right."

Sadie nodded. Had Sara's guess been right and Greg moved the skeleton to another part of tunnel before the authorities arrived?

Sadie took another step, then felt her ankle twist. She grasped on to Edwin's arm as the ground shifted beneath her. Edwin grabbed on to her with both hands.

"Are you all right?" he asked.

"I'm fine," she assured him.

"This isn't safe, Sadie—"

She felt the ground shake. Rocks tumbled from the ceiling above them and down the sides of the tunnel. Dust swirled around them, filling Sadie's lungs as a section of the tunnel collapsed in front of her.

Sadie fought for air as she took a step backward, only to knock into the wall. The flashlight she'd been carrying fell, taking with it any remaining light as it shattered against the ground. Sadie blinked, unable to see anything, including Edwin, beyond a sliver of light coming from the entrance of the mine behind them.

She pressed her hand against her mouth and coughed. "Edwin? Where are you?"

"Get back, Sadie! Out of the tunnel."

"Edwin!" Sadie tried not to panic at his muffled voice. She reached out in front of her. There was a pile of rocks in the middle of the tunnel. Was he caught on the other side? "Edwin?"

Sadie felt her heart beat faster as she waited for Edwin to respond.

"Covered in dust but okay." His voice sounded muffled through the wall of debris. "But I'm going to need help getting out of here."

Sadie felt a wave of relief sweep through her, but the danger was still far from over. "I'll be right back, Edwin. I promise."

Sadie pulled her phone from her pocket and slowly made her way toward the mine entrance, trying not to imagine what *could* have happened.

Trying not to imagine what would happen if the mine collapsed further.

Please, Lord, protect Edwin…

Greg and Evelyn were making their way down the path toward the mine. Sadie let out a breath of relief.

"Sadie," Greg said. "We didn't expect to see you back today. Most of the crew has left."

"Greg…Evelyn…The mine has collapsed. I've got to call the sheriff."

"I don't think so." Greg snatched the phone out of her hand. "Why did you come back, Sadie?"

"Because I know the truth," Sadie said, realizing she was still holding the bone in her hand. Greg stared at it. Sadie took a step forward, not caring any longer about what they were hiding. "Listen. Edwin is trapped in this mine. We have to call the sheriff."

"Can't do that." Greg's frown deepened as he stepped in front of her, blocking her way.

"What are you going to do? Let him die in there?"

"You couldn't stop digging, could you?" Evelyn's normally friendly smile was missing. "I told you she'd find out, Greg."

"Be quiet, Evelyn."

"I know there's plenty you don't want the sheriff finding out about," Sadie said. "Starting with the fact that you moved Raymond's skeleton, presumably to ensure no one discovered you'd found more than just a dead body. What did you find up here, besides Raymond's skeleton? Silver? Gems?"

"Diamonds," Evelyn said.

"Evelyn!"

"What does it matter anymore, Greg? She clearly figured out what was going on."

"And you don't know how to keep your mouth shut!"

Sadie turned to Evelyn. "The warning notes were all a part of your plan, as well, weren't they?"

"It was supposed to be a publicity stunt. A bunch of strange things going on up at the mine…people forced to wonder if it really was Abigail herself not wanting questions of the past asked. The Denver paper was just the beginning. I was getting calls from across the state for exclusives to the story."

No doubt those tips had originated from Evelyn, Sadie thought. They'd both had quite a balancing act to pull off, between hosting the TV show and keeping the news of their diamond find a secret.

Greg clenched his teeth. "Evelyn—"

"It doesn't matter, Greg. We haven't done anything illegal."

"Illegal?" Sadie said. "That's yet to be determined, but you certainly crossed the lines of what is ethical. What about Nicole's car?" Sadie asked.

"We just wanted to scare her. She didn't get hurt."

"And your brother?" Sadie continued. "I'm assuming he has no idea about the worth of this mine."

"My brother has everything he's ever wanted," Greg said. "He'll never miss it."

Sadie glanced behind the Winstons and saw the sheriff and his deputy making their way down the path.

"Sheriff...Officer Kenmore...Edwin's in trouble. The mine collapsed."

"Greg, Evelyn, step out of the way, and then stay there." Mac Slattery gave the couple a stern look. "We heard enough to bring both of you in for questioning."

"How did you know to come?" Sadie asked, hurrying behind them.

"Edwin asked us to meet you here. We got here as soon as we could," Slattery said.

Sadie hurried inside the mine behind the officers, thanking God for their timely arrival. Leave it to Edwin to err on the side of precaution.

Sheriff Slattery turned to Sadie. "I want you to stay here, Sadie, until we can determine the extent of the collapse."

"I—"

"Trust us, Sadie."

A few minutes later, Edwin emerged from the mine into the sunlight with the sheriff and Officer Kenmore behind him. Relief flooded through Sadie.

"Edwin!"

"Thankfully, the cave-in wasn't too extensive," the sheriff said. "Didn't take long for us to get him out with his help."

Sadie threw her arms around Edwin and kissed him. "You're okay."

"Breathed in a a little dust, but yes," he said, smiling back at her. "I'm definitely okay."

"Sadie, would you make sure our esteemed mayor pays a visit to Doc just to make sure he's all right?"

"I'm fine, Sheriff—"

"He's right, Edwin." Sadie shook her head, then turned to the sheriff. "Of course I will."

"Looks like we need to do some questioning of the Winstons in order to wrap up this case."

Sadie started up the path behind the lawmen.

"Before we go, I have something for you," Edwin began.

"What is it?" she asked, brushing off the dirt caked on the object he handed her. "It looks like a . . . silver flask."

"I found it in the rubble. It looked like a cool antique for your collection."

Sadie rubbed her fingers against the front to reveal a set of initials.

R.B.

Could it be? *Raymond Butler?*

Sadie felt her heart pound as she examined the flask. She looked up at Edwin in anticipation, then back down at the flask. She twisted the silver top and looked inside.

"There's something inside it." Sadie pulled out a brittle piece of paper and unrolled it. "It's a letter." She began to read. "From Raymond to Abigail."

Sadie held the letter under the beam of the flashlight and read it out loud to Edwin.

My dearest Abigail,

I have decided to write down my thoughts in this letter, hoping that I have the chance to talk to you in person, but fearing that I might not be able to. If I don't meet you tonight, it isn't because I don't long to see you. Or that I don't love you. In fact, my mind can barely take in the thought of not being able to be with you any longer. And writing it down with pen and paper only seems to make it all the more real.

I do not know what your father has told you about me, but I must confess that I have not always been honest with you. But please believe that I didn't start out to deceive you. In fact, I didn't come to Silver Peak to fall in love. I came to make money. I've done it a dozen other times, in a dozen other small towns. But I never—in all of that time—met anyone like you.

But I did meet you, and you have changed me. You made me want to settle down, marry you, and start a family. And perhaps, even, walk the straight and narrow.

Which is why I must confess the truth to you. I know your family believes that my love for you isn't real, but as you read this letter, please know that this isn't the truth. I do love you. And no matter what happens, my love for you will never lessen.

My heart, I fear, will never been the same, though perhaps it is justice, and everything I deserve. I fear I have broken your heart and I am deeply sorry for that.

You wrote once how you wondered what would have happened if you hadn't decided to walk into the restaurant that Saturday afternoon. If you hadn't let Julia convince you that you both needed an ice cream sundae to beat the intense summer heat that hung heavy that July afternoon.

What would have happened if you hadn't looked across the rows of tables and diners and noticed me. I never regret anything that happened between us.

By the time you finish reading this letter, there is a good chance that I will be gone—because I have agreed to meet your father tonight. I don't know what he wants to say to me. I fear he will demand that I leave. I can't live a life on the run with you. I love you too much for that.

I am sorry, Abigail. Sorry for loving you. Sorry for hurting you.

Raymond Butler

Sadie shivered as she turned to Edwin. "He really did love her."

"It would seem so."

"Do you know what else this means?" Sadie asked. "It wasn't Philip who killed Raymond. It must have been his father. And Abigail probably never knew the truth. Only that the man she loved left her."

"Perhaps that was the reason Philip started drinking. He must have known what his father had done, and tried to protect him."

Sadie stared at the letter. There had been much sadness that should have been avoided. So many treasures that had been lost here on this earth, because they hadn't been stored in heaven.

Edwin wrapped his arm around Sadie's waist as they started back up the path toward their car. "After I get cleaned up, how about a quiet meal together? Just you and me. No TV crews, threatening letters, or talk of murdered skeletons."

Sadie looked up at Edwin and smiled. It might be too late for Abigail and Raymond, but it wasn't too late for her and Edwin. "Sounds perfect. Absolutely perfect."

Epilogue

Two months later…

Sadie carried out a large pitcher of lemonade onto the back deck of her home where Edwin and Roscoe were cooking hamburgers on the grill. She'd decided to throw a small party with Edwin, Alice, Theo, Sara, Roz, and Roscoe to watch *American Treasure Chest*'s episode of Abigail and Raymond. It might not be completely accurate, but it had brought back a lot of memories.

Sadie poured a glass, then took it to Sara, who was staring out over the mountains as the sun began to set, casting a golden glow against the clouds.

"Would you like some lemonade?" Sadie asked.

Sara smiled up at her grandmother. "Thanks."

"You're welcome."

Sara took a sip of the drink, then rested it against the edge of the deck.

"You were awfully quiet in there," Sadie continued. "What did you think about the episode?"

"I guess I was surprised they didn't cut me. My friends were planning to watch it."

"I guess it would have been embarrassing if you'd told them you were on television and they'd cut you."

"Yes, but..." Sara took another sip of lemonade. "I've learned a lot since then. I shouldn't worry so much about what everyone thinks of me. I just need to stay true to myself and what is important."

"And what is important to you?" Sadie asked.

"I guess I'm still figuring that out." Sara looked up to catch Sadie's gaze. "It's still hard, but I don't want to do things because of what everyone else thinks. Mom's always telling me that I need to make decisions ahead of time, so when that moment of temptation hits, I won't have to think twice, just do what's right. But sometimes that's still hard. Just like it was for Abigail."

"That's pretty wise thinking." Sadie pulled her granddaughter into a hug. "I'm proud of you, Sara. We all make mistakes, but what's important is that we learn something from the experience and grow from it."

Alice walked up to them. "What are the two of you gabbing about?"

"How much your daughter is growing up," Sadie said. "I think she just might make it through these rocky teen years after all."

"I, for one, never had any doubts," Alice said with a grin.

"Never, Mom?" Sara raised her brow.

Theo walked up to them, saving Alice from having to answer.

"So what do you think about your sister's sleuthing, Theo?" Sadie asked. "Despite her injury, she helped come up with a few crucial pieces to the puzzle."

"Looks to me as if we might have our own Sherlock Holmes," Theo said, shoving a lock of his dark brown hair out of his face. "Maybe we could call you Shirley for short."

"Very funny, Theo. Though if I'm Sherlock, I guess you'll have to be Watson…Doc." Sara shot her brother a wry grin.

"You're the funny one." Theo nudged her with his elbow. "But seriously, you did good, sis."

Sara beamed. "Thanks, Theo."

"Burgers are ready," Edwin called out from across the deck. "Grab yourselves a plate, and we'll serve them up."

Alice lingered beside Sadie while Sara and Theo headed for the table. "I've always found it interesting how the two of them can fight like cats and dogs, and then eat up the praise from the other one."

"Sibling rivalry is an interesting phenomenon. Look what it did to Greg," Sadie said. "He was so jealous of his brother, he was willing to trick him out of his half of the mine, and do whatever it took to get away with it."

"The Winstons' court date is coming up, isn't it?"

"Next week. I'm not sure how the judge will rule. No one was hurt, but that might not matter." Sadie turned to her daughter, glad to be able to put the secrets of the mine behind her. "You're blessed, Alice. Despite the ups and downs every parent goes through, you've got good kids."

"I agree." Alice nodded her head. "They've both volunteered to help out at the vacation Bible school next month and Theo's even talking about going on a mission trip."

Sadie smiled. *Storing up treasures in heaven.*

"The two of you'd better come get your burgers," Roz said as she walked up to them with a burger with all of the fixings. "The men have outdone themselves."

"If it tastes as good as it smells, we're in for a treat," Sadie said, as the three of them started for the grill. "By the way, I meant to tell both of you that Priscilla called me today."

"She finally was able to meet her sister?" Roz asked.

Sadie nodded. "It turned out to be a wonderful blessing for both of them. I think the only regret they have is that their mother never got to know Melanie. And one other thing." Sadie turned to Sara, who had just finished fixing her burger. "Priscilla asked me to thank you for helping to find out the truth. It really meant a lot to her."

Sara beamed at the compliment.

Sadie watched those closest to her laugh and enjoy the evening and felt her heart swell with gratitude, reminded once again of the importance of friends, family, and faith.

About the Author

LISA HARRIS IS A CHRISTY AWARD WINNER FOR *DANGEROUS Passage*, a Christy Award finalist for *Blood Ransom*, and the winner of the Best Inspirational Suspense Novel for 2011 from *Romantic Times*. She has sold over thirty novels and novella collections. She and her family have spent over ten years living as missionaries in Africa where she works with the women and runs a nonprofit organization that works alongside their church-planting ministry. When she's not working she loves hanging out with her family, cooking different ethnic dishes, photography, and heading into the African bush on safari. For more information about her books and life in Africa, visit her Web site at lisaharriswrites.com or her blog at mybloginthe heartofafrica .blogspot.com.

Read on for a sneak peek of another exciting book in Mysteries of Silver Peak!

Time Will Tell

"THANK YOU ALL FOR COMING THIS EVENING." SADIE SPEERS smiled encouragement as Mayor Edwin Marshall rose to address the group gathered around him. They were the very first passengers on the newly formed Silver Peak Scenic Railway. Edwin leaned forward slightly and grasped the padded mohair seats on either side of the aisle for support as the train chugged through the mountains. "When the Mountain Crest Railroad closed in the 1940s, no one knew for certain if these magnificent engines would ever run again. Tonight, we are pleased to welcome the Silver Peak Scenic Railway as part of our town's flourishing tourist industry."

Sadie added her applause to the rest of the passengers in the packed railroad car, clapping her kid-gloved hands until Edwin waved for silence. Her heart surged with pride. She and Edwin grew up together and dated in high school, but life had taken them in different directions. After the passing of both of their spouses, however, they had found their way to each other once more, and in Edwin's company, Sadie was content. He looked so debonair tonight in his tuxedo, more at home in 1930s attire than in the casual outfits she encouraged him to wear throughout the week as the mayor of a thriving mountain community.

"As you know," Edwin continued, his dignified baritone voice ringing through the train car, "this 'maiden voyage' begins a week of festivities centered on Silver Peak history in the 1930s, when the Mountain Crest Railroad was in its prime. We have old-fashioned games planned for the children, a gospel music concert, and a film festival with a special tribute planned for Collin Malloy, the opera star turned Hollywood star."

Sadie smiled at the mention of Collin Malloy. When the investors in the Silver Peak Scenic Railway had approached the Historical Preservation Committee for festival ideas, Sadie had spent hours brainstorming with Edwin, trying to come up with events that would reflect the town's heritage throughout the Great Depression. It was her idea to pay tribute to Collin Malloy, who, while not a native of Silver Peak, had gotten his start as a performer at their opera house. Collin had been a particular favorite of Sadie's mother, and what better way to rekindle the glamour of that era than to pay homage to Silver Peak's most successful adopted son?

Edwin's steel-blue eyes twinkled in her direction before he turned his attention back to the passengers. "I'd like to say more, but the conductor would like to give everyone one last chance to sample the refreshments before we arrive back at the station. So if you want to hear more about a little surprise I have planned, linger for a few moments after we depart the train. I'll give you all the details before we head over to the Depot for the reception."

Sadie applauded with the crowd once more, her curiosity piqued. What surprise had Edwin planned for this week? She thought she knew all the events of the Railway Festival, from this inaugural train ride to the film festival.

She couldn't suppress a grin as she gazed at her reflection in the window beside her, which showcased a dusky Colorado sky. Her salt-and-pepper hair, normally styled in a simple way, had been coaxed by her daughter Alice into marcel waves. Her hairstyle, crushed velvet gown, and lace stole made Sadie feel as though she'd stepped out of another time.

As she glanced around the railway car, she recognized several familiar faces even though everyone was dressed in period costume. Her best friend Rosalind, whom everyone called Roz, sat just behind and across the aisle from her. Somehow, Roz's normal bohemian style melded perfectly with 1930s glamour, and she sported a turban with an ostrich feather as naturally as her straw gardening hat.

Across the car and up a few rows, Spike Harris looked more dapper than she'd ever seen him, wearing a tuxedo, his long hair slicked back. Spike usually wore a leather jacket and jeans, which felt natural for a musician and the owner of the Silver Peak Music Emporium, but tonight he could've been an extra in a Hollywood film.

She caught glimpses of other familiar faces here and there—Pastor Don Sweeting and his wife Jeanne, who sported chandelier earrings so dazzling that light glinted off the prisms, and Roz's husband Roscoe, owner of the town's hardware store, looking slightly upholstered and uncomfortable in a subdued suit.

But it was also heartening to see so many new faces in the crowd. Silver Peak was a small town and Sadie had lived here all her life, so she knew practically every member of their community. Just about everyone in town supported and encouraged both historical preservation of the town and the development of the tourist trade so vital for its survival. Seeing so many familiar faces here tonight was to be expected, but many tourists had shown up as well, and all of them in costume.

She glanced around the car and caught the eye of Roz, who gave her an enthusiastic thumbs-up. By any measure, this event was a success. Purely in terms of the number of visitors it brought to Silver Peak, it had already accomplished its goal, since the whole purpose of the railway was to attract tourists from the neighboring ski resorts.

She glanced at the man sitting beside her in the aisle seat. The train seats had been assigned as tickets were bought, and as result, a nice mix of locals and tourists mingled together.

Like everyone else in the car, her neighbor was dressed elegantly in a period-appropriate tuxedo, but he kept his top hat on, tugged tightly over his head, his dark hair curling out under the brim. He was in his fifties, she guessed, and had a thick, full beard and a magnificent mustache. Sadie couldn't help thinking he looked like a cross between a mountain man and a Civil War general. The effect was undercut somewhat by a pair of wire-rimmed glasses with thick lenses. Despite the glasses, though, his piercing blue eyes were striking.

Sadie had tried to engage him in conversation early in the trip, but he had politely sidestepped all her comments and questions. She'd given up after ten minutes and knew no more about him now than she had when he'd sat down. He hadn't even told her his name.

As Sadie peeked at the stranger again, a vivacious brunette wearing a vintage uniform wheeled a cart up the aisle. She paused at each row, offering steaming cups of hot chocolate to the passengers. Sadie had met her during the planning for the train's first ride. Her name was Darcy Burke, and, like a few other part-timers on the train's staff, she was from a neighboring town. She also happened to be the niece of Jack Fitzgerald, the train engineer, and she shared her uncle's enthusiasm for the antique train.

As Darcy approached, the man sitting beside Sadie turned to her. "Would you like something?"

"Yes, I would. Thanks." Sadie smiled at him.

"Two, please." The man took the cups Darcy offered and looked at them in surprise. "Well, this is a luxury. Real china, just like in the old days."

"Oh yes." Darcy smiled at him. "Thanks to Mrs. Speers here, we have all the authentic things we need, right down to the hot chocolate mugs."

Sadie gratefully accepted her cup from her seatmate and grinned at the young woman. "The Antique Mine is always happy to lend a helping hand—or in this case, a few antiques. Are you enjoying your work here, Darcy?"

"I am. Being around all these antiques sure makes it beautiful." Darcy peeked into the silver-plated chocolate pot. As she lifted its lid, her elbow knocked one of the ceramic mugs off the cart. It bounced off the cart's wheel and then shattered into a dozen pieces on the floor of the train.

Sadie felt her heart wrench at the sound and the sight of one of her beautiful Fire-King mugs destroyed. Passengers all around gasped and Darcy cried out and crouched down, her shaking fingers clumsily picking up shards of mug.

"I'm so sorry!" she said, her voice high and shrill. "Oh, your beautiful mug! I'm so, so sorry, Mrs. Speers! I can't believe I did that!"

Sadie's neighbor slid out of his seat and helped Darcy pick the final pieces off the floor.

Sadie watched them in dismay for a moment before shaking herself out of it. It was just one mug, after all, and Darcy was near tears.

"It's okay, it's okay," she said, trying to soothe the young woman. "Worse things have happened. You haven't done any serious harm."

Darcy dumped the pieces of mug onto a lower shelf of the cart and nodded jerkily at Sadie's neighbor, who resumed his seat. "I don't know how to apologize enough, Mrs. Speers. You can ask Uncle Jack to take it out of my paycheck. It's only fair." She took a deep breath and seemed to gather herself. When she opened her eyes again, she fixed them with a shaky smile. "There'll be a table set up as you get off the train. Just set your cups down, and we'll take them to be washed." Darcy shot a nervous glance in Sadie's direction. "I promise to take good care of them. Truly. But if you'd rather someone else washed them, I'd understand."

"I'm not too worried, Darcy. They're Fire-King mugs. They're built to last." She looked at the pieces lying on the lower shelf of the cart and fought a smile. Well, maybe not *that* one. "This is just a fluke, I promise."

Most antiques were meant to be used, Sadie believed, which was why she'd lent the mugs and chocolate services to the train station for this event. Putting a beautiful object behind glass and never letting anyone use it again—what a waste. Obviously some artifacts were too fragile to withstand everyday wear and tear, but most antiques were more practical than people thought.

With a small wave, Darcy moved the cart up the aisle, stopping to chat here and there with other passengers. Sadie could see her slowly regain her equilibrium.

The man beside Sadie offered a charming smile. "You must own an antique store. What a great job."

"Yes—" Sadie began, but a shrill whistle rent the air.

Thundering groans rose from the many wheels and gears and machinery beneath them, and the train's momentum slowed.

Sadie looked around. A man across the aisle just behind her held his phone to his ear. "I can't hear you," he hollered. "Just a second." He rose, moving into the aisle. Beside him, a woman dressed in silver lamé clutched at her fox fur stole and began to follow him.

Darcy waved her arms from the back of the train. "Sir, please sit down. We'll be in the station in moments."

The woman in silver lamé tugged at the man's sleeve, and with a disgusted grunt he sat back down, running his hand through his dark hair. "Ridiculous. Can't even get a clear signal," he announced to the car in general.

The train shuddered to a stop with a final *whoosh* of the brakes. Sadie settled back into her chair with a happy sigh. Now that the ride was over she could join Edwin, who had been seated at a place of honor as the mayor and so he could easily address the group, and find out what surprise he had in store for the town.

Turning toward the window, she noticed the brass tag screwed into the mahogany wall next to her. It read "13-C" in Art Deco lettering. How perfect. She ran her fingertip along the tiny brass plaque. Every detail of the train had been preserved and restored back to its 1930s glory, when it had so briefly been the main transportation between Silver Peak and Denver.

Beside her, her seatmate stood to exit the train, but the aisle was full of passengers. Neither he nor Sadie was going anywhere for a few minutes.

Sadie began gathering her things to leave. She tried to arrange her lace shawl about her shoulders, but a corner of the fabric had gotten shoved down between the seat cushion and was caught on something. She gave a gentle tug, a gesture borne of many years of working with delicate fabrics, and pulled the shawl free. But it was heavy, tangled with something that glittered.

She unwound the fabric and smothered a gasp as the soft light from the light above her revealed her find. A million prisms sparkled off the surface of a gentlemen's pavé diamond pocket watch.

Sadie straightened and held the pocket watch out in the palm of her hand. Her antique-expert mind took over, and she examined the watch to see if it was authentic. She angled it carefully so the prisms would catch the light. The sparkles were so bright they hurt her eyes. It certainly passed the brilliance test. Would it stand up to a fog test? She held the watch up to her lips and breathed on it, a trick she'd learned while scouting antique jewelry. Real diamonds didn't fog up; fake ones, even very well done fakes, always did.

These diamonds didn't fog.

Who would simply leave a treasure like this on a train? This was no mere prop that had fallen from one of the train staff's pockets. Someone must have lost it.

"What a stunning watch." The stranger beside her ducked back into his seat, peering intently at her hand. "Is it yours?"

"No. It must have been dropped by someone else." She clasped her hand around the watch. "I should notify the staff." Someone, somewhere would be missing this watch.

"Of course. Here, I'll get out of your way." With one fluid gesture, the man moved out of his seat and into the aisle, holding back the exiting passengers so that Sadie could slip out of her seat.

As Sadie stepped into the aisle, all the lights on the train went out. A wave of gasps and muffled exclamations swept through the car. Her shin hit something in the sudden blackness and she fell to her knees.

"Here." From the shadows, a hand grasped Sadie's gloved wrist. "Let me help you," her seatmate murmured in her ear. She was lifted back to her feet with a single graceful pull.

A few seconds later, the lights in the car flickered back on.

"Sorry about that, folks!" Darcy shouted from the back of the train car. "Everything's fine! Please continue exiting the train."

Sadie turned to thank her helper, but he was gone. Behind her, a column of passengers stood, all of them impatient to press onward. Where had the man who was sitting next to her gone? He couldn't just vanish into that crowd of jostling passengers.

"*Excuse me.*" The woman in the silver lamé gown pushed forward, eyeing Sadie as if she were the sole person in her way. "I'd like to get off this train, if you don't mind."

"Yeah. I'd like to return that call sometime this century." Her companion, tall and dark, rolled his brown eyes and sighed in exasperation.

"Oh, sorry. Of course." Sadie turned and started walking up the aisle. Then she paused and looked down at her hand.

The dazzling pocket watch was gone.

A Note from the Editors

We hope you enjoy Mysteries of Silver Peak, created by the Books and Inspirational Media Division of Guideposts, a nonprofit organization that touches millions of lives every day through products and services that inspire, encourage, help you grow in your faith, and celebrate God's love in every aspect of your daily life.

Thank you for making a difference with your purchase of this book, which helps fund our many outreach programs to military personnel, prisons, hospitals, nursing homes, and educational institutions. To learn more, visit GuidepostsFoundation.org.

We also maintain many useful and uplifting online resources. Visit Guideposts.org to read true stories of hope and inspiration, access OurPrayer network, sign up for free newsletters, download free e-books, join our Facebook community, and follow our stimulating blogs.

To learn about other Guideposts publications, including the best-selling devotional *Daily Guideposts*, go to ShopGuideposts.org, call (800) 932-2145, or write to Guideposts, PO Box 5815, Harlan, Iowa 51593.